EXPC

A completely unputdownable gritty
and gripping gangland thriller

CASEY KING

The Dublin Thrillers Book 2

Joffe Books, London
www.joffebooks.com

First published in Great Britain in 2023

© Casey King 2023

This book is a work of fiction. Names, characters,
businesses, organizations, places and events are either
the product of the author's imagination or are used
fictitiously. Any resemblance to actual persons, living
or dead, events or locales is entirely coincidental.
The spelling used is British English except where fidelity to
the author's rendering of accent or dialect supersedes this.
The right of Casey King to be identified as author of this
work has been asserted in accordance with the Copyright,
Designs and Patents Act 1988.

Cover art by Nebojša Zorić

ISBN: 978-1-83526-189-7

CHAPTER 1

Danielle Lewis knew for a fact that everyone who'd posed a threat to her was either fucked up, locked up or dead. Yet that knowledge did little to quell her thudding heart, or the feeling that the world was about to explode around her. So she shut herself away, waiting until she could be certain whom to trust.

But after a month of isolation in her Dublin penthouse apartment, she had little choice but to re-enter the world. Things had reached a stage where her supplies had run out and the supermarkets had no available delivery slots. She herself could make do, but the baby needed proper sustenance, and her own milk had dried up a decade ago.

At eleven weeks old, the baby had Danielle wrapped around her little finger. She had learned that a certain cry would bring a cuddle, another would bring food. And she was crying that way now.

The investigating officer was due to phone and arrange a time to take her statement. Being on this side of the law was a new experience for Danielle, but it came with a benefit. If she complied with the authorities now, one of the threats to her would be conveniently removed. They'd be spending years in a prison cell, and she would stay alive, providing care for the baby.

The unseasonal mid-October warmth meant that she wouldn't be able to conceal her identity beneath scarves and a woolly hat. She would have to do what she could with a light bandana pulled up to cover her mouth, and a baseball cap to hide as much of her hair as possible.

Danielle draped a crocheted blanket over the roof of the buggy to keep the early morning sun off baby's little face. An inner pocket at the side of the buggy held a Beretta Pico handgun — not your standard accessory for a baby carriage, but Danielle needed to carry some form of protection.

Preparations made, Danielle was as ready as she'd ever be to leave the sanctuary of her Clonliffe View home and head out. The local shop was just minutes away, and if she took it at a jog, she'd be there and back in less than twenty minutes.

Outside, Danielle stood close to the wall and took stock of her surroundings. By now, these were familiar enough for her to notice anything out of place.

She smiled down at the blanket covering the buggy. 'It's just you and me, sweetheart. Don't worry, I'll keep you safe.'

Cautiously, she stepped forward. A sudden breeze, strong enough to lift the blanket, caught the bandana and nearly whipped it from Danielle's face. She adjusted it and put the blanket back. The baby stirred but didn't wake. An empty beer bottle rattled towards the front wheel of the buggy. Danielle kicked it aside. A green taxi, empty of passengers, drove slowly by, the driver staring through the windscreen. She hung back and watched the taxi disappear from view before continuing.

Her runners tip-tapping on the pavement, she made the last few metres to the store at a run.

She pushed in through the door, the shrill ring of the bell making her heart stop for a second. She always forgot about that damn bell. She caught her breath and headed for the aisle holding baby products.

A young fella, barely the height of her chest, wearing a jacket that was far too warm for the weather, eyed her up and down as she bent to pick out a tin of formula.

Why was he looking at her?

He opened the jacket. She caught a glimpse of the torn lining as he tucked a multi-pack of chocolates and a packet of custard creams inside it and ran. The bell at the door told her he'd succeeded in making his getaway. Too late the owner shouted after him.

'Excuse me.' A woman leaned forward, her warm breath brushing Danielle's ear, making her jerk back in fright.

'Oh, I'm sorry. I just need to get at the bleach.' The woman pointed to a pink bottle on the bottom shelf.

'Here, let me get it for you.' Danielle handed it to her.

'Ah, look. What a dote. Congratulations. What's her name?' The woman reached an outstretched finger towards the baby's cheek.

At once, Danielle's hand was around the woman's wrist. 'If you don't mind, I've just gotten her to sleep.'

'Sorry, I didn't mean . . .'

Danielle's grip had left a pink mark on the other's wrist. The woman stepped back, clutching the bottle of bleach to her chest. 'I'll leave you to it, so. Thanks for passing this.' The woman backed away and then turned and hurried off to the cash desk.

What's her name? The question they all ask, but Danielle didn't have an answer. She called her sweetheart, pet, baby names. How could she not have named her?

'Can I help you with anything?'

The shop assistant's words yanked her out of her thoughts. 'I have all I need,' she answered brusquely.

'Right.' Some of the packets of custard creams toppled over into the aisle. The shop assistant sighed as he bent to pick them up. Damaged goods to discount, on top of what had been lost to the tiny thief.

She lifted four formula tins from the shelf and placed them by the baby's feet, along with a large packet of nappies and some wet wipes. Then she headed to the cash desk.

Danielle stood behind the woman with the bleach, shuffling from foot to foot while the woman painstakingly counted out her coins. Danielle wanted to scream. Already she'd been

3

out longer than she'd intended. She chewed on her thumbnail, watching a bus go by, the passengers all looking half asleep.

'Are you paying for those? Excuse me. Are you paying—?'

'What? Christ, yes, of course. Sorry.' Danielle hadn't realised that the woman had left with her bottle of bleach. She put one tin on the counter. 'I have three more and a packet of these.' She displayed the barcode for the cashier to scan, then the packet of wipes.

'Anything else.'

It sounded like a command, so automatically Danielle snatched up a bag of salt and vinegar crisps along with a bar of minty Aero. 'Here. And this.' She threw in a packet of chewing gum.

She paid, stuck her card in her pocket, and headed out through the door, where she collided with the bleach woman. 'Excuse me. Can I get past you?'

The woman stared at her vacantly.

'Will you get the fuck out of my way?'

Only then did the woman step aside.

Danielle half ran. Her heart leaped at the sound of thumps, hisses, and beeps coming from her left. A rubbish collection lorry pulled up at the kerb. The man in a reflective jacket shouted something at her. She paused briefly, until she heard his mate answer from behind.

It was as if the city had been lying in wait for her, only coming to life when she left the apartment. Just what she had been hoping to avoid.

She reached under the blanket and felt for the reassuring shape of the small Beretta. Again, she had to halt while the man in the hi-vis jacket thrust a couple of bins onto the pavement in front of her. Meanwhile, the baby sucked happily on her soother, oblivious to the action— *Shit!* There was no spare soother in the apartment. Where the fuck was her brain? Too late to go back to the shop though. She just wanted to get home now.

At the entrance to the apartment complex, she stabbed the pin number for her card into the keypad instead of the code for the electric gate. Her ears pounded. She tried again, struggling to recall the correct sequence of numbers. Finally, the gate opened with a clunk and she rushed inside.

'Only three more entrances and we're home,' Danielle said to the baby. 'Let's lock the door and not leave again for at least another month.' Her throat was parched.

She was metres from the main door when the ground rose up to meet her. Grit and gravel tore into her cheek, her knees. The buggy rolled forward as if it had a life of its own. She pushed herself up and looked around, dazed. There was just time to register a pair of dark red sneakers before something was pressed against her back and she was pushed back to the ground.

The baby started to yell. Danielle moved instinctively towards the pram, but a hand at the back of her neck held her, face in the dirt.

'Stick the soother back into her gob and grab her. Take the lot.' The woman's voice was that of a stranger.

Someone was pulling at the handle of the packet of nappies, still looped around her wrist. Her fingers scraped the gravel.

She tried to scream. Maybe the refuse collectors were still nearby, maybe the taxi was passing back this way. Maybe if she could get at the gun. Maybe . . . The pressure on her neck lessened slightly. Maybe if she could stand . . . She pushed herself off the ground and cried out for help, hearing the beep of a vehicle reversing. She called out again.

Danielle was almost on her feet when she felt a sharp pain in her side and fell back onto her knees. The foot then connected with her face like a demolition ball. She rolled to the side just as the vehicle came in through the gate. She groaned — not in pain but in sorrow. She'd promised to keep the baby safe, and she'd let her down. Not content with leaving her where she'd fallen, one of them returned and gave her a final kick. She surrendered to darkness.

CHAPTER 2

An hour before sunrise on a cold October morning, Dwayne Flynn stood outside the red-brick two-storey house, his bag at his feet, and for a moment, expected his brother to be inside, waiting for him. But no one was waiting for him. His brother was dead, a lifeless body, one of all the other lifeless bodies laid out in the funeral home, waiting to be disposed of, Dwayne didn't know how — cremated or buried. They'd never spoken about death — not their own, anyway. Everyone knew that brought bad luck.

There had certainly been plenty of bad luck in the four months Dwayne had been away cementing the Flynn business connections overseas. Bad luck or some serious fuck-ups. Now he was back to put things right.

A bell rang. The Luas tram was about to depart from Ranelagh. Dwayne watched it pass, with its smattering of early commuters off to work in the city centre. A lone woman jogged by, buds in her ears, oblivious to her surroundings. Dwayne turned away with a shrug. She obviously believed herself perfectly safe — little did she know. All it needed was an opportunity and a person with a mind to take advantage of it. Nowhere was truly safe.

Dwayne slung his bag over his shoulder and keyed in the code. The electric gates slid silently open. He looked up and saw that the curtains at the bedroom window were closed. Did Bird not open them before he left his house for the final time?

The front door key in his hand, Dwayne mounted the steps. He unlocked it and pushed. A chain lock held him at bay.

He swore and crunched on the gravel around to the back door, where he was greeted by a cardboard box full of empty wine bottles. The back door led into the kitchen, which someone had painted green. They'd also set a couch against the end wall beneath a giant clock with Roman numerals. In the few months Dwayne had been away, his brother had made some changes. Dwayne wasn't sure if he approved.

A handbag sat open on the kitchen counter. Inside were a book, tissues, a make-up bag and a bar of Dairy milk chocolate. He ate two squares and rummaged through the bag, but it held no indication of who its owner might be. Had his other brother, Jason, been staying here? Had he had a woman here, before his brother's funeral? Dwayne grunted. The dead deserved respect, at least until the body was consigned to earth or ashes.

Bird's post-mortem had bought Dwayne time to finish up his business dealings in the Caribbean. Good old Bird. He'd always understood about making money, and what Dwayne had been setting up would make them a lot of money. Not wishing to alert the cops to his movements, Dwayne had kept his return quiet. The undertaker, thanks to a hefty cash payment, had readily agreed to hold off on the burial until he could be there. Everything had gone smoothly, and only now he was back in Dublin did the reality of Bird's death hit him. The sweet taste of the chocolate turned bitter on his tongue.

Above his head, a shower pump activated. The muted tones of a nineties ballad about heartbreak floated down from one of the rooms upstairs. Fucking bullshit. Who the hell was occupying his dead brother's house? Dwayne needed to see what state the business was in and take charge of the few who remained to work it. First, however, he needed to evict whichever cuckoo had made its nest in his brother's house.

Dwyane crossed the hall and marched into the living room. A jacket and blouse were thrown across the back of the couch. He tutted, picked them up and tossed them out into the hall. They landed in a heap beside the hall table, which held a vase of flowers — a "woman's touch."

He sat on a chair which gave him a view of the hall and waited. The shower was eventually turned off and it wasn't long before there were footsteps descending the stairs. Marion Aherne appeared, wearing a white fluffy dressing gown with the letters "BF" embroidered in gold on the pocket. She carried a wine glass and an empty bottle.

He watched Marion's face take on a look of confusion as she caught sight of the clothes on the floor. Shaking her head, she picked them up and carried them into the kitchen. He followed silently. Ahead, he heard the fridge door open, followed by the glug of liquid being poured.

When she turned, he was leaning against the doorframe. It was barely seven in the morning.

'What do you think you're doing, Marion?' Dwayne said calmly.

The glass slipped from her hand and smashed on the tiles at her feet. She stepped forward and made a grab for the counter, stumbling across the splinters of glass. Her blood pooled on the floor along with the white wine. She clutched the dressing gown to her chest with her free hand.

'You've made quite a mess there, Marion. I hope you're going to clean it up.'

'Jesus Christ, Dwayne. I never heard you come in.'

'So I see.'

Marion raised the injured foot. 'Can you help me here, Dwayne, please?'

'No.'

He remained leaning against the doorframe, watching her hop to the kitchen drawers and grab a couple of clean tea towels. From there, she hopped to the couch in the living room, dropped down beside Dwayne's bag and began to pick splinters of glass out of her foot. Her blood was deep crimson against the white of Bird's dressing gown.

'You didn't answer my question.'

'What question, Dwayne?'

'What are you doing here?'

'I live here now.' Marion dabbed at her foot with a towel.

'No, you don't.' He scratched his beard. Bird had never said anything of the sort to him.

She winced. 'Oh yes, I do. We moved in together.'

Her dressing gown fell open, revealing a lacy nightdress. Dwayne stared for a moment, then looked away. 'When?'

'When what?'

'Did you and Bird move in together?'

'As you know, it's been on and off for a number of years, but I officially changed my postal address about seven or eight weeks ago.'

'Hmm. Really.'

She narrowed her eyes. 'Yes, really.'

'I don't believe you.'

'Well, it's true. I swear on my son's life.'

Dwayne let out a sinister laugh. 'Well, I've no way of checking, do I, now that Bird is dead.'

Her bottom lip quivered. 'Don't be cruel, Dwayne.'

'I'm just being realistic.'

'As realistic as having everything delayed until you got back?'

'There was business to be done, Marion.' He swept his hand around the room. 'How do you think all this gets paid for? Not by lying on your back for a dead man.'

She stared at him, her mouth open.

'That is what's cruel, Marion.'

'Stop saying that word, Dwayne, please.'

'What word? Dead?'

She nodded, tears wetting her chest, her lap.

'I can say whatever I want. He was my brother, my blood. What was he to you?'

'He was the love of my life,' she sobbed.

'Who wouldn't love a fat wallet and a nice house?'

'I'd have done anything for him.'

'Then get the fuck out of his house.'

'Look, it was overdue anyway, we'd been together for years.'

Dwayne shrugged. 'So what. You've no right to be here now.'

'Of course I do. I gave that man the best years of my life. I don't have any children with him, because he kept telling me to wait until he was ready. Well, I waited, and now he is dead, so I deserve some kind of compensation for the years I wasted.' She covered her face with her hands and wept.

'Your choice. You chose to stay with him. More fool you.'

She looked up at him. 'I am nobody's fool, Dwayne Flynn, and don't you come back to Dublin thinking you know it all. If I'd married him, we'd be related now.'

Dwayne gave her a tight smile. How, in the months he'd been away, had the likes of Marion Aherne grown balls enough to even think about speaking to him like this? 'Really? Still not blood relations, though. Anyway, he'd never have married you.'

'He was going to ask me, I know he was.' Marion choked back a sob. 'I've asked you, now I'm begging you, Dwayne. Don't be cruel.'

'Ah, Marion, what are you talking about? You have your son.'

'You know full well that Brendan is an adult now and has his own life. You can't do this to me, Dwyane, not now, just before Bird's funeral. I am heartbroken.'

'I can. And I'm heartbroken, too.'

'Really? You have a funny way of showing it, being awful to the woman your brother loved. Please be reasonable.'

'Loved? Really?'

'Yes, really.'

He sighed. Hysterical women were hard to reason with. 'As next of kin, the property belongs to me now, and I don't want you in it.'

'Maybe it was willed to me.' She screwed up her red, blotched face and glared defiantly at him.

His jaw tightened. Christ, he hadn't thought of that. He would have to make tracks to the solicitor pretty damn quick. Dwayne just hoped his brother hadn't been stupid enough to sign the house over to Marion before he died.

'I doubt it.' He paused. His mouth was dry, but he wasn't going to the tap to get water. Never show weakness. Their father had beaten that into them. This needed to be sorted. With an effort, he eased the tension in his jaw.

'I seem to remember you swore on your son's life earlier.'

'What do you mean?'

'His life. What I mean is, what is it worth to you? Is it worth fighting me on this?'

'Dwayne, don't—'

'Get someone to collect you and your stuff. I want you out, today.'

'But my foot's pumping blood. It might need stitches. I'm in no fit state to pack up and move.'

'Not my problem. I didn't drop the glass, did I?'

'No, but you sneaked in here like a cat burglar and scared me. You made me jump and caused me to drop it.'

'Exactly. You dropped it, not me. And you wouldn't have been scared if you'd been in your own house, would you?'

'This is my home, Dwayne.'

'Don't make yourself look any more pathetic than you already are by begging.'

'Just give me until after the funeral. I'll be packed up and gone by the following Monday.'

Dwayne shook his head. 'That's too long.'

'It's a traumatic time for me. If I'm to uproot and move, it would only add to my trauma.'

11

'What's in it for me?' he said.

She sniffed, then wiped her nose with the sleeve of the dressing gown. 'I can tell you what Bird was last working on.'

'How do you know I don't know that anyway?'

'Fine. If you know where over seventy kilos of pure cocaine are being stashed, then you don't need me to tell you.'

'What are you talking about?' Dwayne did a rapid calculation. Seventy kilos were worth over five million euro.

'Before he died, Ged Lewis brought it down from the north. All you have to do is check your contacts to confirm that.'

'Go on.'

'Hazel Brady's niece, Kym, she's living with Ian Gallagher.'

He took a breath to calm his excitement. 'So what's that got to do with it?'

'He drives — rather, drove — for Ged Lewis. It was him given the job to bring the consignment from the north.'

'How do you know this?'

'Kym was the only one of the family that bothered to visit Hazel after she had Ged's child. She told Hazel that Ian was doing a big delivery job that was paying out a nice few quid. They'd planned to emigrate with it, set up somewhere else.'

His excitement over the unexpected windfall faded. 'So this Ian isn't even around now, and without him, there's no information, is there?'

'That's the thing. He never got paid after Ged died.'

We're still on a winner here. 'Where do they live?'

'An apartment near Spencer Dock.'

Dwayne whistled. 'No shortage of money there, so.'

'It's one of the Lewis Holdings apartments. It's not costing them a penny.'

Marion was staring at him.

'What?'

'So, will that information buy me a little more time in this house?'

Well, why not tell her what she wanted to hear? It wouldn't make much difference to him. 'Okay, I'll check your information out. Stay here until after the funeral. But then I want every trace of you gone from this house.'

'Right, okay. Thank you, Dwayne. I always knew you weren't as bad as you make yourself out to be.'

If Marion Aherne thought he was going soft, she was in for a shock. He took a breath. 'You'd want to get that foot looked at there. It looks nasty. You might need stitches.'

Marion side-eyed him. She pulled her phone from the dressing gown pocket and froze. Dwayne loomed above her. Then he reached for his bag.

'Relax,' he said and grinned.

She inched away from him as she dialled a number. He listened as she spoke to her son. Brendan, she called him. He remembered she was the only person to use the fella's full name. She was telling him to come and get her. She told him a story to explain the cut on her foot without mentioning Dwayne.

'What about Brendan?' she said when she'd ended the call.

'What about him?'

'Will you leave him out of this, please?'

'Of course, once you're gone. And he still works for us, so there will be plenty to keep him busy.' He held out his hand for the phone.

She turned pale.

'Just in case you try anything.'

'I won't. Er, would you mind leaving?' Marion said, her voice shaky. 'Please, Dwayne, while I get sorted?'

'Of course I will.'

And he did leave. But he wasn't gone for long.

CHAPTER 3

Danielle could just make out the blurred figure of a woman. Faces that loomed and receded, yellow and green shapes. She reached out, but the woman she thought she'd seen faded away.

'Can you hear me?' It was a man speaking.

Danielle tried to nod, but it made her head pound like someone had taken a hammer to it. There was more pain in her side, where she seemed to have swallowed a cinder-block.

For a moment, the blur cleared and she saw the woman from the shop, the one with the bleach, looking down at her. Danielle reached out again.

'Do you know this person?' It was the same male voice.

'No, I don't,' the woman said. 'I'd forgotten to pick up some bread. I knew there was something else I needed when I was still in the shop, but I couldn't think what it was. It wasn't until I was halfway home that I remembered. So I turned to go back to the shop and that's when I saw her, here, on the ground. I came in through that gate there.' She turned and pointed.

Danielle tried to open her mouth to speak, but a terrible pain seared through her jaw. She coughed, bringing up phlegm and vomit. The ground spun and she closed her eyes.

'Right, we'd better get you stabilised and moved.'

The earth stopped spinning and instead began to rock, as if she were on a boat. They were carrying her somewhere. For a brief moment, she opened her eyes and saw the underside of the archway to the apartment complex. She heard beeps, and then the voices faded and she surrendered to oblivion.

* * *

Danielle woke wearing unfamiliar clothes, in a bed that wasn't hers, to the sounds of machines bleeping and background chatter. Metal scraping against metal and the swish of someone pulling aside the curtain around her hospital bed. She brought her arm up to shield her eyes and a sharp pain sprung from her chest.

'How are you feeling?'

'Like I've been hit by a truck.' She started to ease herself upright, but lay back again with a grimace.

'Don't try to move until we've done a proper examination.'

'Jesus.'

'Do you remember your name?'

'Danielle. Danielle Lewis. My head feels like it's cracked open. What's happened to it?'

'You suffered a mild traumatic brain injury.'

'What?'

'A concussion.'

'Where's the baby?' Danielle asked, struggling to rise. The need to find the little one was stronger than the agonising pain.

'What baby?'

'The baby that was with me when I was attacked.'

Again, Danielle tried to haul herself upright. Again, a gentle hand guided her back down.

'You need to keep still. Are you saying your baby's been taken?'

'No.' Oh fuck, this was like speaking through mesh, and how would she explain? 'She's not my baby, but she was with me, and whoever attacked me took her.'

15

'So, you're the baby's guardian?'

'No.'

'Then who exactly are the baby's parents or guardians? Who were you minding her for?'

'Ged Lewis,' Danielle said. She took a breath. 'He's deceased and her mother is Hazel Brady, who is . . . not around at the moment.'

'Are you the baby's foster mother or guardian?'

'No. Well, yes, a type of guardian. I was looking after her in the absence of her parents.'

'Do social services know about this, er, arrangement?'

Shit. That was not a route she wanted to go down. 'Not yet.'

'What's the baby's name?' The doctor was writing on a notepad.

Oh hell. Only one name came to mind. 'Er, Sam.'

'As in Samantha, or just Sam?'

'Um, Samantha.'

'Date of birth?'

'First of August. She's nearly three months old.'

'Okay. There are guards here to speak with you about your assault, but I'd like to examine you first.'

'But the baby! She needs to be found.'

'I understand your concern, but I need to check you out. If you cooperate, I'll make it as quick as I can.'

Danielle nodded.

Every poke and prod ached, but she tolerated the pain just to get it over with.

'Hmm, you've a scar on your rib cage.'

'It's a gunshot wound.'

The doctor made no comment, merely continued to examine the scar.

'Isn't it in my files?'

'How long ago were you treated for it?'

No questions around how or why. Danielle was grateful for this doctor's tact — or was it indifference? 'Over ten years ago.'

'And was it in this hospital?'

'What hospital am I in?' Danielle asked.

'St Vincent's.'

'Oh no, I wasn't treated here.'

'Right. Well, I'll make a brief note of it for your file.'

As soon as the doctor was finished, two men in Garda uniforms appeared by the bed. Danielle didn't catch their names. All she could think about was the baby and the random name she'd given her in the heat of the moment. But of course, it wasn't random. It was the name of her son.

'We're here to take details of what happened to you this morning,' one of the guards was saying.

'What time is it now?' Danielle asked.

The one who'd spoken looked at his wristwatch. 'Nearly a quarter past two.'

Fuck. 'So I've been here all morning?'

'That's right.'

'It was not long after seven a.m. I had run out of a few things, so I went to the shop—'

'Danielle Lewis, is that your name?'

'Yes, and I was attacked, from behind. Anyway, I went to the shop and I'd just got back when — bang. Next thing I know, I'm in here.'

'Can you recall anything about it? The smallest detail can be relevant.'

The guard doing the talking had a thick ginger beard. The other one flipped open a notebook and glanced at his colleague, pen hovering. His blond hair looked bleached, reminding Danielle of the woman in the shop. Hadn't she been there?

'The bleach . . . the woman . . . what about her?'

Blondie flicked back through his notebook, found a page and showed it to Ginger-beard.

'A woman called Frances Neenan rang the three nines. She was headed back to the shop and found you lying just inside the gate. Luckily it had been propped open with a piece of timber, otherwise it would have been a problem getting to you.'

'Did she see them? Maybe she saw them running away.' She looked from one guard to the other.

'Frances says she saw you lying on the ground, but not what happened,' Ginger-beard said.

'Really, that's it?'

Blondie looked up from his notes. 'That's what she said.'

'And the baby?'

The two guards looked at each other, puzzled. 'What baby?' Ginger-beard said.

'The people who attacked me took the baby. Fucking hell, where is she?'

'You had your baby with you?'

Danielle sighed. 'Well, she's not mine. She is the daughter of a deceased relative, my uncle.'

'And her mother?'

Fuck. Here we go again. 'She's not around at the moment. The baby was staying with me for a while.'

'Age?'

'Thirty-four.'

'Not you, Danielle, the baby.'

'Nearly three months old. She was born on August first — the bank holiday.'

'What was she wearing?'

'Who?'

'The baby.' Ginger-beard was showing signs of impatience. *What the fuck?* 'A babygrow and a nappy.'

'Colour?'

'She's white.'

He raised his eyebrows.

'Oh, the clothes, you mean. Green, with white bunnies. The buggy was a City Select, easily folded, red and black, the kind you'd slot the maxi-cosi car seat into straight from the car. They also took what I'd bought. Four tins of formula, a multi-pack of wipes and nappies . . . there was also a packet of Tayto and a mint Aero bar. Oh, and she had a white fleece blanket over her, with little yellow ducks on the edge.'

'What are the parents' names?'

'Ged Lewis and Hazel Brady.'

Both guards stared at her. 'You mean Ged Lewis, married to Ann Lewis and father to the late Dean Lewis?' Ginger-beard said faintly.

'Yes, that's exactly who I mean.'

'And he fathered a child with this Hazel Brady?' Blondie asked. 'Did he and Ann divorce?'

Danielle and Garda Ginger-beard both looked at him.

'Oh, yeah,' Blondie said. 'Hazel and Ged . . . yeah. Forget I asked.'

Ginger-beard turned his attention back to Danielle. 'And you've guardianship?'

'No. Look, it's all unofficial. Stuff needed to be sorted out. Shit hit the fan in the past couple of weeks, as I'm sure you're well aware, or at least, should be anyway, if you're doing your jobs properly.'

'We sure are,' Blondie said. 'On all counts. And now the baby is missing?'

'Yes.'

'What's her name?'

'She doesn't have one.'

Ginger-beard made a face. 'Nearly three months old and she's no name?'

'I was going to call her Sam, but I don't know . . . Sam is my son's name, so maybe Samantha or something like that would be nice.'

'What would your son think of another Sam in the house?' Blondie said, with a tight smile.

'I don't really know, and I can't ask him. He's no longer with me.'

'Is he with his dad, so?'

'No, he's buried in Glasnevin Cemetery.'

'Oh.' Blondie's expression softened. 'I'm sorry.'

Danielle was sorry too. She hadn't been fair. 'Thank you. How long have you been a guard?'

'Five years.'

'All that shit was before your time, so. It's over a decade ago I lost him, after I was shot at while visiting my mother's grave.'

He nodded solemnly.

Ginger-beard coughed. 'Are you okay to carry on with the questions?'

'I am. I want to know where she is and if she's okay.'

Ginger-beard nodded to his colleague. Blondie hesitated for a second, then brought the radio attached to his stab vest to his lips. He walked away while he spoke into it.

'Control is checking PULSE,' Blondie said, regaining his seat.

'What was that?' Danielle said.

'Sorry, it means that the members in the control room are looking into any extra details on our system, called PULSE, that may help get us a few answers,' Blondie said.

'Well, why didn't you just say that?' Danielle put her hand to her forehead. 'Fucking headache. And my face. Jesus.'

'Are you okay to keep talking to us, Danielle?' Garda Ginger-beard asked.

'Yes, yes. The baby. We have to find the baby.'

Blondie's radio crackled. He walked away. Danielle strained to listen to what he was saying, but all she heard were his shoes squeaking and the murmur of his voice.

'Did you get a look at your attackers? Anything that may help identify them?' Ginger-beard asked.

'Hard to see from where my face was — planted in the ground.'

'Right.' He stood up.

'Wait,' Danielle said.

He paused. 'Go on.'

'Red sneakers. Adidas, I think. A woman's voice, but muffled. I didn't see the other person.'

Blondie returned and flipped the notebook open again.

'So you remember that there were two attackers,' Ginger-beard said.

'More than one, anyway. It could have been a gang, for all I could tell. Also, there's this.' She pulled the hospital gown open to show the officer the two small scorch marks just behind her ribs. 'I think I got tasered. It hurt like fuck. That's when they got the better of me. I tried to get up, and next thing there was this terrible pain in my side.'

'Can I take a snap of that?' Garda Ginger-beard asked.

'Go for it,' Danielle said.

'And your face?'

'How bad is my face?'

'Enough for us to tell that you met with quite a few punches, kicks, or both,' Ginger-beard said.

'Great,' Danielle said. No wonder it hurt so much to talk.

The guards held a whispered conversation. Blondie showed Ginger-beard something in his notebook. They exchanged a look, and both turned to face Danielle.

They regarded her in silence for a second — long enough to make her stomach churn.

'For fuck's sake, will you stop giving each other these looks and tell me what is happening,' Danielle said.

'A car called to the Brady residence — that is, the baby's maternal grandparents' house, and spoke with Frank and Alice,' Blondie said. 'They say Chloe Hazel Brady is currently with them and safe.'

'What? How? It wasn't them who attacked me, surely?'

'Tell us again how you came to have the baby with you?' Ginger-beard said.

'Hazel needed a sitter. I minded the baby for her while she went to her nephew's removal, and she never returned to pick her up.'

'Really? And did you report Hazel missing?' Ginger-beard said.

'No.' Danielle ached all over. 'I just thought Hazel had gone on a bender and would show up whenever. That was her style.'

'Did you try to contact her family, Danielle?'

How to explain it? 'Hazel was estranged from her family. They didn't like the idea of their daughter being Ged's bit on the side.' She glanced at the young Garda, who was obviously relishing every word of this juicy gossip about the Lewis family. 'They ended all contact with her when she got pregnant. Look, I've tried to speak to them several times, but they wanted nothing to do with the baby.' This was a lie, but what could she say? That she didn't want them to have the baby?

'The guard who called said they seemed happy enough to have her with them.'

'Maybe they're interested now because she comes with a trust fund that Ged set up for her after she was born. That would prompt some people to be very forgiving. God only knows what kind of conditions they have her in.'

'We will follow up with that, to check on her welfare,' Ginger-beard said officiously.

'Unless there is a risk to the child's safety, we have no grounds to remove her from her family home,' Blondie added.

'But she was with me. I was looking after her in my home.' Danielle's throat was parched. 'Can you at least let me know how she is?'

'Not unless her family allow us to. It would be up to her grandparents.'

'But if she's in danger — could you get her back for me then?'

'It would depend on the risk to her. After that, it would come down to who is next of kin and is entitled to custody of her. There are procedures that must be followed.'

'Even though they may have attacked me to get hold of her?'

'We will investigate all angles,' Blondie said.

'They have to be behind it.'

'We'll look into that,' Ginger-beard added.

'And how long is that going to take?'

'I can't say. We'll need proof, of course. But I assure you, we will personally call to Hazel's parents' address to check on the welfare of Chloe. I will contact you to let you know,' Ginger-beard said.

At least he was prepared to bend the rules a little. 'You will?'

He nodded.

'Thank you. Oh, I don't have my phone. They either took it or it got damaged in the assault.'

'Your address, then?'

'Okay.' Ginger-beard wrote it down in his notebook, an identical one to his colleague's.

'How long do you claim to have been looking after the baby?' Blondie asked.

'I'm not claiming anything. I *was* looking after her.' Anger made her face flare in pain.

'Right, so how long was that?'

'Since she was about a week old. It was the evening of Jake Brady's removal on eighth August, so what's that — ten weeks or so?'

'So just to recap, you're saying you've been minding a baby that isn't yours since she was one week old? She's what, your cousin?' Blondie sounded sceptical.

'Yes, so I'm her family too.'

'But you're not her *immediate* family,' he said.

How dare he? He knew nothing about her, or her family. He knew nothing about the love she'd poured into that baby. Danielle wanted to weep — but she wasn't going to give him the satisfaction.

'And her mother has been missing since she dropped her to you to look after about ten weeks ago, and you didn't report it to anyone?' Ginger-beard said.

Fuck. 'I . . . no. I collected the baby from Hazel's house. Wait a minute, should her own *immediate family* not have reported her missing, then?'

'You said yourself that she was estranged from them,' Blondie said.

'Yes. And now they have custody of a baby that they didn't give a shit about up until now. And I'm not sure I'd give them a self-service checkout to look after, never mind a baby. I remember her aunt Audrey. She worked in one of Ged's pubs and was never sober. And another thing. How was the car able to call to their house so fast?' Danielle asked.

'They were patrolling in the area,' Blondie said.

'See? They want to raise a baby in a place that needs constant Garda presence,' Danielle said.

'It was on a routine patrol. Nothing out of the ordinary,' Blondie said.

Ginger-beard frowned at him. 'Either way, you should have contacted a social worker at least.'

'So, let me get this right. Chloe, or whatever they've called her, is safe?'

'Yes.'

'And how did they say she got there?'

The guards looked at each other. 'They got a call to say she was being left nearby,' Blondie said.

'What?' Danielle wanted to leap from the bed and shake the information out of him.

He nodded. 'Well, in the buggy. They didn't see who left her there.'

'The phone number, maybe you could trace that and get to the bottom of who attacked me?'

'Private number, so they told the officer,' Blondie said.

'Great,' Danielle said.

'They also said they were just happy she was back. They weren't interested in how she got there, just that she was home. And they've submitted an official missing person's report for Chloe's mother, Hazel. It sounds like you were the last person to have seen her.'

'I doubt that. She's probably off getting pissed somewhere.'

'Possibly.'

'Wait. I was attacked and she was kidnapped, and the Bradys aren't interested in how she got there?'

'I don't think the officer who called to the address told them about the circumstances,' Blondie said, with a glance at Ginger-beard.

24

'Jesus Christ.'

'It's never a good idea to reveal too much about an investigation,' Ginger-beard explained. 'Especially in the early stages when we're dealing with potential witnesses.'

'Well, can you get back to them and delve a little deeper?' Danielle pressed her hand to her forehead and closed her eyes for a second.

'You've clearly been assaulted and suffered a concussion—'

'What did the witness say, the one who rang it in, the woman with the bleach?'

'That she found you barely conscious. She said nothing about any baby,' Ginger-beard said.

'Jesus. The baby had been with me for the past ten weeks. The Bradys would hardly even know what she looks like at this stage.'

'You have a photo of her?' Ginger-beard asked.

'Yes — in my phone. I took a selfie with her this morning, and I have plenty of others.'

'Didn't you say your phone is missing?' he said.

Danielle sighed. 'The photos should be backed up. Once I get a new phone, I should be able to access them again. Then you can make sure that the baby they have is really her. Anyway, what about the fact that I've been caring for her since she was a week old? Shouldn't that count for something? She can't be just whipped away from me all at once, like she was this morning.' Danielle's face had begun to burn.

'Look, Miss Lewis . . .' Ginger-beard began.

'Fuck off with your formalities. Just give me answers, would you?'

'Danielle, the point is you don't have legal custody of her. Whether she was with you is neither here nor there. Look, you've received a nasty head injury, on top of being present at a pretty horrific and shocking incident at a loved one's funeral recently—'

'Just get the fuck away from me. Get out.' The words caught in her dry throat. She began to choke. The officers took a step back.

She heard someone say, 'That's enough.'

The pain ripped through her side, her face, her body. Tears ran down her cheeks. It was all going to shit, and she had no one to turn to.

CHAPTER 4

Dwayne had learned at a young age that if you acted like you belonged in a place, people believed that you did. He had also learned that it was child's play to break into that place.

Apartments were the best. There was always someone rushing out of the main door without giving a shit that they'd left it unlocked. He waited outside the block of apartments off Spencer Dock until one of those very people hustled from the building pulling a suitcase. Probably off to the airport, guessed Dwayne, giving a 'Cheers,' as he passed him on his way in.

The third-floor corridor was empty. Dwayne pulled on gloves and made his way to flat five. The lock gave easily as Dwayne picked his way in.

Removing a handgun, he set his bag down just inside the front door and followed the sound of snoring to the bedroom. The door stood ajar, and Dwayne eased in. He pushed the clothes from the bed and sat on a chair to wait, the handgun across his knees. The naked man and woman slept on, oblivious to his presence.

It was the woman who stirred first. She had been lying on her stomach and reached out for the glass of water on the bedside locker without noticing the man in the chair.

Only when she turned slightly to put it back did she catch sight of Dwayne. The glass landed soundlessly on the carpet. Only when she'd covered herself with the bedclothes did she scream, waking her companion, who shot upright.

'Tell her to shut up, would you?' Dwayne said evenly.

'Shh, Kym, please. It's all right.'

'There's nothing all right about some guy with a gun in his hand, staring at the two of us naked. I hardly recognised you with the beard.'

'What did Ian say your name was — Kym? Yeah, just do what your man told you to do.'

'What are you doing here, Dwayne?' Ian asked.

'Looking for answers, Ian.'

'How would I have answers for you?'

'You work for the Lewis family — or what's left of them — don't you?'

'Well, yes.' He glanced at the woman beside him who had her eyes fixed on the gun, which was now pointing straight at Ian. She needn't have worried — Dwayne was perfectly conscious that if he used it in one of these apartments, the guards would be here within minutes.

Dwayne glanced towards the sliding door to the balcony. It was open a couple of inches. Dwayne went over to it and thrust his head outside, glancing left and right past the table and its empty bottles of cider. One other apartment still had its lights on, but the others were in darkness. No witnesses here. He closed the door and stood with his back to them.

Ian rubbed his eyes. 'Will you let me put some clothes on, Dwayne?'

'What do you need clothes for, Ian? It's stupid o'clock and we're not heading out anywhere. This conversation will be over as soon as you tell me what I want to hear. So just keep your balls covered and you'll be fine. It's been a long day, and I don't want the sight of them keeping me awake when I go to my bed.'

'Okay. What do you want from me?'

'You did a little job for Ged Lewis at the beginning of August, if you remember. You collected something from up north that may not have reached its final destination. Is any of that ringing a bell with you?'

'I'm not sure what to say, Dwayne.'

Dwayne sighed patiently, stepped forward out of the light and pointed the gun towards Ian. 'A pillow across your face would be enough to soundproof a bullet. Just the one would be enough . . . And another one for her.' He pointed the gun at Kym, who whimpered.

'Don't worry, darling, you won't feel a thing.' He clicked his fingers. 'Just like that. Lights out.'

Tears began to stream down her face. She turned to Ian. 'What's going on, Ian? Tell the man what he needs to know, for fuck's sake.'

'Good girl, Kym, you tell him. I can see who's the boss in this relationship.' Dwayne smiled, keeping the gun aimed at Kym.

'All right, all right. Yes, I know what you're talking about.'

Dwayne lowered the gun. 'There. That wasn't so hard now, was it?'

Ian said nothing.

'I have reason to believe that the drugs in that van never made it onto the street,' continued Dwayne.

'I know nothing about that,' Ian said.

'Well, I do, because it was over seventy kilos. That's five million euros' worth. If that much coke had made it onto the street, there wouldn't be the shortage there is now. And given the shortage, it's working out that much more valuable. Supply and demand, Ian.'

'I get you. Yeah, I remember it. I was told by Ritchie Delaney that Ged wanted me to collect a van full of linens and tableware that had some precious cargo in with it.'

'Go on,' Dwayne said.

'I collected it at Belfast Port and drove it to Dublin.'

'And?'

'That's it. What else do you want to know?'

'What I want to know is where the fuck is it now?'

'Jesus, Dwayne, that was over two months ago. Mid-August, I think.'

Dwayne fingered the gun. 'Do your best to remember.'

'Right, look, I swapped vans with Ritchie Delaney near Coolock Garda Station.'

Dwayne burst out laughing. Kym jumped. 'You swapped a van loaded to the hilt with drugs near a fucking Garda station? Are you serious?'

'Yeah. Doing a thing in plain sight can often be the best way to get away with it.'

'Jesus, Ian, that's clever. And where are the contents of the van now?'

'I don't know where he brought it after swapping with me. I never got that information.'

'Well, get the information.'

'But Ritchie's dead. How am I supposed to get it?'

'Figure it out.'

'Yeah, but how?'

Dwayne put the gun in his pocket and ran his fingers through his hair. After a moment's thought, he left the bedroom, retrieving a different weapon from his bag. He scratched his beard as he took a breath, then returned.

Neither of them had budged from the bed. Sitting ducks. He moved towards Ian and grabbed his left wrist, forcing his hand down onto the locker at the side of the bed. The knife had a leather handle and a blade the length of the handle.

Dwayne held the knife over the back of Ian's hand. 'You have one more chance to tell me.'

'I've no idea. I swear, I don't—'

The knife descended, pinning Ian's hand to the locker. Ian roared. Kym screamed, backed out of the bed and scurried towards the balcony door. Ian's body bucked.

Dwayne stepped back, leaving the knife embedded in Ian's hand. He looked down at his handiwork and sighed. It was going to be difficult to pull it out without doing serious damage. No point letting Ian bleed out. *Shit.* These kinds of violent reactions always cost him. Fuck it, he'd have to leave it where it was and get himself another one.

'I don't like those kinds of answers, Ian. A person needs to be straight when they talk to me. I think you do know how to come by that information. If you don't, then you have the means to find out. The Lewis family have property all over the place. So which one was the van brought to?'

'I . . . I can find out. Fuuuuk. Take it out, Dwayne, please. Jesus.'

'Ah. Well, we have a bit of a problem there. If I pull that knife out, you'll bleed like a stuck pig. You'd be better pulling the knife from the locker and leaving the blade in your hand. So. How can you find out?'

'There are a few . . . storage yards and sheds Ged used . . . fuck.'

'You're saying it could still be parked in one of them?'

'Yeah.'

'A ball of drugs just parked in a shed somewhere, unsold. Christ, that is a sin.' Dwayne shook his head. 'Right, I'll be off. You have forty-eight hours to get the info on the van to Bosco Ryan.'

'How?'

Dwayne took a small mobile phone from his pocket and tossed it onto the bed. 'There. You can get him on that. There's just one number there.'

'But—'

'But what? What will happen if you don't get it within forty-eight hours? Is that what you want to ask me, Ian? Is it?'

With a groan of pain, Ian nodded.

'Here's how it will go. Either me or someone acting for me will come back here when you're both sound asleep. They'll wake Kym here, or whoever is beside you, and they'll cut you into little pieces while she watches. Then they'll decide what to do with her. Because if you can't get the information, you are of no use to me. Is that clear?'

'Yeah . . . yeah, Dwayne. It is.'

Dwayne turned to face Kym. 'If I were you, love, I'd be doing what I could to help my man get what I asked him for.'

Kym sat on the floor, knees raised and her arms around them, gazing into nothing.

'Oh, and I'd get that cut seen to, Ian. It looks a bit nasty. And another thing, if you tell anyone I was here or you report what happened, you are both dead.'

He stared at Kym until she gave a slight nod, still without looking at him.

'Oh, and Ian. I don't need the knife back. You can keep it.'

Dwayne picked up his bag and left, closing the door quietly behind him.

CHAPTER 5

Though she had given up for the sake of the baby, Danielle woke longing for a cigarette. One of the nurses had given her a *Frankie Says Relax* T-shirt and a pair of grey tracksuit bottoms that were at least two sizes too big, from who-the-fuck-knows where. She was afraid to ask. The guards had taken her clothes as evidence, since the extent of her injuries was sufficient to warrant an investigation. They said they'd contact her later for her statement. One of the guards had given her a card with his name and contact details. Garda Ginger-beard turned out to be Garda Cameron Cashman. She stuffed the card into the tracksuit pocket.

A lady at Patients' Services phoned for a taxi for her. It pulled up in minutes, no doubt delighted to have a fare on a quiet morning. Thankfully, she still had her bank card — retrieved before it was consumed by an evidence bag — and could pay the fare.

'My machine's broken, so it's cash only, love.'

'Okay,' Danielle said. The driver would have to wait until she got to her destination to get paid, but she wasn't telling him that until he'd got her safely there.

Danielle eased herself painfully into the back seat. The car had a pine fragrance tree hanging from the mirror, a scent she'd always disliked. Her face, still bruised and swollen, had the driver glancing at her in the rear-view mirror. She was tempted to tell him to fuck off but was unable to summon the energy. They'd kept her in for the night for more tests and observation, and had sent her home with mild painkillers instead of the drugs she really wanted. A few phone calls to the right people would have got her what she needed, but she didn't have any numbers.

At last, they were pulling up at the apartments. 'If it's cash you're taking, I only have my card on me, so you'll have to hold on while I get it for you.'

He didn't respond, so she began to ease herself from the taxi.

There were three unfamiliar cars parked in various spots outside the main entrance. The other apartments in the complex remained unoccupied. Ged had claimed it was safer that way. He had a point. You never know what kind of randomer you'd bump into in an apartment block.

The code for her flat wouldn't work. As she tried, the main door opened and a man appeared.

'Hello?'

The man looked in her direction for a moment. Then he shook his head and continued to one of the cars.

'What's going on?'

The man closed the boot and began to shrug on a jacket, which had three large letters across the back: CAB.

Jesus Christ. What the hell?

She knew what those letters stood for and what they signified. Every organised criminal gang dreaded a visit from the Criminal Assets Bureau.

With her hands around the cold metal bars of the closed gate, she shouted to him again, 'Hey, this is my place. What the fuck are you doing? What about notice? You've no right to be here.'

He paused.

'Hey, excuse me, I'm talking to you. My stuff is in there.'

He turned and began to walk towards her.

Don't piss him off. Yet. 'About time,' she muttered, though she knew she shouldn't. He didn't seem to have heard her.

He approached the gate and stared through it at her. She took a breath, telling herself to think before she spoke. 'Look, this is my place and all my things are in there. I'm not able to get in. If you could please explain what's going on, I'd appreciate it.'

'And your name is?'

'Danielle Lewis.'

He regarded her through narrowed eyes. 'And you say this is where you've been living?' He looked beyond her for a moment.

'Yes. I need to pay my taxi fare. My phone was stolen or destroyed, and I have cash in there.'

'What happened to you?'

In her panic at finding herself locked out, she'd forgotten about her injuries. 'Oh, this.' She pointed to her face. 'I was assaulted here yesterday morning as I came back from the shop. I'd only popped out for a few minutes. I made a report. Here . . .' She rummaged in her pocket and took out the card. 'This was given to me by your colleague who came to the hospital. I've just got back from there, and now I find . . . this. Someone is setting me up, playing a cruel joke.' She was struggling not to cry.

'Do you have a bank card, or was that taken too?'

'What? No, I mean, yes, I do, it wasn't taken.'

'The taxi driver should be able to take the payment that way.'

'His machine is broken.'

'Is it now?'

'It is.'

'Okay.' He looked beyond her towards the taxi and back to her. 'First off, you're not getting in, so you can get the details of the taxi driver and pay him at a later date.'

'What? But should I not have been given notice? I mean, the Criminal Assets Bureau can't just rock up and seize my stuff without some kind of warrant, surely? I mean, this is my home. There's no criminal activity going on here. It's all above board.'

'You think it is, do you?'

'Is what?'

'Above board.'

Did she, really? Ged would never have left her in such a vulnerable position, would he?

While she turned over possible answers that wouldn't implicate her in anything, a noise drew her attention. It was that empty beer bottle again, rattling across the footpath, as if it was taunting her. How had the bin men not seen it? Would someone not have picked it up by now?

Danielle heard a sigh. The CAB officer was becoming impatient.

'Yes, everything I own is legit. And I live here. It's my home. Currently.'

'You're not the owner, though.'

'But Ged told me this place is mine. You could have at least waited until his body was cold. He was only buried a month ago. Jesus.'

'He's not the registered owner.'

'Then I am?'

'Only if you are Ann Lewis. But you're not, are you?'

'What?'

'She has been the owner for a number of years. There is some doubt about the source of the money she bought it with. That's all I'm saying.'

Fuck. Ann knew. That sneaky bitch knew this was coming and had kept it to herself. There was no way Ged would have said it was Danielle's home if he hadn't intended it to be. Maybe she'd misinterpreted his words. She'd just landed back in Dublin and was still in shock after the way she'd been manhandled when she was brought here.

The CAB officer was turning to go.

'Wait.'

'I've already said too much.'

'So, I can't get a thing from there. My money, my passport, nothing?'

'Not while we are compiling the inventory of items on the premises.'

'And how long will that take?'

He shrugged.

'Sorry. But you must understand, this is very stressful for me.'

'Okay, I understand. But I can't say. Each job takes as long as it needs to take.'

'Ah, shit. Are you serious?'

'Whatever you can identify as your property, you can get back, so long as you can prove it is yours and not obtained illegally.'

'Right. Who do I contact?'

The officer glanced behind him. 'Gavin Kelly was a colleague of mine, so the contact you already have will sort you out.'

'Thank you.'

She knew exactly who he meant, and it wasn't Gingerbeard. But with her phone gone, she had no contact details and she couldn't exactly rock up to a Garda station and ask to speak to Detective Garda Saoirse Kelly. Besides, she wasn't even sure which Garda station Saoirse was working out of now.

While she considered her predicament, the officer walked away.

She sighed. With not a penny in her pocket, she'd have to owe the fare. So, as fast as her injuries would allow, she returned to the taxi. 'I don't know what the hell is going on in there, but I've been told I can't get in to fetch my money. Give me your details and I'll get payment to you. That's what the officer instructed me to do. So, it won't be an offence not to pay you, because it's beyond my control.'

'You have it all worked out, Danielle. You think you can buy your way out of anything, don't you?'

'What, no, I . . . How do you know my first name?' She looked closer at him. He looked vaguely familiar, but she had no idea where from.

'Oh, how the mighty have fallen.'

'Look, who are you?'

'It looks like it really isn't your day, is it?'

She glanced at the dashboard. The place where his identification should have been displayed was empty.

'Listen, don't worry about the fare,' he said. 'Don't worry about your apartment and most of all, don't worry about the baby. She is where she is meant to be. Just like you.'

'What the fuck?'

'The minute I saw your surname come up as needing a taxi, I made sure I was the one who picked you up. I hadn't seen you in years.'

'But we've never met.'

'We did, a few years ago. I knew your mother.'

'How? When? I don't remember you.'

'A long time ago, Danielle. Better times.'

She stared at him. 'Tell me more.'

'Not now, Danielle. There's too much going on.'

'If you knew my mother, you must have known Ged, too.'

He squeezed the steering wheel and stared straight ahead of him. 'When my daughter hooked up with Ged, she allowed him to destroy her life, strip away any dignity that she may have had.'

'Wait. You're Hazel's dad?'

'Yes. Frank Brady.'

'Frank, your daughter loved Ged and hoped he'd leave Ann for her. He set her up in a nice place where she could have lived pretty comfortably.'

'She was no homewrecker. He took advantage of her. '

Danielle couldn't imagine anyone taking advantage of Hazel Brady, who seemed to know exactly what she was doing when she hooked up with Ged.

'She had brains, could have been something. But he had her working like a skivvy in one of his bars.'

'I don't know what she told you, but she was managing a lucrative business for Ged.'

'Do you think I'm stupid?'

'No, of course not.'

She could see the pulse at his temple. 'You'll not muddy her name.'

'I'm not trying to.'

'She was running a knocking shop, for Christ's sake. Of course it was lucrative. Hazel wasn't brought up that way.'

There was no point in arguing with him. 'How is, er, Chloe?'

'She's with family now, so she's fine.'

'I'm her family, too.'

At least he didn't disagree. He didn't respond to that at all.

'You could have spoken to me, you know, about Chloe. We could have worked something out. I tried to get in touch, but no one answered me.'

He turned to face her. 'Oh? How?'

'I contacted your sister-in-law, Hazel's aunt Audrey.'

'She never said. Are you sure?'

'Yes. I rang her and she said not to bother. As far as you're concerned, the baby is now a Lewis, so she's our responsibility.'

He shook his head. 'Doesn't make sense to me. Why would she not say that she'd spoken to you?'

'Well, maybe you should ask Audrey yourself.'

'Don't tell me what to do when it comes to my family. You've interfered enough.'

'Sorry, I didn't mean . . .'

'Was she sober?'

'I was sure she was.'

'Hmm.'

'I understand that Chloe is where she belongs, with her family. But I did care for her. You'll need to know her little quirks and habits. She might only be little, but already her sweet personality is shining through.'

'I want nothing from you, do you understand?' he said, through gritted teeth. 'Any getting to know that baby will be done our way.' He put the car into gear and indicated to pull out.

'Wait. Look, there was no need to set the heavies on me, beat me up. I was terrified something had happened to her — Chloe.'

He took the car out of gear again. 'What do you mean, set the heavies on you?'

'I was attacked. Chloe was taken from me during the attack. That's why I ended up in hospital. Are you saying you didn't know anything about this?' She pointed to her face.

'No.'

'And these are only the injuries you can see. I got tasered, too. The woman who found me thought I was dead.'

His expression softened briefly. 'I knew nothing of this.'

'And now that you do?'

He shook his head. 'Whatever I think of you, Danielle, you're a Lewis, and your family has always meant trouble. Chloe is safer with us, where she can be raised in a proper family.'

'I still didn't deserve this treatment.'

'No, you didn't, but that was nothing to do with me.'

'Can I do anything to persuade you to keep me in Chloe's life?'

'Well, you can give me a straight answer to this question — do you know where Hazel is?'

Danielle swallowed. 'No, I don't know where she is.' That, at least, was true.

'Do you know if she has come to any harm?'

'Look, Frank, she took drugs—'

'Stop.' He raised his hands. 'I've heard enough. Stay away from us and from Chloe. We want nothing to do with you.'

'I'm still related to her. Please, let me help with her care.'

'As far as she's concerned, you don't exist. I mean it, Danielle, stay the hell away.'

The window slid shut, the engine revved, and Frank Brady drove away.

Danielle stood at the kerbside, wearing a stranger's clothes, without a clue as to where to go or what she should do.

CHAPTER 6

It was midnight before Dwayne finally arrived at Jason's apartment, having stopped en route to buy a pizza. Dwayne crashed at his brother's, rather than return to his apartment, where Marion would still be in residence. He managed a couple of hours' sleep before making his way on foot from Phibsborough to Capel Street. The short walk gave him space to think, time to breathe. He wasn't yet ready to share the information or his plan with Jason. First he needed to assess how to use his younger brother to his best advantage. He did tell him that they were burying Bird sooner than planned, as his body had been lying in the mortuary for long enough. Jason didn't object. It would have made no difference if he had.

Hunger drew him towards the Centra shop on Capel Street in Dublin's city centre after a stop at the barbers for a much-needed trim. He was ready to part ways with the beard. He sat by a window with a view onto the street, with its multi-coloured picket fences, the tattoo studio beyond, next to the shop selling dartboards and pool cues. He sipped his tea, watching the pedestrians pass by, some in a hurry, others ambling, staring at their phones. Cyclists raced by, making the most of the absence of traffic. Unlike the passers-by, Dwayne had nowhere in particular to be, though he had plenty of business to take care of.

On his way to Capel Street, Dwayne received a photo of Lola from Bosco, who always looked after her while he was away. He smiled down at his screen. She looked lovely. She'd been by his side for the past two years, and he couldn't wait to see her again. Her puppies would be worth a fortune. He really should get her with a male, but somehow, none he'd seen so far seemed suitable.

The waitress brought his crispy chicken sandwich to him. He was chewing on his second bite when Brenno Aherne went past the window. He came in and made his way slowly over to where Dwayne sat.

'You were looking to talk to me, Dwayne?'

Taking his time, Dwayne continued to work his way through the sandwich, washing it down with a mouthful of tea. Brenno remained standing by the table until Dwayne nodded to the seat opposite him.

'You're late.'

'When I got your text, I was at home. Made it in twenty minutes on the motorbike.'

'You're still late.'

'I swear I got here as fast as I could. Ma cut her foot on some glass yesterday morning. It was still bad today, so I had to take her to the doctors to get patched up—'

'Not my problem.'

'Yeah, right, of course. Look, sorry for being late. I meant no disrespect, Dwayne. Sorry for your loss and all that, too.'

'Yeah, right. Tell me something.' He finished off his sandwich, wiped his mouth with the tissue, and brushed crumbs off his hands. 'You're still working for us?'

'Of course, Dwayne. I wasn't sure where I stood after, you know, Bird. But, yeah, I'm up for whatever you need.'

'Good to hear. I have a job for you later.'

'Okay,' Brenno answered. 'What is it?'

Dwayne said nothing.

Brenno looked up, beyond Dwayne, and his face turned pale.

'You alright there, Brenno? You look a bit worried.'

'Nah, I'm the finest. Don't worry about me.'

'I'm not worried, but you looked like you were about to faint. I can't have you going all stupid on me in front of people. Fuck that, I have a reputation to maintain.'

'Yeah, I'm grand.'

Bosco Ryan dragged over a seat from the next table and sat astride it between Brenno and Dwayne. Brenno shifted back on his seat. Bosco glanced at him briefly, then turned his attention to Dwayne.

'Hello, boss,' Bosco said.

'Meet your new right hand there, Bosco,' Dwayne said. 'You already know each other.'

'We sure do,' Bosco said.

'Fine, so no foreplay needed here, just straight in, no kissing. Brenno, you do everything Bosco tells you to do. No questions. You are either working with us or you don't exist. Is that clear?'

'Y . . . yes, Dwayne, it is. Crystal clear.'

'Good.' Dwayne looked out through the window. None of the passers-by paid the slightest attention to their little meeting, and he didn't see any cops. 'Now, next bit of business. What about that buddy of yours, Brenno?'

'Which one, Dwayne?'

'That Anto fella, Doyle.'

'What about him?'

'He owes us a few hundred thousand euro.'

'I thought that was gone—'

'Why? Because Bird is gone?'

Brenno's knee began to jerk. He looked from Bosco to Dwayne. 'Well, yeah.'

Bosco laughed.

'It doesn't work like that, Brenno. The debt is still owed,' Dwayne said. 'I want to know where he is.'

Brenno shook his head. 'I haven't seen him.'

'When did you last see him? Was it days? Weeks? Come on, when?' Bosco asked.

'Few days,' Brenno answered, avoiding Bosco's gaze.

'Ring him and tell him you want to meet,' Dwayne ordered.

'What? Now? As in this minute?'

'Am I speaking to you in a language you have difficulty understanding?'

A red flush crept up Brenno's neck. 'No, Dwayne, no, not at all. I just want to be clear about what you want me to do.'

'Want me to write it down for you? Get your phone out now, ring Anto, and tell him to meet you.'

His knee twitching at a furious rate, Brenno took his phone from his pocket and made the call. Anto answered immediately.

'Hey, lad, I'm here with—' he cleared his throat and hunched forward, '—Dwayne Flynn.'

Dwayne could just make out Anto saying, 'Yeah, go on.'

'We're to meet up, you and me.'

'Where?' Anto asked.

Brenno looked at Dwayne.

'Go to Temple Place in Ranelagh, park in the supermarket car park, and I'll meet you there.'

His face creased in confusion, Brenno repeated the instructions, adding, 'He has a job for us.'

'In an hour,' said Dwayne.

'Yeah, got that,' Anto said. 'Just the two of us?'

Hearing Anto's question, Dwayne said, 'Four. Me and Bosco will be there, too. Bring your car, Anto.'

'Yeah, sure thing. I'll be there. Supermarket car park, Ranelagh, an hour.'

Dwayne nodded and Brenno ended the call.

'Am I going with you two, or . . . ?'

'You head away. Take your motorbike or hop in with Anto, I don't care. Just be there.'

'Course, yeah, Dwayne.'

'Right, fuck off then, and don't be late.'

Brenno stood, his chair scraping. 'Yeah, Dwayne, I won't. See you then.'

Dwayne and Bosco watched Brenno walk past the window and out of sight.

'Can we trust him, Dwayne?'

'In about an hour, we'll find out exactly how trustworthy he is.'

'Yeah, whatever you think. But won't the likes of those lads stand out a bit in an upmarket suburb like Ranelagh? What's the plan you got going there?'

'The plan, Bosco, is a surprise eviction; a test, if you like. We'll see how he carries it out.'

'Right. And he doesn't know?'

'All Brenno needs to know is that I am the boss.'

'Yes, Dwayne, we all know you are the boss.'

'That I am, Bosco. That I am.'

CHAPTER 7

Danielle waited at the gate to the apartment like a stray kitten with nowhere to go. The CAB detective was clearly not going to return. The bins that had been emptied that morning were scattered haphazardly along the footpath, one open, another's lid banging in the breeze. At least they gave her something to lean on as she made her way forward, with no idea where she was heading. She was weak and hungry, having eaten little of the hospital breakfast. Since Ged's funeral, she'd cut everyone off, even Linda, who, to Danielle's surprise, had proved to be a valuable ally. It seemed the safest thing to do, since she no longer trusted her judgement of people.

A dark car drove towards her. The row of lights above the front windscreen showed it to be an unmarked squad car. Off to join their compatriots in the search through her knicker drawer, no doubt. Bastards. She kept her eyes on the ground. The car reached the end of the road, turned and drew up beside her. What the hell did they want now? *Christ.* She was sick of Gardaí who asked questions while providing her with little or no help.

'Get in.'

Danielle leaned on one of the bins, ready to tell them to piss off. She couldn't see the driver, whose voice sounded familiar.

Leaving the engine running, the driver hopped out, ran to the rear and opened the door.

'Jesus. I didn't think I'd ever see you again.'

Was Saoirse Kelly her friend in need? At this stage, Danielle wasn't sure if she could even trust Saoirse, despite the CAB officer's words.

'I got a call that you were in a bit of a shit situation,' Saoirse said.

'That's one way of putting it.'

'Get in the back seat there and we'll talk.'

'The back seat of a squad car? Now there's an invitation I can't refuse.'

With a glance at her surroundings, Saoirse pushed her in and slammed the door.

'Jesus. Go easy, would you?' Danielle said. 'My whole body is in bits.'

'Sorry. Force of habit. I just wanted you in quickly, so we can get out of here.'

'Sounds like you're kidnapping or arresting me.'

'I can assure you I'm doing neither.'

As she drove away, Saoirse looked at Danielle in the rear-view mirror. 'Frankie says relax, eh?'

Danielle pulled at the ends of the T-shirt, reading the words upside-down. 'Well, beggars can't be choosers.' Even the slight laugh hurt. 'I wouldn't recommend the beautician I went to either.'

Saoirse's eyes were back on the road. 'You got some going over, didn't you?'

'You sound like you know something about it.'

'Cameron gave me a buzz — one of the officers you spoke to in the hospital.'

'Ah, Garda Ginger-beard.'

'You didn't say that to his face, I hope?'

'No.' A dart of pain made Danielle squirm. 'Why would he bother to contact you? And how would he have known about me, especially from ten years ago? He's a guard only a wet week.'

'His father is in the job. He's a superintendent now. Terry Cashman.'

'But still, why would Cameron even be interested in a shooting that happened ten years ago?'

'Research. It's his thing. He likes to look into gangs and the various families implicated in illegal goings-on. He'd make it his business to know. Nosiness is a great attribute to have in this job. He's destined for great things.'

'I didn't click with the surname.'

'Why would you? I think you were a bit busy with being in pain after getting the shit kicked out of you.'

'It was decent of him to get in touch with you.'

'He wasn't the only one. I was actually on the way to the hospital to meet you when one of the lads on the CAB search also rang me. So, I knew I'd most likely find you here.'

'The people who attacked me tasered me, too.' Danielle lifted her T-shirt to show her the scorch marks.

Saoirse stopped the car at the entrance to the Belvedere rugby grounds car park. She turned to look at the marks. 'Jesus, they gave you a right going over. Did you get a look at them?'

'Why are we parking here?' Danielle asked.

'Because it's usually quiet when they're not training. And you wouldn't want anyone from your world spotting you in a squad car.'

'With the state of my face, I doubt they would recognise me. I'd certainly scare the baby anyway.' *The baby.* The words caught in her throat.

Saoirse turned right round and reached between the seats. She rested her hand on Danielle's for a second or two before drawing it back again. Her touch felt comforting.

'Are you okay to continue talking?'

'Yeah. Where were we?'

'The attackers?'

'Oh, yeah. I told this Cameron fella and his colleague the truth. I didn't see my attackers; it all happened so fast. The thing is, whoever kicked the shit out of me took the

49

baby. She's with Hazel's family now. I suppose at least she's safe, but I don't know how much they care about her. They never bothered to ask me about her after she was born.'

'Who did you speak to about the baby?'

'The only one of them I could remember — Hazel's aunt Audrey. She was married to this guy who raced greyhounds. They were always in the pub. He used to hang around with Ritchie Delaney.'

'Well, Audrey has plenty of money for drink these days. Her husband manages a few taxis and buses now for his brother, Frank, Hazel's father. So, what did Audrey say to you?'

'I rang her to see if she or any of the family wanted to be in the baby's life, but she said no way. I'd never seen her sober before, but the day I contacted her she was clear as day. She was categorical that the family wanted nothing to do with the baby.'

'And she claimed to speak for all of them?'

'Yes. In hindsight, I suppose I should have contacted Hazel's parents themselves and heard it from them, and not the drunkard auntie.' Danielle sighed. 'They didn't need to beat the crap out of me, though. I'd have met them and discussed who should have custody of the baby.'

'So you're coming round to the idea of it being Hazel's family behind your attack?'

'Look, it was most likely them, but I'm not a hundred percent certain. Hazel's father drove me back from the hospital.'

'Really?'

'Yeah, he seemed surprised when I told him how I came by these injuries. Like it was the first he'd heard of it.'

'It doesn't sound like his style. Those taxis of his and the fleet of minibuses seem perfectly legit. He's never come to our attention.'

'Look, they've been through enough. Their daughter's missing. They seem to hate the Lewis name enough already, without me making an issue of it.'

'Well, if that's what you want to do . . .'

'Frank said he knew my mother and Ged when they were younger,' Danielle continued. 'It went down very badly when Hazel hooked up with Ged.'

'I can just imagine the reaction.'

They watched a car pull out from the rugby grounds car park.

'Yeah,' Danielle said. 'It was decent of that Cameron fella to make contact with you.'

'It was. Tell me something. Would you have given her back if they'd tried to speak with you?' Despite the losses they shared, despite even the plan, Saoirse was above all else a detective. Danielle wouldn't fob her off so easily.

'I didn't know they gave a shit.' *I didn't enquire too deeply either*, she thought. 'Why didn't they go through social services or something? Why do this to me?'

'Who knows? There's no logic to it. So you're not going to make a statement about the attack?' Saoirse persisted.

'For a start, I didn't get a clear look at them, and making statements in this world—'

'Is dangerous. I know,' Saoirse said. 'I get you, but just think how bad it would look for the Brady family if they want to retain custody and are found to be behind a serious assault on you.'

'The more I think about Frank's reaction, the more certain I am that he can't have known,' Danielle said.

'Of course, Hazel could always return and take her back, then it's all academic anyway,' Saoirse said.

But Hazel is never coming back, Danielle thought. Avoiding Saoirse's gaze, Danielle stared out through the side window. There was nothing to see there but a concrete wall. 'You're right, it wouldn't look good for the family. Chloe, or whatever they called her, would be better off with me.'

Saoirse had twisted round to face her again. 'Do you really want that burden? She's not yours.'

Christ, as if I need reminding of that. Her whole body was exhausted, weighted down by a huge girder of tension across her shoulders. 'Oh boy, do I know that.'

'You're not . . . you know, using her as a substitute for your own loss, are you?' Saoirse said tentatively.

Danielle sighed. 'Of course not. That would be weird. She's not Sam.' *Sam.* The first name that came to her when that guard had asked what the baby was called. She could have given Chloe the middle name of Sam. That would have been nice.

'I understand,' Saoirse said. 'I hope you didn't mind me asking.'

'It's fine. You, of all people, know what it's like.'

Saoirse's eyes took on a faraway look. 'Unfortunately, yes.'

'Thanks for caring enough to ask, though.'

Saoirse smiled. 'Look, Danielle, making the statement could ensure that there is input from social services, and that they check on her welfare.'

'Only if it can be proved that they were involved.' *Shit, I never thought to ask Frank about the anonymous caller. Maybe he recognised the voice. It may not have been Frank they spoke to.*

'And you've been looking after her how long?' Saoirse asked.

'Since Jake Brady's funeral.'

'Jesus, that's—'

'Over two months ago. She was only a week old.'

'Right.'

'She's grown so much, too. Her own little personality developing. I took a photo of her every day.' Danielle looked down at her hands folded on her lap. 'They were on my phone, which has gone missing since the attack.'

'Were they backed up?'

'I'll know when I get a new phone and log into my account. But they'll only prove that she was with me and well cared for — it won't be enough to make them give her back to me, or even let me see her.'

'True. So, the apartment. What's the story there?' Saoirse asked.

'I thought you might be able to tell *me*, Saoirse. It was a complete shock to me when I came back from the hospital and found I couldn't get in. Even the code for the keypad had been changed.'

'Hmm. And there's not a hope of me getting that info. CAB keep everything within themselves. And given our connection, I couldn't risk asking. It was a lot to have even received that call.'

'Listen,' Danielle said, 'I wanted to ask you, why is a completely different member looking to speak with me over the incident at Ged's funeral last month? I thought I'd be dealing with you. When I asked, all they said was that they were dealing with me now. The one I spoke to was a bit curt, to be honest.'

'Ah, that. Well, the arrest was literally snatched out of my hands and taken over. I can see their point, though. I'm way too close to you. But the way they did it was a bit under-handed. The commissioner wasn't impressed with how we went about our own investigation, off the books and all that, but I bet she was delighted with the results.'

Danielle made a face. 'Is anything in your job straightforward?'

'No, and it's getting more and more complicated by the day. What I will say is that Sinead Teegan is a good detective. She's young, ambitious and has guts. Get on her good side, and you'll have her undying support.'

Danielle wasn't sure she gave enough of a shit to try being on anyone's good side. 'So you don't know what is happening at all? Even though you are all in the same job.'

'Nope. I can't even check something on our computer system without it creating an alert.'

'You mean that Garda PULSE thingy?'

'Yes. How come you know about that?' Saoirse asked.

'One of the guards at the hospital mentioned it. He was checking PULSE for something or other.'

'Well, once you check it, there's a digital footprint. If you do a search for anything you're not a part of, you get a fairly terse request for a written report as to your reason for doing so. Now, if I happen to meet up with one of the lads, that's a different story. That superintendent I mentioned, Terry Cashman, is involved, along with Dave Richards, who's a sound guy, and they keep me posted informally.'

'Via that non-talk and saying-everything-with-looks bullshit you all do?'

Saoirse laughed. 'Something like that, yeah. Though I don't know Sinead Teegan well enough yet to chat to her that way.'

Great. 'I thought you'd promised to keep me out of it. Wasn't I supposed to do what I could to get the evidence into my shooting and your husband's murder, and leave the rest to you? Now I find that I'm more caught up in it than I intended, and may even have to make a statement.'

'Trail of evidence. If you hadn't found that SD card . . .' Saoirse sighed. 'Look, you did, and we got answers. At last.'

'Yes. But can't you just shut the prison door and throw away the key?'

'Everyone's entitled to a trial — innocent until proven guilty? Remember that?'

Danielle grunted. 'At least that fucking psycho was refused bail.'

'True. And all outside contact and jail visits are closely monitored.'

'Good.'

'Who knows? We might get a guilty plea,' Saoirse said.

'You know, I always thought that when I got answers, I'd get closure, but that hasn't happened. Don't get me wrong, Saoirse, I have no regrets about what we did, or the way we did it.' Danielle looked out of the window. That concrete wall still let no light through. 'I feel . . . I dunno, not quite as horrible and scared as I did when I knew nothing, but not a heap better.'

Saoirse let out a long sigh. 'I hear you.'

'There are days when I don't know what the fuck to do. I feel lost.'

Saoirse met her gaze. 'You've lost a lot.'

'Having the baby with me made me feel I could make a difference to someone, especially when I thought no one else wanted her. I was surely a better option than a foster home. Ged would have turned in his grave if he knew a Lewis wasn't being looked after.'

Saoirse shook her head slightly. 'If you want my advice, leave Hazel's baby with her family.'

'It's hard, though. We had a bond. I at least need to make sure she is happy and healthy.'

'I understand,' Saoirse said. 'But look at the shit caring has drawn down on you. Losing a baby is something I'll certainly never get over and I know you feel the same. Christ, it's how we bonded in the first place. It's something you and I will carry with us until the day we die. What matters is *how* we carry it. Don't let it get in the way of your future happiness. You can drown in the torment of it if you're not careful, and you deserve better than that.'

Danielle swallowed. 'You're right.'

'Caring for Chloe would limit your choices. I honestly thought you'd head back to the UK. You've business interests there still, and they're doing well.'

'I guess so, but at the moment, I just feel wretched.' She took a breath. 'So, wasn't it great catching up?'

The two of them dissolved into laughter.

'Ow.' Danielle put her hand to her face.

'There's something else I wanted to talk to you about,' Saoirse said, serious again.

'Oh?'

'You've mentioned her a few times — Hazel Brady. She's been reported missing. You may have been the last person to speak to her.'

Shit. Suddenly Danielle wished she were anywhere but here.

CHAPTER 8

At Brenno's direction, Anto reversed into one of the spaces beneath the shrubs and trees at the far end of the Supervalu car park at Temple Place. From here, they had a clear view of the vehicles entering and leaving. Soon, a motorbike rumbled in and drew up next to the BMW. The driver's face was masked by a helmet, but behind him, Dwayne lifted his visor and gestured for Anto to follow.

Once out in the traffic, the motorbike proceeded sedately, allowing Anto to keep up. Soon they came to a halt outside Bird's house. The driver took off his helmet to reveal the face of Sal Fogarty. Behind him, a car drew up. Bosco got out.

'Fuck, no,' Brenno said, rubbing his hands nervously on his jeans.

'What the hell are we doing here?' Anto said.

'Dwayne said it's an eviction,' said Brenno. 'He must be throwing my ma out on the street. Shit, Anto, I'm not even going to get a chance to warn her.'

Anto's stomach was in knots. 'And you know what Dwyane is capable of if we refuse to do it.'

'Yeah, I do. At least Bird would give you a good beating and be done with it, but Dwayne? Nah, Dwayne would fucking wipe us off this earth.'

'This is a test, Brenno; you realise that? He wants to see how far we'll go for him.'

'I know. But family. My own mother. Jesus Christ. She was Bird's woman, and after all she done for him, this gets done to her. Fucking psycho.'

'At least if we're here, we can prevent them doing anything sinister.'

'What do you mean, *sinister*?' Brenno's breath was coming heavily. 'I don't like this, none of it. Have you anything on you?'

'What, like a gun?' Anto watched uneasily as the three men conferred. 'You must be joking. With this lot, I'd be off my head to even let on I was armed. They'd take it from me and beat me to death with it.'

'Fuck it, Anto, what can we do?'

'Sweet Fanny Adams, Brenno, that's what. We are screwed. Damned if we do, dead if we don't.'

'Shit.'

Slowly, the gate creaked open.

'Let's go,' called Dwayne.

The two of them got out and followed the others around the back of the house. His hand shaking, Brenno took out his phone and found his mother's number.

'Mam, Dwayne's coming to kick you out, and he's making us help do it.'

Anto could hear her say, 'What are you talking about?' He snatched the phone from Brenno and shouted, 'They're coming in, right now.' He ended the call and handed Brenno his phone.

'Come on, lad. We have to make sure this is done as soft as possible.'

Leaving Brenno hesitating outside in the back garden, Anto went in.

Dwayne was unrolling a pack of black refuse sacks. Bosco had disappeared from sight. Sal remained outside.

'I want all traces of her gone,' Dwayne said.

Taking two refuse sacks, Anto hurried upstairs, just in time to see Bosco hauling Marion across the bedroom floor, the bandage at her foot unravelling. Bosco gave her a shove, sending her down between the dresser and the stool in front of it. He threw a black bag at her.

Anto watched, helpless in his fury. This was no way to treat a grieving woman. The gun inside his jacket seemed to throb. What wouldn't he give to take it out and shoot the bastard. But they were outnumbered.

'Hey, Bosco, that's enough.' The words escaped before he could stop them.

Bosco charged towards him and pushed his face into Anto's. 'What did you say to me?'

'Sorry,' Anto said, averting his face. 'I meant leave it to me. I'll help Marion pack up in here.'

Bosco spat on the carpet at Anto's feet and stalked out of the room.

Anto waited until the door closed and released a breath. 'Christ. Look, Marion. Me and Brenno had no idea they were going to do this. They just said we were to meet them, nothing more. We'd no chance to warn you.'

She turned to face him. 'Brenno's here too?'

He saw that her nose was bleeding. 'Yeah, he just rang you.' He realised she was drunk, totally out of it. He sighed. 'Come on, Marion, let's get you home.'

'But I am home.'

'Dwayne wants you out.'

'But the funeral? He said—'

'He wants you out now.'

'Now, like this minute?'

'Yeah.' He pulled her up onto the stool at the dresser.

'He can't do this.'

Anto rested his hand on her shoulder. 'Marion, love, I know, but he's downstairs. He'll do us all a lot of harm if we don't do as he says.'

'But he said I could stay till after the funeral. I don't understand.'

'We can't believe a word he says, Marion. But his threats, they're another story. He's not afraid to carry them out. Come on, love, work with me. Let me and Brenno get you out of here with as little fuss as we can. You'll be safe back at home.'

Tears cascaded along her face and onto Anto's hands. 'Brendan's here?'

'Yeah, they made him come along.'

'Is he okay?'

'He will be, once we get you packed and out of here.'

She was calmer now, but still looked bewildered.

'Now, let's sort this for you.' Anto took a tissue from his pocket and gently rubbed the dark streaks from Marion's cheeks. 'Dab that on your nose, too, while I get you more.'

He took a wad of tissues from the en suite, which she took from him and began to wipe her face. He brought the glass of water from the bedside locker, smelling it first to make sure it really was water. She gulped it thirstily and got to her feet. She made it to the en suite quite steadily. He began to empty the dresser, filling the refuse sack with her clothes.

She emerged from the bathroom, her face no longer streaked with tears and mascara. Wordlessly, she began to stuff her remaining belongings into the other sack.

When it was done, Anto said, 'Do you want to go and sit in my car? It's just outside.'

She stared out of the window, then back at him. 'Bosco drove my face into the locker. Is this what I'm reduced to, treated like a trespasser in my dead partner's home?' She began to sob. 'I invested my whole life in that man. Finally, I got him to take me seriously, I moved in and then . . . This.'

Anto burned with rage and pity. *Jesus Christ.* Why were they treating her like this? Marion was fuck-all threat to Bosco or Dwayne. All she'd done was love Bird Flynn.

Glancing at the door, he whispered, 'Right, how's about we sail past them pricks without a word? Show them . . . show them you haven't lost your dignity. Me and Brenno will bring your stuff.'

Slowly, she nodded. Anto gathered up the two refuse sacks and followed her down the stairs. Brenno was waiting at the bottom with another few bags. Dwayne had his back to them, talking on his phone. There was no sign of Bosco or Sal.

'Do you think we have everything, Mam?'

'We do, Brendan, we do.'

'Here, Mam, I got you this, too.' He handed her a framed photo of the two of them, her and Bird, Bird with his arms around her. She was still gazing at it as Anto drove them away.

CHAPTER 9

Danielle may not have been the last person to speak to Hazel, but she was probably the last person to see her — or what was left of her.

'Hazel surely met someone after she left the baby with me?' Danielle waited while a man appeared, closed the gates to the rugby grounds and hopped into a car parked a little further up the road. She and Saoirse watched as he drove away. From her pocket, Danielle took out one of the pain-killers the doctor had given her.

'Is there any water in this car?'

Saoirse opened the glove box. Nothing. She got out and found a sealed bottle of still water in the boot, which she handed to Danielle.

Danielle waited for Saoirse's next question, hoping her injuries would help conceal any *tells* that might give her away.

'Two lads living on the street were found dead last week,' Saoirse began. 'One I knew well; he'd just agreed to go into a programme. He was avoiding a prison sentence, but I didn't mind. He was still trying to get clean. I won't go into the gory details of the post-mortem, but basically, he and the other lad had injected dodgy heroin. A woman staying in a nearby shelter ended up in hospital around that time, and eventually

61

admitted to taking some she'd found in a bag discarded in one of the lanes. One of the other addicts mentioned a warning that had been doing the rounds about some dangerous crap on sale. He said he'd heard it had been pulled, the dealers recommended to dump it. Another source told me about a party at a house near Leopardstown or Cabinteely, maybe Foxrock, about two months ago. Apparently, one person injected it and died soon after.'

'Who was the person that died?' Danielle asked, trying to sound casual.

'We've no official intel on that.'

'Unofficial?'

'It was a woman, in her early thirties, linked to someone in the criminal fraternity.'

'And?'

'And it happened around the time Hazel went missing.'

'Right.' *Fuck.* 'Okay. But what has that got to do with me? Shouldn't you be going back to your source?'

'I should, but I wanted to check with you first. There is a house nearby, in Foxrock, registered to Lewis Holdings.'

'So it's assumed that it happened there?'

'No. I don't make assumptions. I'm looking for facts.'

Danielle shrugged. 'The Foxrock area has lots of houses. It could be any one of them.'

'Not many are registered to Lewis Holdings, though. And let me be straight here: Dean was distributing drugs to the dealers. Now, whether your uncle was aware of the way Dean was getting his money, we'll never know. But I'm putting a few pieces together, and I'm beginning to get a good idea of the picture.' She held up her hand. 'I am fully aware that you were out of the country while this drugs business was being built up, and you had nothing to do with it.'

Saoirse looked straight at Danielle. Danielle returned her gaze as steadily as she could, wondering what she was supposed to say. Shit, she'd nearly forgotten about the five million euros' worth of coke that Ged was bringing down from Belfast. Where the hell did that end up?

'Right. Well, I'm glad you don't tie me to whatever shit Dean was into. Have you enough grounds to get a warrant and check the place?'

'I'm not sure if it is that house. Were you ever there?' Saoirse said.

Danielle's mind was whirring. If the cleaners had done their job properly, there should be no trace of her anywhere in that house. But could she be sure? Maybe someone saw her. Maybe there was surveillance on that house. Maybe Saoirse was testing her. Maybe . . .

'Like I said, I haven't been anywhere since his funeral, so . . .'

'Before Ged died?'

'Ged never got to show me the place.' That wasn't a lie. He hadn't. 'But I was there once.' *Safer to tell at least a part of the truth.*

'And?'

'It's not rented out or anything.'

Saoirse smiled. 'Jesus, who'd afford the rent on a place like that?'

'True.' *And the person would want to love wallpaper with leopard prints.*

'If we find out it was that house and we don't get a warrant, do you have a key, or know where we'd get one?'

'Would it not be better to get a warrant?' Danielle asked.

'There may not be enough grounds. And you didn't give me a straight answer about the key.'

'With CAB taking over the apartment I thought was mine, I'm not sure if I'd be allowed.' *The Foxrock place could be in Ann's name too, for all I know.*

'That's still not an answer. Do you have a key for the place or not?' Saoirse's tone was unexpectedly sharp.

'Sorry. I think I do have it somewhere. But it's back there, in my apartment. I'd have to get in to find it. I'd have no objection to you going in to look. If it is my place to have no objection, that is. I need to talk to the family solicitor, in case everything is gone to shit.'

'If you tell me what the keys look like, I can get my hands on them.'

'I thought you said you weren't supposed to have anything to do with me?' Danielle asked.

'That's absolutely true. But if you were registered as a source, it would be a different matter.'

Official source, also known as a rat. Saoirse is off her head if she thinks I'm going on the books. 'I don't think I'd be happy with that, Saoirse. The only thing worse than a rat, in my world, is a paedophile. Both have a hit price of zero on their heads; whoever chooses to do so has free rein to kill on sight. I do not want to be in that position.'

'Okay, I understand. And you could also be put with a different handler to me. No, it wouldn't be worth the risk. I'll just have to find another way. Maybe they haven't logged everything they've found, and I can get hold of them. If we do get in and anyone challenges us, I'll find a way to work around it.'

There's a reason she's no ordinary guard, but a detective. 'Wait, wouldn't the CAB officers be wondering about that house too, and they decide to seize it or something?'

'Not if it's not on their radar, or if its acquisition was completely above board.'

'I see. Actually, Ged's father owned that land. He kept horses there. And Ged built that house.'

'The house should be okay, so if the money he used to build or renovate it wasn't the proceeds of any illegal activity.'

'I don't think it would have been.'

'It's safe then.'

That was handy to know. But was it a good idea to let the guards just wander around in there? 'Will you get my passport and a few quid for me, too? And give me back the keys when you are done? I need identification for the bank, as well.'

'If I did get you your passport, Danielle, would you use it to leave the country?'

'Leave the country? What's that got to do with anything?'

'You know what will happen if you stay. You're a Lewis, and that name has a reputation, because of Ged and what Dean was up to in the past decade. Just look at what's happened since you've been back, what you've learned about your family.' Saoirse shook her head. 'It'll be hard to pull away from.'

This from the woman who wanted me to register as a fucking Garda source. 'I could stay here and go legit.'

'How long would that take?'

Danielle shrugged. 'Any threats to me have been neutralised.'

'Really? Have you looked in a mirror lately?'

'I know, but that was different.'

'How can you be so sure? It could have been someone with an issue, who happens to be close to the Brady family. Someone who knows that losing care of the child would hurt you badly. They'd be getting at you through her.'

'Do you really think that?'

'Who knows? It's like this, if you hang around, you'll be involved in a battle for control of the city whether you want it or not. And,' she sighed, 'if you stay, our contact has to sever. Then I won't be able to help you. We'll be nothing more to each other than detective and civilian. And you're a civilian who may draw the attention of the law through her association with the Lewis family. CAB are already closing in. If you leave, you have some chance. What about the life you made for yourself in London? It took a hell of a lot of determination to achieve what you did. You always said you planned to return as soon as you had answers. Well, you got them, but you're still hanging around.'

Yeah, on the street to be picked up in an unmarked squad car, Danielle thought. 'I can't go. Not now. You even said yourself, Saoirse, that statement is important to prove the trail of evidence. The SD card, the finding of it and all that.'

'You can always travel back for the trial if you are needed, and then, as an essential witness, we can protect you.'

'So, why can't you protect me now?'

'You haven't made a statement yet. Until then, your best option is to put a lot of distance between yourself and Dublin.'

'Hmm. Maybe I don't want to go. Maybe I want to stay and manage things here. We've shared the same dream for a decade, and now that we have answers, that's it?'

'It has to be, Danielle.' Saoirse's phone rang. She glanced at the screen and let it ring out. 'Shit, I'd better get back to this guy. Right, where will I drop you?'

Danielle hadn't a clue. 'That's it? You're just kicking me out?'

'What else do you want me to do?'

'I suppose you've no spare room going in your place?'

'Could you just imagine?'

They both laughed at the idea of Danielle Lewis sharing the same house as a Garda detective.

'I meant what I said, Danielle. It's up to you, but there are consequences if you stay. In the meantime, I'll get try to get hold of some of your belongings. How will I get in touch with you?'

'I'll text you when I get a new phone. I'm due a cash injection from the business in London in three days. I'll get one when that lands.'

'What have you to get by on until then?'

Danielle scrunched her lips. 'About forty-five flipping quid.'

'Shit.'

'Yep.' Danielle sighed.

There was a brown envelope in the centre well, with a harp inscribed on it. Saoirse scribbled the number on it and handed it to Danielle, who tucked the envelope inside her bra.

'Classy,' Saoirse said.

'Saves losing it out of this piece-of-shit tracksuit pants. The keys you're looking for have a pink furry pom-pom attached to the keyring.'

'Here.' Saoirse held a fifty in her direction.

Danielle grinned. 'I thought bribery went the other way around.'

'Watch it. It's just until you get sorted, and you can pay me back. Didn't you say you hadn't much cash?'

'Yeah, thanks, I do appreciate it.' Danielle shoved that into the other cup of her bra.

'Drop me to Berkley Street . . . Shit, I've no keys for there either. I know. Take me close to Lindsay Road. There's someone I know there who might have a spare bed for a few days.'

'If I get the keys to the house on Brennanstown Road and get them to you after, it wouldn't be a bad place to stay.'

Yeah, if it wasn't flipping haunted, Danielle thought. 'Like I said, if you get my stuff, give me those keys, too. It'll give me the option. And I'll pay you back as soon as I'm sorted.'

'Right.'

Saoirse pulled into a spot outside a red-brick house, just down from a hairdressers, along a quiet lane to the back of the busy Lindsay Road junction.

Danielle didn't tell Saoirse that some of her fifty quid was going on a few shots of tequila to ease her pain.

CHAPTER 10

Without a thought for the traffic violations he was committing, Anto sped to Marion's house. He wasn't even sure that Brenno had been calling from there — but where else would he call from? All Anto knew was that Brenno sounded desperate, and he needed Anto's help.

There was no one outside Marion's house. Anto parked and got out, his hand on his gun, which he'd shoved down the back of his jeans. He ran up the path and banged on the front door. No one answered.

He leaped over the fence and round to the back. The kitchen window was open, so he climbed in. On the floor above, he could hear Brenno calling out to his mother.

Anto took the stairs two at a time and stood on the landing, panting. The sound of someone whimpering came from one of the bedrooms. Inside, Brenno was on his knees cradling his mam, pills scattered across the carpet.

Anto took a breath. 'Hey, lad, what's happening?'

'She's gone, Anto, she's gone.'

'Are you sure?' Recalling what little he'd learned of first aid at school, Anto reached out and placed two fingers on her wrist. Nothing. He felt around. Still nothing. He looked up at Brenno.

'Dwayne's fucking puppet, Bosco Ryan, sent her a message to say she wasn't welcome at the funeral. Bird's funeral. Jesus Christ, Anto, that fucking animal. They're all animals.'

Anto thought of how Marion had been manhandled and assaulted yesterday. *Bastards.* He dialled triple nine and told them they'd find the back door unlocked. The woman on the other end asked him if he could do CPR. He racked his brain. *I can only try.*

'Okay, Brenno, ease up your hold now. Lay her down for me. The woman on the phone will tell me what to do.'

Brenno stared at him as if he hadn't understood. Gently, Anto prised Marion from her son's embrace and laid her out on the floor. Following the woman's instructions, he began to press, rhythmically, counting as he worked. He felt weird, as if he were floating, watching the scene — himself and the woman — from somewhere up near the ceiling. He kept going until she told him to check for a pulse. There was a faint beat. The sound of sirens drew near. The woman on the phone told him to roll Marion onto her side, keeping her airway clear. Brenno, very white, watched from the doorway.

After what felt like hours, Anto heard the thump of feet on the stairs. Two lads in yellow and green uniforms pushed past Brenno. One began to check Marion.

Apparently satisfied, the paramedics had Marion loaded onto a stretcher that seemed to appear from nowhere. One of the paramedics bagged up the scattered pills and container, and they bore her off down the stairs.

'Come on, let's get you to the hospital after her,' Anto said. Brenno looked bewildered, as if he didn't understand what was happening. 'They're taking her to Blanch hospital. I've the car outside, and I'll have you there in minutes.'

Anto was obliged to fasten Brenno's seatbelt for him before he took off.

'There was a pulse, lad, I swear. She's like my second ma. Never bothered when I stayed over with you unannounced. Makes the best fry this side of Dublin, so.' He glanced at Brenno. 'Come on, lad, snap out of it. Your ma needs you.'

Anto meant it. Brenno was his best buddy. No way should any man have to find his mother like that.

As Anto pulled into the set-down area at the hospital, Brenno seemed to jerk awake. He unfastened the seatbelt and ran in, while Anto set about finding a parking space.

No wonder this had happened. Marion had been dealt blow after blow, and what for? Brutally kicked out of the place she'd shared with Bird, and then told — by text message of all things — that she was barred from saying a final farewell to the man she loved. Bird's funeral was to take place in two days' time. Neither Dwayne nor Jason Flynn would miss him. Right now, Anto considered it more important to support Brenno. He'd had enough of those Flynn bastards and their cronies. They seemed to think they owned Dublin . . . well, they were mistaken. They didn't own him. It was time to show his mettle. Time to stand up and defend a good woman's honour.

CHAPTER 11

Danielle woke in a strange bed that smelled of stale alcohol. Unwilling to face the daylight streaming in through the curtains, she patted the locker until she felt the cool curve of a glass of what she hoped was water. Slowly, painfully, she turned her head to the side. To her relief, she was alone. The last thing she remembered with any clarity was ordering a whisky and cranberry juice. After that, a vague memory of chatting to a barman, and someone loading her into a car. At least she hadn't woken up in a poxy cell at the Garda station. Danielle pulled herself upright and gulped down the water.

A siren sounded. For a moment it seemed to have stopped outside the room, then it faded into the distance. She kicked off the duvet and went to the window. The room she was in was a few floors up. There was a church to her left, a fruit and veg shop to her right and a constant stream of cars heading in both directions.

Jesus Christ, she was in the Berkley Street knocking shop. She hoped to fuck that the sheets had been changed since the last client. They did look clean, and only smelled of someone who'd been on the piss, meaning her.

71

Danielle went to the bathroom and splashed water on her face and looked into the mirror above the basin. 'Mirror mirror on the wall,' she muttered. 'You look like shit.'

The bruise on her cheek had turned purple, and the one at the side of her jaw was a blend of red and yellow. Her long dark hair was a mess. She cast about her for something to fix her face — after all, the place was supposed to be a beautician shop — but the bathroom was pretty basic. A generic shampoo and conditioner in the press. Nice smelling shower gel, though. Fresh towels. But where were her clothes? The fifty quid that Saoirse had donated was well gone, and she couldn't find the envelope with her mobile number on it. She found a fluffy bathrobe hanging at the door and put it on. She shook the duvet and the harp-crested brown envelope flew into the air. It was a relief that she hadn't lost it. Folding it smaller, she stuck it into the dressing gown pocket. A search of the house might get her a few answers, as well as something decent to wear.

The door wouldn't open. She rattled the handle, pulled and pushed, but it wouldn't budge.

What the fuck is going on?

Her chest tightened with the beginnings of panic. She tried slowing her breathing. *Come on. Think.* Maybe in her drunken state she'd accidentally locked herself in. But no, there was no key.

Danielle hammered on the door, shouting to be let out. She heard the lock click, and the door opened.

Danielle found herself face to face with Linda Bradford, the woman who had run the brothel and who had become her friend. Until Ged's funeral, that was. Danielle had shut everyone out after that.

Danielle pushed past her and made for the stairs.

'Danielle,' Linda called after her. 'Are you still pissed or something?'

Danielle, already several steps down, turned and looked back up at her. 'You had me locked in a room, for Christ's sake. I knew I couldn't trust anyone, and you've just proved me right.'

'What do you mean? Danielle, wait.'

'What do I mean?' Danielle cried. 'Why the fuck did you have me locked up? And where the hell are my clothes?'

'I suppose you're talking about the man's tracksuit bottoms and the eighties throwback T-shirt.'

'They're better than nothing,' Danielle muttered.

'Were you going to head out the door in that dressing gown?'

'For fuck's sake, Linda, will you just tell me what's going on?' Danielle said, her rage beginning to subside.

'I will, if you make your way calmly to the kitchen and let me make you a strong mug of coffee. Besides, I need to open the window in here and let some air in. The room reeks of stale booze.'

'Right.' Danielle sighed, and continued down the stairs. Posters advertising beauty treatments were still displayed in the reception area. In the hall, she noticed a small pile of smashed glass in a shovel.

Linda joined her in the kitchen. 'Not even going to switch on the Nespresso machine or boil the kettle, eh?'

'No, I . . . you said you'd make me one.'

'What is it to be, your majesty?'

'Fuck off with that shit, Linda. A cappuccino . . . Please.'

'Coming up.'

Soon Linda and Danielle were seated at the kitchen table, with steaming mugs of caffeine in front of them. A clock ticked, loud in the silence that had fallen. Danielle was surprised that it was nearly eleven.

'This place was so busy that you never used to hear that clock,' Linda said.

'Have you not been running the place?' Danielle asked. 'Keeping it ticking over — oh, excuse the pun.'

'No, I shut it down after Ged's death. I figured with all the attention on the Lewis family, we couldn't risk even offering the legit services. Sunbed, anyone?' Linda laughed. 'Plus, those outfits I had to wear squeezed the hell out of me. Shoving all my curvy bits in here and there.'

'Yeah, I barely recognised you in the yoga pants and sweatshirt. The highlights through the auburn suit you. When did you get glasses?'

'I always had them; they just didn't suit the look if I was covering the front desk. What you're seeing is more me that you've ever witnessed before.'

'I like it. You look . . . normal.' Danielle smiled.

'Thanks, I think.'

'So this place has been closed down, so there's been no income from here?'

Linda shook her head. 'No, nothing.'

'How have you survived?'

Linda shrugged. 'Phone sex and BDSM classes.'

'BDSM classes?'

'Yes, I have a huge client list. A lot of frustrated young mummies. You should see some of them go when they really let loose. One-to-ones, obviously.'

'So, no getting your hands on the clients.'

'Exactly,' Linda said, sipping her coffee.

'Are those BDSM outfits not more uncomfortable than the front-of-house dresses?'

'Surprisingly, no.'

'I'll take your word for it. And how come I ended up here, in my underwear, locked in a room?'

'I had to lock you in. You were insisting on heading out — fucking clubbing of all things. With the state of you, the only place you'd have ended up would've been a Garda cell, you mad bitch.'

'Did you take my clothes off me?'

'Nah, you as good as fell out of them and onto the bed. I just helped to make sure you didn't do yourself an injury in the process. You'd fallen a few times.' Linda pointed at Danielle's leg.

Danielle looked. She could see a few bruises forming — as if she needed any more.

'Edge of the bed, that one,' Linda said. 'You'll probably have one on your arse, too, as you backed into the hall table.'

'Hence the glass on the floor?'

'Yeah, you knocked the vase off. I didn't get a chance to dump it because you fell up the steps and I had to help you.'

'If I was that drunk, then why take me all the way up to the top floor?'

'Oh, you insisted on going to that room as no one — and I quote — "would have been riding in that room." You remembered that it was kept for any of the girls who got caught to work late. It was safer for them to stay.'

'Did I remember that now? And did I just rock up at the door? Have you been staying here?'

'No and no. You ended up at one of the bars the Lewis family owns, the one that was set on fire. Your welcome home party. I was there that night.'

'Shit, Linda, you never said. I didn't see you there.'

'Ah, it never came up in conversation. No one could get near you anyway. You were knee deep in chat with Ann. We were all lucky to get out, with the way that fire took hold. Anyway, you know the bar I'm talking about. Same bar manager. He recognised you straight off.'

'You mean despite no make-up and the state of my face?'

'Yes. There is no disguising a Lewis. Anyway, it was only right that he did. He works for you. Jesus. Anyway, he got you into one of the snugs, let no one in to bother you, then rang me. By then you were totally hammered.'

'Oh, fuck, very professional.'

'Absofuckinglutely not the thing to do in your position. He stayed with you to make sure you were okay. Said you lay on the seat and wanted to go to sleep, then would pop up insisting on shots of vodka. He gave you water, and you were too pissed by then to know the difference.'

'And you swooped in to rescue me?'

'Basically, yes.'

'Well, cheers for looking after me.'

'What's happened to you, Danielle? You completely cut me off after Ged's funeral, even though all I ever did was support you.'

'I just wanted to keep me and the baby safe. I wasn't thinking straight. I holed up in the penthouse at Clonliffe View and refused to see anyone.'

Linda shook her head. 'Not healthy.'

'I know that now.'

'I heard you got attacked and ended up in hospital, and now the baby is with Hazel's parents,' Linda said.

'Where did you hear that?'

'That barman is friends with Ian Gallagher and Lee, the lad working in the gym.'

'Who's Ian Gallagher?' Danielle asked.

'You should know him; he works for you. He's one of the drivers. He's going out with Kym Brady, Hazel's cousin.'

'And this Lee fella?'

'You'll meet him another time. Forget him for now.'

'Right. You didn't happen to hear who assaulted me, by any chance?'

'Unfortunately not,' Linda said. 'So, what's going on with the apartment?'

'CAB seized it. Apparently it's in Ann's name. She must have known they'd be coming, but she never told me.'

'I don't think that crowd exactly announce themselves,' Linda said.

'They need a court order to seize property. There had to be some warning.'

'And you're completely out of the loop?' Linda asked.

'That's one way of putting it. But, yeah. Homeless, too. Not broke, but cash skint. All I have is what's in the account, and I still have the bank card.'

'Come on, Danielle, you're nowhere near homeless. What about all the Lewis Holdings properties?'

'What? Like the place in Foxrock on Brennanstown Road, you mean? I haven't been there since . . .' Danielle stopped herself.

'And all the others, Danielle? I thought you knew what Ged had.' Linda stared at her. 'You really have no idea of what he owned, do you?'

'I was in no rush to find out. After everything that happened, I just wanted to shut out the world and look after the baby. She was the only thing that mattered — her, and staying safe.'

'I understand.'

'Can you make me a list, Linda?'

'Of course, but I don't know the full extent of it. I did a lot of the paperwork and accounts, if you remember. But he had other business dealings I know nothing about. Everything went through his solicitors. I can get you an appointment with them if you want.'

'Please. And give me what you do have,' Danielle said.

'The thing is, Ged changed a lot of the passwords before he died. He said you'd know what they were.'

'What? How the fuck would I know?'

'Dunno, but you'd want to have a think. Could he have changed them to something connected with you?'

Danielle shrugged. 'My date of birth?'

'Nope.'

'Can't you hack it or something? You're good at that kind of thing.'

'To a point,' Linda said. 'He was fairly tech savvy himself. It was how come he saw my potential and got me out of having to dress up to welcome clients. I wasn't impressed when I had to cover for Hazel and get back into that role.'

'Wow, okay.'

'We do need to start checking all the properties. Don't forget that there's over five million euros' worth of cocaine in one of them.'

'We still have that?'

'Yes, of course; why wouldn't we? It was collected in the north around the time Ged went up to fetch some of the Eastern European girls. The time he . . . well, you know. Ian Gallagher drove it so far, and Ritchie Delaney took it from him and stashed it. Him and Ged were the only two who knew where it was.'

'Would Ann have known, seeing as—'

'She might, but do you really want to go and ask her?'

Danielle made a face. 'Fuck no. Any other way to find out?'

'Leg work. But we'd have to make sure there's no one keeping an eye on it. And we daren't have anyone follow us.'

'I didn't think of that,' Danielle said, wishing she wasn't so hungover.

'Someone else may have got wind of the delivery and seen that it never made it onto the street,' Linda said.

'How come you didn't look before now?' Danielle asked. 'You could have found it and distributed it yourself. You'd have made a fortune.'

'Oh sure, if I had a death wish. I'm curves, brains and beauty, me. Clever at the tech, and beauty here, but not brawn. Besides, I'm not a Lewis. Without that name behind me, I'd be laughed at or robbed of it, and probably killed.'

'Makes sense.'

'Think of it, Danielle. That amount of coke would keep the Lewis family right at the centre of Dublin's drug dealing business. The city would be yours, just as it was Ged's at the height of his power. It's just sitting there, waiting for you to claim it.'

Danielle frowned. 'I'm not sure if I want that life.'

'That's up to you to decide.' Linda looked at her watch. 'I have a BDSM lesson in ten minutes.'

'Here?'

'Yeah, I'll be an hour. Stick yourself in the room, have a nice long shower and I'll give you a shout when I'm done. And, here—' Linda reached into her bag — 'I got you a new phone, and I'll give you some cash to tide you over.'

'When did you get me that?' Danielle slid the phone closer.

'I went out first thing this morning. You were still passed out. Don't even think of putting on those clothes you'd on last night.'

'With CAB searching the apartment, I can't get back in, Linda. They're all I have to wear.'

'I left a spare set of clothes on the chair for you. They're mine, so a size or so bigger than you'd take. They also might cover a bit more than you're used to. But they'll do. I can pick up a few more bits at the shops later, whatever you need. Just give me a list. That way you can lay low for a bit longer.'

'That's really good of you, Linda. I appreciate it.'

'Did you back up your photos?'

'What? Yes, I think so. Hang on and I'll check.' Danielle took the new phone from Linda and put in her details. 'Yes, they are backed up.'

'Great. I put my phone number in there, too. Send me a picture of you and the baby.'

'Why?'

'Jesus, Danielle, there's some attitude. Because I want to do something nice for you, all right?'

'Oh, okay. Sorry, and thanks again.'

Slowly climbing the stairs back to the top floor, Danielle thought about Saoirse and the conversation they'd had. If she took over the helm of Dublin's drug dealing business, they'd be on opposite sides of the law. It would certainly bring an end to any relationship they may have had.

If I had control over that cocaine, the Flynns couldn't get their evil hands on it.

But did she really want to go down that road? If she got caught, she could kiss goodbye to the baby. She'd never see her again. She had a lot of thinking to do, but right now her brain was too fuzzy to decide what direction she wanted her life to take.

CHAPTER 12

Having spent the night in his car in the hospital car park, Anto woke to the hoped-for message. Marion was doing okay, he read. She'd had a comfortable night and the psychs would be coming to assess her. The next message was a request for coffee and something to eat. Poor Brenno; he was starved. Anto climbed stiffly out of the car straight into the pouring rain. Head down, he made his way into the hospital to pick up a breakfast roll and an Americano at the cafeteria.

He was about to text Brenno to let him know he was bringing his supplies, when he spotted Ian Gallagher standing just inside the hospital doors.

The first thing Anto noticed was Ian's bandaged hand. The second was that he was clad in nothing but a polo shirt and jeans. Ian, playing the hard man, coatless in the freezing October piss-fest.

'Ian, bud, what's the craic?' Anto nodded at the bandaged hand. 'What happened to you? Hope that's not your *important* hand.' Anto made a jerking-off gesture and laughed.

'That new boss of yours, Dwayne Flynn, that's what happened,' Ian said, through clenched teeth.

'Woah. Wait up there now.' Anto raised his hands, breakfast roll aloft in one and Styrofoam cup in the other.

'He's no boss of mine. He thinks he has me onside because of Brenno. And Brenno's working for him because he worked for Bird — Dwayne's not letting him go. I can't turn my back on the lad. You don't do that to your mates, ever.'

'Oh. Right. Sorry, Anto, my mistake. Don't mind me, my head's been all over the shop since this . . .' He lifted the bandaged hand.

'That's all right. The bastard's also saying I owe him a few grand and have to work it off. But that's a load of bollocks. And I'll tell you this for nothing — I'm biding my time, waiting for my chance. There's a lot about to happen. You wait and see.'

'I don't doubt you, Anto, but watch your back. That Dwayne Flynn is a monster.'

'You can say that again. But don't you worry about me. I'm a survivor.' Anto nodded at the bandaged hand. 'Spill. What'd he do to you, that you ended up like that?'

Ian glanced around, Anto followed suit. 'Go on,' Anto said.

Ian lowered his voice. 'The bastard drove a blade through my hand and threatened to kill me if I didn't supply him with some information he was after.'

'What information?'

'He wanted to know the whereabouts of a stash of over seventy kilos of blow,' Ian said.

What the actual fuck? What a haul. Anto's future flashed before him. He had a vision of himself lying in the bath, balls naked, immersed in cash, all five million of it. Ian needed to elaborate further.

'Are you telling me you know that there's over seventy kilos of blow just sitting somewhere? Fuck me, that's over five million's worth.'

'I don't know. That's the problem.'

'Okay, let's rewind there, Ian, lad. Five million worth, yeah? And Dwayne thinks you know where it is. How come he thinks that? There must be some reason.'

Ian sighed. 'He knows I haven't a clue where it is, but he thinks I can find out. What's more, he has threatened to break into the apartment some night and kill both me and Kym if I don't. And I am one hundred percent certain that he'll carry out his threat.'

'Was Kym there when he . . . ?'

'Yep.'

'Did he hurt her?'

Ian shook his head. 'No, but he did frighten the shit out of her. He said I had forty-eight hours to get the information to that sidekick of his, Bosco Ryan.'

'Jesus Christ. Is Kym here with you?'

'Nah, I just came in for a check-up.'

'Wait. You said you had forty-eight hours?'

'Yeah, they expired last night. I've been looking over my shoulder since. When you appeared, I nearly shit myself.'

'I'd never do you, Ian. You're a mate.'

'Yeah, but a few grand debt is a few grand debt. Things happen when a fella owes that kind of money.'

Anto didn't doubt the threat Dwayne posed, but there was no way he was staying under his thumb. If he did, no one would go near him. 'I'd almost be offended, if it wasn't Dwayne Flynn we were talking about.'

'Yeah, look, I meant no offence, Anto, but a fella has to watch his back.'

'Wait, you say the forty-eight hours is up. So, did you manage to get your hands on the information?'

'Not a hope. I didn't even know where to start.'

'Shit.'

'Yeah.'

'Where's Kym now?' Anto asked.

'At her mother's. She's helping out with minding her cousin Hazel's baby, Chloe,' Ian said.

Anto nodded. 'Oh, right. Hazel's still missing, isn't she?'

'Yeah, the family finally made an official report.'

'Right.'

'We can't even sleep in our apartment, in case Dwayne or Bosco break in.'

'But what are you going to do? Are you going to keep looking for the stash?' Anto asked.

'I'm doing my best. I was going to maybe talk to Jason, see if he can get his brother to give me a little more time.'

'Would that work?' Anto said dubiously.

Ian shrugged. 'A lad's gotta try.'

'I hear you.'

'Tell me, what do you know about this stuff?' Anto asked.

'It belongs — belonged, I mean — to Ged Lewis. So, I guess it belongs to Danielle now, but she's gone off the radar, and no one seems to know where she is. Apparently, CAB took the apartment she was staying at. Kicked her out. I heard she was attacked too, assaulted outside the flat. Ended up in hospital.'

'Jesus. Who'd tackle the head of the Lewises?'

'No idea. They took the baby from her and left her in a right state, so they say.'

'Danielle Lewis has a baby?' Anto asked.

'No. It's Ged's baby. The one he had with Kym's cousin, Hazel,' Ian said. 'The one Kym's helping look after.'

'Jesus Christ.'

'Anyway, I drove the stash down from the north, which is why Dwayne thinks I know where it is. I was meant to meet one of Ged's right-hand men — Mark something. Stocky fella, tattoos — but instead, I met Ritchie Delaney. I swapped vans with him and he took it away, but I've no idea where to.'

'So it's likely to be stashed at one of the warehouses or sheds belonging to the Lewises, then.'

'Maybe. That's the thing. I have no idea.'

'Do you have a list of them places, or know from past experience where they stored the likes of that?' Anto said.

'No, it was my first time on that kind of job.'

Anto's mind was starting to race. 'We could narrow it down, and make a plan for it, like—'

'Like what, Anto? Get the stuff for ourselves?'

'Yeah. Why not? Do you have any idea what that would do for our standing in this town?'

'Are you off your fucking head? You're on something, aren't you? We'd have no standing. We'd be dead, is what we'd be.' Ian shook his head.

'Well, I'm dead sober.' Anto set down the cup and roll on one of the chairs and held both hands out. 'Look. Not even a tremor.' He took Ian by his elbow and guided him to a chair, seating himself beside him. 'We could do this, you know.'

'You think we could really go against the Flynns *and* the Lewis crew?'

'Give me a reason why we shouldn't at least think about it.'

'I'll give you a million fucking reasons. Because that animal Dwayne Flynn wants it. And another thing, Bird might be heading for six feet under, but there's still Jason, and when he sees red, we're fucked. Have you seen my fucking hand, Anto? This is what Dwayne did by way of asking me to find the information. Can you imagine what he'll do to me if I not only fail to deliver, but take it? Jesus. Sal and Bosco are ruthless. Then there's Danielle Lewis.'

'Who has she got to back her?' Anto said.

'No idea, and that's worse,' said Ian.

'How?'

'No info is worse than bad info. And suppose she gets in the way, are you prepared to take her out, Anto? You know someone that is? She hasn't even been around for the past few years. Who knows what contacts she has in the UK that could turn up and take us when we least expect it.'

Anto was chewing on the inside of his cheek. 'Someone has to know where it is.'

'Did you not hear a word of what I just said?'

'Yeah, yeah. Whatever, we need to do something about Dwayne. Getting at Sal or Bosco first would be the best move.'

'Ah, here, I'm not listening to this.'

Ian was halfway out of his seat when Anto caught hold of his arm. 'No, sit. Hear me out. Dwayne has to be stopped.

Marion Aherne is up there in HDU after taking an overdose. Dwayne not only kicked her out of Bird's house, but he made Brenno and me help him do it.'

'Jesus. That's low. Her own son?'

'Yeah, he threatened to kill all three of us if we didn't cooperate. Then, on top of that, Bosco sent her a message to say she wasn't welcome at Bird's funeral.'

Ian shook his head. 'No way. Her partner for all those years. That's wrong, lad, so wrong.'

'He's only back in the country three days. Can you imagine how dangerous he'd be with several million euro behind him, after he's sold all that blow?'

Anto watched Ian's face. His determined expression had begun to relax a little. 'Any thoughts on my proposal now, Ian?'

'Okay, I see your point. I'm happy to brainstorm if you like. But that's as far as I'm agreeing to go, for now at least. We need to find out exactly who we have on our side.'

Anto held out his hand. Ian took it. They shook solemnly.

'Not here, though,' Anto said. 'Let's head somewhere we won't be seen.'

'You're right. I must hit the jacks first, though,' Ian said. 'Drain the snake.'

'I'll get this stuff to Brenno.' Anto picked up the coffee, now cold, and the roll. 'We can head in my car. It's pissing down outside, and all you've got on is that polo shirt.'

'I had a jacket, but some prick stole it,' Ian said.

'Stop. No.'

'Yeah, I'd it on the chair in the waiting area. My new Canada Goose jacket, a neat royal blue one. Jesus, place is full of scumbags. I must report it at reception. Surely someone will have seen it. I'll be back in a shake.'

Ian went to the reception counter. After a few minutes' conversation there, he disappeared from Anto's sight, presumably heading for the jacks.

Brenno yawned. He was pale, slumped onto the chair in the corridor outside Marion's room. Anto sat beside him. 'She's doing okay. Thankfully.'

'That's great to hear. Christ, I thought we'd lost her.'

'No. Thanks for what you did too.'

Anto pursed his lips and nodded. He could hardly believe what he'd done himself.

Before he could tell Brenno about his chat with Ian, he heard a voice from overhead him. 'You shouldn't be up here,' a passing nurse said.

'Yeah, 'course, sorry. I'll head out of your way now.'

She nodded and continued along the corridor.

'Here, lad, text me or ring if you need anything.' Anto stood and left his buddy staring at the wall opposite. His food uneaten and coffee untouched.

Anto found a seat by the wall facing the entrance and amused himself watching the nurses come and go. Most looked young and easy on the eye. A woman in a different uniform to the nurses hurried by, rifling around in her handbag. Anto noticed the dark circles under her eyes and guessed she'd come off a night shift. As she passed, she dropped a set of keys, so Anto bent, picked them up and handed them to her. She gave him a weary smile and thanked him.

Among the visitors and staff pushing through the revolving doors, one guy stood out. He wore a blue jacket with the familiar logo embossed in red on the sleeve. It had to be Ian's jacket. Of course, Anto couldn't be sure, but what were the chances? He looked around. No sign of Ian yet. Anto wondered what to do. They had bigger fish to fry right now but still, you don't steal a man's jacket, and especially not from a hospital. It could belong to a nurse or a doctor, or someone with a relative in the throes of death.

Anto stood up to see which way the guy was headed. He took his mobile out and took a snap, but the guy's face was hidden beneath a hood pulled up over a baseball hat. If he didn't know that Ian was in the jacks, he'd swear it was him; yer man was the same height and build. If Ian didn't get a move on, he'd never see his jacket again, because the fella was just about to disappear.

Anto looked back towards the toilets. It was killing him to let this guy off. Where the fuck was Ian?

Just then, Ian appeared, strolling in his direction.

'Here, Ian, quick, I found it, your jacket,' Anto called and beckoned. Ian didn't seem to have heard him, so Anto left him to follow and ran towards the door.

An almighty bang sent Anto diving for cover. People screamed, and there was a crush at the door as people tried to get out. Anto looked back. Ian was on the floor. Had Dwayne got someone to follow him to the hospital? What a scumbag to try to off him here. Anto needed to get to Brenno and warn him. From where he cowered, half under a chair, all he could see were feet, running to and fro. Anto decided it was safer to stay on the floor and play dead.

Two more shots rang out.

CHAPTER 13

After a night spent at Blanchardstown Hospital being puked and shit on, Lisa had had enough. She pushed through the throngs of people milling about in the reception area, but every time she tried to make headway, someone else blocked her path. It was crazy. Her oldest was due at rugby training, and he needed his breakfast. Her husband was supposed to be at work for ten. At least she'd had a chance to read a bedtime story over the phone to her youngest during a brief break from the night's madness.

The lining of her handbag had swallowed her car keys. She rummaged around, trying to pull them free, only to drop them. They skittered across the floor, landing at the feet of a young man in cream jeans and a black jacket. He picked them up and handed them to her with a smile. She gave him what she hoped was a smile in return and hurried on.

Now the woman in front of her stopped suddenly, blocking her way. Lisa pushed past, only to be stuck behind a guy pushing a patient in a wheelchair. Finally emerging through the exit doors, she needed her phone, which meant another deep dive into her handbag. As she felt around for its rectangular outline, something floated from the pocket of a guy wearing a blue jacket who had just shoved her out of his way. She stooped to pick it up.

'Excuse me.'

The words had just left her lips when a loud bang rent the air. She froze, still bent forward, one hand on the glass panel beside her. An intense sterile smell filled the air and a bitter taste settled on her tongue. She spat and glanced up. The sanitiser dispenser had exploded.

Another two ear-splitting cracks. She fell to her knees and put her hands over the top of her head. The guy in the blue jacket fell to the ground, landing on his back in front of her, blood spewing from his throat. Her ears ringing, she shouted for help. Her voice sounded very faint. She pressed on his wound while he gasped and choked. To her left was the woman she'd passed, collapsed against a chair, holding her arm, a crimson stain slowly spreading across her jacket. The wheelchair careered into the path of an oncoming car, hit the kerb and tipped over, throwing the patient out in front of an ambulance.

A man in overalls, wearing a baseball hat, stood and looked down at the woman who'd fallen from the wheel-chair. Lisa was about to call out and tell him not to move her when she noticed what he was holding. A gun. He started to walk towards where she knelt, vainly trying to staunch the wound at the stricken man's throat.

She looked up toward the man wearing overalls and back to the man whose life she was trying to save. She wasn't about to abandon him. As the man in overalls drew near, she saw that his face was half hidden by a scarf — and, yes, the thing in his hand was a gun.

She watched, mesmerised, as he paced forward, bran-dishing the weapon. Around them surged crowds of panicked people, all of them intent on saving themselves. Muffled screams filled the air.

All Lisa saw was his boots, which she noticed were cov-ered in plastic, on the other side of the wounded man. The gun was aimed in her direction, the muzzle inches from her forehead. The young man's blood kept pumping through her fingers. She held on and pressed, the gun at her face.

Her arms were clamped so tight her muscles hurt. She tried to resist, but was jerked backwards. Her fingers slipped from his neck, she was dragged across the ground, then let go. She rolled onto her side, intending to push herself up, to go back and help, but slumped back down, all her strength gone. No one could help the young man now.

The gunman took aim and squeezed the trigger. The blast sent hair, blood, and shards of bone in every direction, splattering the panel Lisa had steadied herself against just minutes ago. Remnants of his brain snaked down the glass.

The man in overalls turned and walked away, as if he'd just stopped to make an enquiry and had received a satisfactory answer. As he went, he brought his phone to his ear and spoke for a moment. Then he broke into a jog, the weapon still in his hand.

CHAPTER 14

The bass was turned up high. Kym could feel the beat in her chest. It pulsed through her body. For a short while she let it take her into oblivion, a million miles away from Dwayne Flynn's sinister ultimatum. It was midnight. The forty-eight hours he had given them was up. And Ian hadn't found the information.

Leaving Ian bleeding, Kym had run to her parents' house, only to be welcomed by a drunk mother and a million questions about where she had been and who with. Kym spent the day looking after Chloe, which had kept her distracted. But then she had the night to deal with, and Kym wasn't about to spend another night anxiously jumping at the slightest noise. So she went out to what had started as a hen party, and ended up with Kym totally out of her head at Lee Thompson's house.

She found herself on the couch alongside one of the girls she'd come with. Someone — Lee — was bending over them from behind and kissing her friend. Then he climbed over the back of the couch and onto the girl beside her. After a while they stopped kissing, and both stared in her direction. Kym moved across and soon all three of them were a writhing mass of tongues, hands, flesh. Briefly, Kym thought of Ian. Lee wouldn't have let Dwayne Flynn break into the apartment and put a knife through his hand. Lee was strong; he ran the gym.

Then again, Ian was the safer bet. She began to feel guilty at the way she'd treated him. The feeling grew. What was she even doing here? She pulled her dress down and struggled to her feet, knocking the phone from Lee's hand. Was he recording? He liked to do that sometimes, 'just for me, to relive the pleasure,' he'd say.

She needed a drink. Water. She found the kitchen, where someone handed her a glass of what turned out to be vodka. She groped her way to the sink, put her head under the tap and drank. She let the tap run, her mind going back to days at the beach with her gorgeous cousin, Hazel. They were the best. Hazel always made time for Kym, helping her with her hair, her nails, so she'd impress the lads.

Even when Hazel was fucked up on drugs she'd looked out for Kym. She'd met Ian when she was out with Hazel. Then her cousin hooked up with Ged Lewis, the bastard, and the good times came to an end.

Kym returned to the living room and found her handbag stuffed behind a cushion on the now empty couch. Lee and her friend had disappeared, no doubt to finish what they'd started. In the hall mirror, a girl stared at her, her face streaked with mascara, lipstick smudged. Jesus, it was her own reflection. *Shit.* She found a bathroom and did her best to make good the damage.

Kym remembered that she'd agreed to mind her baby cousin for an hour at midday. Her aunt and uncle were like new parents with the little one. They named her Chloe Hazel. She was no substitute for Hazel herself, though. Where the hell had she gone? Hazel needed to get back here and mind her kid.

Chloe was nearly three months old. They'd only had her back a few days, but she seemed happy enough, a contented little kid. Danielle Lewis must have done a good job minding her, but there was no way Frank and Alice would give their granddaughter up to a Lewis. No way. Thinking of Danielle Lewis, an idea began to form. Maybe Danielle could help with the Dwayne problem? Danielle was now in charge of the Lewis businesses, so she must know where those drugs were being kept. But how would she get in touch with her? Kym had heard that the cops had taken the apartment she was meant to be staying at. And what would she even say to her? Fuck it. It was too much to process, the state she was in. She'd deal with it another time.

She stumbled out of the house and immediately fell to her knees. Muttering imprecations at Ged Lewis, she picked herself up, kicked off her shoes and, barefoot, continued on until she found herself at Mulhuddart Cemetery.

Dazed, she looked around. This was where some of the Lewises were buried, wasn't it? It must have been thoughts of that bastard Ged that had brought her here. She tried to send a video message to Ian, but had no idea if it had sent, so she sent a text as well, though she couldn't read what she'd written.

Traffic sounded in the distance. A breeze whipped around her. She dropped her bag, extended her arms and raised them to the moon, which had just appeared through a break in the clouds. *Hazel, where are you?*

She picked up her bag and started to walk. In her confused brain, the thought took hold that if Hazel was anywhere, she'd be here, hiding among her family's graves. The grass was damp from the day's rain and her feet squelched in the muddy ground. She squinted, trying to make out the names carved into the granite headstones. Where was Hazel hiding? Where the hell was the plot?

She fell onto a mound of freshly dug earth. *Hazel, is that you?* Hazel was not dead. She'd just fucked off somewhere because she couldn't deal with the responsibility of a baby.

Typical. No way is she gone from this earth. She'll come back, eventually, for Chloe. She has to.

Kym tried to picture Hazel the last time she saw her. She was all dressed up, heading to a party, and Kym wasn't invited. Then nothing. Phone dead, contact broken. Kym missed her cool older cousin with every bone in her body. The almond and cocoa smell of her perfume. If she was dead and buried, at least they could visit sometimes. This not knowing was way too painful.

She pushed herself to her feet. Stumbling, she passed grave after grave until she found it, the place where Ged Lewis was buried.

At the bottom of her handbag was the gun, zipped into the inside pocket. She'd found it in a pouch attached to the buggy the baby had come in. Pity it hadn't been to hand when Dwayne broke in. How ironic, to have shot Dwayne Flynn with a gun belonging to Danielle Lewis. She laughed out loud, and the sound of it made her jump.

She gripped it with her right hand. At least she knew not to point the thing at her own face. Aiming at the grave, she said, 'I'm making sure you never come back, prick.' And pulled the trigger. The bullet sent earth and gravel flying into the air. The slide hit her thumb, bending it backwards, and she let the gun drop. After a few minutes, the pain eased and she felt around on the ground for the gun. *Where the fuck is it?*

The headlights of a car blazed though the bars of the entrance gate, blinding her.

'Fuck.'

She crouched behind a headstone.

'Kym. Are you in there?'

It was Ian.

'Kym?' Wasn't that Anto's voice? What the hell was he doing here with Ian?

'Are you okay? Your message was weird.'

She heard them muttering to each other. *Fuck. Maybe she isn't here at all. You'd better not have dragged me out at this hour of the night for nothing.'*

'The picture was all over the place, she was real shaky, but I'm telling you, there were graves in the background, and she mentioned Ged Lewis. It has to be here she called from, Anto. We have to make sure she's all right.'

'Fine. We'll hang on for another few minutes.'
'What if she's passed out here somewhere?'
'Shit, Yeah. Come on. Use the torch on your phone.'

Did she want Ian and Anto to see her in this state? She thought about her friend and Lee. They wouldn't come looking for her in the dead of night. Ian and Anto gave a shit, and that's what mattered.

'I'm here,' she croaked.

'Where's here?' Ian shouted.

'Are you here on your own, you mad yoke?' Anto added.

'Yeah.' She felt weak, all her anger extinguished.

Suddenly someone caught hold of her arm.

'Jesus Christ. Are you trying to do me in? Make a little noise or something, would you, Ian, if you're going to grab me.'

'I have been.'

'Yeah. Sorry.' She lowered her voice. 'What the hell did you bring Anto along for?'

'How was I meant to drive here and bring you back with only one hand? And me and him were together all day. Planning.'

'Oh yeah. Planning what?'

'Leave that with me for now. I'll share it when we have a solid one. Did you not hear about the shooting at the hospital?'

'What hospital?'

'Blanch.'

'No, not a thing.'

'Some poor fucker wearing my jacket was annihilated. Anto reckons it was meant for me. I had a lucky escape, Kym.'

'How can you be so bloody calm about it?'

'Because I'm not dead. Anyway, I thought they'd got hold of you. You weren't answering my calls or texts. I wanted to tell you to keep a low profile. Where were you anyway?'

'At a hen party.' *Busy getting off my face on anything I could snort or drink.*

'Oh?'

'Yeah, then we went on to a party.'

'Where?'

'Lee Thompson's house.'

'That dirtbird?' Ian said. 'I bet he tried to get up on one of your friends. I hope he didn't try to have a go on you?'

'Yeah. You know what his motto is, don't you? There's a gap that my dick will fit, let me ride it.' Anto laughed. 'He'd mount a low flying crow if he could.'

'No, he didn't try to *have a go* on me. What do you think I am, a carnival ride?'

Anto doubled over. 'Did you not hear about the time he tried to finger a wan on the roller coaster? Nearly broke his wrist when the ride twisted and dipped.'

'I thought he was your friend, lads.'

'He is,' Ian said. 'That's how we know what he's like.'

'I'm off for a slash. Don't go digging up any bodies while I'm gone.' Anto disappeared into the dark.

Not wanting to hear any more about Lee, Kym changed the subject. 'I didn't hear anything about the shooting. Any idea who it was?'

'Dwayne. Who else? The forty-eight hours is up, after all. He could have given me more time.'

'Shit, Ian.'

'Yeah. Shit. And what are you doing off your head, wandering around graveyards in the early hours? I've never seen you in this state. For a start, it's not safe.'

She sighed. 'It all got too much for me.'

'What did?'

'Hazel being gone, and Dwayne fucking Flynn threatening you to get information on something you can't possibly know. And now someone nearly killing you. I'm worn out.'

Ian put his arm around her. 'I'm fair knackered myself.'

'Hey, seeing as how you were at the hospital, did you have to talk to the cops?'

'No. It was chaos there. We legged it the first chance we got. Anto pulled one of the doctors out of the way of a bullet, though. A hero, he is.'

'Jesus.'

'Yeah, he wasn't hanging around for any medals though, in case the shooter got a look at us and realised he'd got the wrong guy. And if anyone asks, we didn't see a thing.'

'Oh good God, Ian. I really have had enough. We need to get out of here. Somewhere like Spain, where they've never even heard of Dublin.'

'I know, Kym. And you miss Hazel, don't you? At least now the baby is back where she belongs, and you can look after her. You don't want to leave her, do you?'

He's not getting it. Why is he insisting we stay? He's putting us both in danger. 'I still want to go. I thought when Ged died, you'd have nothing more to do with the Lewis family. And now you're a target because of them.'

'I know.'

'You can't avoid Dwayne Flynn forever, Ian, no fucking way. And if he's behind this . . .'

Anto was back, zipping up his jeans. 'If Dwayne is behind that shooting, he's gone too far. And at a hospital, too. That poor fucker had no idea of the consequences of nicking your jacket. He saved your life.'

'You can't keep working for that animal, Anto,' Kym said.

'I have no choice. He says I owe them a debt of two hundred thousand, and Bird being gone makes no difference.'

'Fuck,' Kym said. In the distance, the noise of the traffic grew louder. Dawn was not far off.

'Yeah. And you should have seen what he got me to do first,' Anto said.

'What?'

'Evict Marion Aherne from Bird's house.'

'No fucking way.'

'Yep, and Bosco knocked her around quite a bit, too. And what was even worse . . .'

'What?'

'Dwayne made Brenno come along.'

'Fuck, no,' Kym said.

'Bastard,' Ian added.

'Ian told me what Dwayne did to him when he broke in and threatened you both,' Anto said.

Kym began to shiver.

'Let's get you out of here,' Ian said. He looked down at her feet. 'Where are your shoes?'

'No idea. I kicked them off back along the road there.'

'Fucking hell, Kym.' Ian shook his head. 'You'll get yourself done in if you wander around in the dead of night like this. And in the graveyard, too. God only knows who'd be here.'

'Only me and the dead people,' she said, with a half-smile.

'No. There's always someone ridin', hidin', or shooting up. Any deserted place is a cesspit of fuck-ups at night, not just here. Come on.'

With Ian and Anto supporting her, she picked her way across the grass. Her bag kept slipping off her shoulder, and every time she pulled it up, she lost her balance and almost fell.

They loaded her into the back of the BMW. Kym lay stretched across the seat with the soles of her feet against the window, smearing the glass. There were blades of grass between her toes.

'Fuck's sake, Kym. Take them feet down. You can be cleaning the marks now. We come out here to rescue you and that's the thanks I get.'

'Did I ask you to come?'

'You did, actually,' Ian said.

As Anto put the car into gear, Kym shot upright. 'Oh no.'

'I swear to fuck, Kym, if you puke in my car, I will kill you.'

'No, I'm not gonna puke. The gun.'

'What gun?' Ian said.

'The one I brought to the graveyard.'

'What did you bring a gun to a graveyard for?' Anto asked. 'And where did you get your hands on one?'

'I found it.'

'Where?' Anto grunted. 'Do I even want to know?'

'So, wait,' Ian said. 'There was a gun just lying around and you found it? Was it in that dirtbag's house when you were at his party?'

'Stop calling him that. And no, I didn't find it there. I found it a few days ago.'

'Then why didn't you use it the other night when Dwayne broke in?' Ian asked. 'It would have been justifiable homicide, as long as you didn't shoot him in the back.'

'Believe me, I would have if he hadn't frightened the shit out of both of us.'

'Stop talking shit, Kym, you don't have a gun,' Anto said.

'Yeah, have a smoke and chill out,' Ian said.

'There will be no smoking in my car,' Anto said. 'Wait till we're home to spark up.' He turned on the ignition.

'No, no, we need to go back. Believe me, Ian, I did have a gun.' *Shit, shit, why didn't I pretend to need to puke? I could have hunted for it and they needn't have known a thing.*

'Kym, you are seriously pissing me off now. You'll find yourself kicked out of the car to find your own way back,' Anto said. 'Gun. You're raving. Why the fuck would you bring a gun to a hen party?'

'I'm not raving. I thought it might come in handy. You know, for protection. I wasn't thinking.'

'No, you were not thinking. That's for sure,' Ian said.

'I could have got you one if you needed protection,' Anto said.

'Thanks, Anto.'

'Right. Back we go.'

Kym fell sideways as Anto swung the car around. Using the torch on their phones, they traced the route she'd taken.

Anto swept his phone torch across the ground. 'Kym, you are crazy, for sure. There's nothing here.'

'See that hole in the earth? That's where I fired it, before it fell out of my hands. Bet you the bullet's in there.'

'Well, I'm not digging for it,' Anto said. 'Are you sure it wasn't some plastic toy?'

'It's true, I tell you. How else would I know it's a Beretta Pico?'

'Jesus Christ,' Ian and Anto said in unison.

'Where did you get your hands on one of those?' Ian asked.

'Never you mind.'

'Jesus Christ, Ian,' Anto said. 'She's like a vault. You'd want to watch her, holding secrets like that.'

They searched for a while longer. There was no sign of it anywhere.

'Are you sure you dropped it here?' Anto said.

'I am.'

'If you are telling the truth, you'd better remember where you had it. You'll be in serious shit if you don't,' Ian said.

'Who from?'

'From whoever used that gun before you. If it has been used and the cops get their hands on it, they'll be able to tell who it was.'

'But will they be looking for it?' she asked.

'Yes, if it has been used in a crime. Find evidence like that, they'd be creaming themselves. Suppose some oul' biddy was visiting a grave, found it and handed it in.'

'Fuck, yeah. But no one knows I had it, so how would the cops connect it with me?'

'So long as you haven't been seen with it,' Ian said.

'No way.'

'I told you,' Ian said, 'never think you're on your own in a place like this. Come on.'

'But we haven't found it,' Kym said.

'It's long gone, I'd say. We'd better put a few feelers out to see what happened to it,' Anto said.

'You know what, just let it off,' Kym said, suddenly tired of the whole thing. 'I shouldn't have taken it. And I didn't use it to kill anyone.'

'No. But you did fire a shot. Didn't you say you shot it off into the grave?' Ian said.

'Yeah.'

'So your prints and whatever else might be on it.' Anto grabbed her hand. 'You've a cut.'

'Aw, balls, that's from the recoil.'

'Jesus, that's your DNA too. Kym, if we don't find that gun, you are screwed.'

'Aw, no, Ian. What will I do? Anto, you know guns better than I do. Any suggestions?'

'What makes you think I know about guns, Kym?'

'Who are you trying to convince?' she retorted.

'Fair point. Look, stick with me,' Anto said, 'and we'll figure something out.'

'We both will,' Ian added. 'I'm not letting my woman go down for something she didn't do.'

'I'll do anything to get that back.'

'Let's come back when it gets light,' Anto suggested.

'Can't we just wait here until then?' Kym asked. 'It's not long till morning.'

'We could.'

Anto parked up at the gate of Mulhuddart Cemetery and they settled themselves in the car to try and catch some sleep.

There wasn't a hope of Kym catching any sleep. Her mind kept going back over the events of the past few days. And where was that gun?

* * *

8.03 a.m. Kym heard birdsong. The sky was a pale grey. The two lads stirred.

'How are we all?' Anto asked, moving his seat upright.

'In bits,' Ian said, yawning.

Kym was glad she'd put her phone on silent. Eight missed calls from Lee. A message asking if she was okay and could she meet him. He'd also sent a video. She opened it. It began with a three-way kiss, her, Lee and another girl. *Fuck.* She shut it down before she saw any more, or, worse than that, before Ian saw any of it.

101

'I've had time to think,' Kym said. 'And there's no point waiting around. I need out of here, Ian.'

'Christ, you want to leave now after we've spent hours kipping in the car?'

'No, not this graveyard. Out of the estate. Maybe out of Dublin too. A different country. Spain, or even Australia. Soon. Before Dwayne comes back to carry out his threat.'

'Not with a conviction for possessing a gun you won't,' Anto said.

'I won't get caught with it.'

'Fine, then be alert. Keep your mouth shut and listen. A wrong word in the right place will give you the answer you need. You too, Ian.'

'Yeah.'

'Okay. I'll do whatever the two of you advise,' Kym said.

Anto was first out of the car. After a minute or so, he returned with the Beretta.

'Oh, Anto. Thank God,' Kym cried.

'God had nothing to do with it. I'd say we walked past it a few times. It was behind the cross at Ged's grave.'

'Good,' Ian said. 'Can we get going now?'

'We can,' Anto said. 'But I've been thinking too. Don't be in such a rush to get out of here, Kym. We have to stop Dwayne.'

'How?' she said.

'Me and Ian spent all yesterday hatching a plan.'

'What kind of plan?' Kym said.

'We find those drugs before he does,' Anto said.

'I can't see how either of you are going to do that,' Kym said.

'Well, for a start, we now have a Beretta.'

'And the hospital gave me back the knife,' Ian added.

This made all three of them laugh. Meanwhile, Kym was making plans of her own. Neither Ian nor Anto took her wish to escape the city seriously, or that she was busy drawing up an actual plan. She could use Anto and Ian as a means to get what she needed. Meanwhile, she would go along with them, help them find those drugs. Then she would see.

CHAPTER 15

Danielle woke with a jerk to the sound of her phone vibrating. Her satin eye mask slid up onto her forehead. Her eyes still shut, she felt around for the phone on the locker beside her bed. In the process, she knocked it onto the floor.

She leaned over the side of the bed to retrieve it, muttering, 'Thanks be to fuck.' The screen hadn't cracked.

She had thirteen missed calls from Linda. She groaned and lay back. Her white vest-top had a dark red stain near her left breast, probably from the full-bodied red she'd laced into last night. Her tongue had acquired a fur coat and her lips were dry. Her skin was clammy and smelled of decay. Her long, usually shiny, locks were dull and the ends were split.

A noise outside the bedroom door sent her reaching for the gun under the other pillow. *Shit.* She'd forgotten she'd left it tucked into a pocket on the buggy, which had been taken along with the baby. The door opened a crack. A hand appeared, with a brown paper bag dangling from it.

'Breakfast. And you'd better not have a gun in your hand, or a dick in your mouth.'

'Linda?'

'Who else?'

'Come in, you wagon. It's safe. And if I had a dick in my mouth, you'd have heard the guy yelling in ecstasy all the way to the entrance hall.'

'Too much information, Danielle.'

'And what about you? Giving a hand job to that guy in the kitchen last night. The image is seared into my brain.'

'A girl's gotta do what a girl's gotta do. But, yeah, sorry about that. I've been a month here on my own, run of the house and all that.'

'I thought you were seeing the guy from the gym — Lee something or other.' Danielle rubbed her face and yawned.

'That was him. I introduced you, but you were obviously so pissed you don't remember.'

'You introduced me to him while you were giving him a blow job?'

'It was a hand job, Danielle. And I introduced you later, when you came back into the kitchen for a bag of salt and vinegar crisps.'

'Fuck, did I?'

'Yeah.'

'That explains the taste in my mouth.'

Linda pushed the door open with her hip. In her other hand was a holder with two takeaway cups. The thought of coffee eased Danielle's throbbing headache somewhat, although it would probably require a pharmaceutical — several — to tone down the pain.

Linda made a face. 'Jesus, the stench of stale wine and empty crisp packets in here. Place reeks of it.'

'Tell me something I don't know.'

'Soak that in salt and cold water.'

'What, my head?'

'No, the top.'

Linda plumped herself down on the bed and rested the cup holder and brown paper bag on the locker. Danielle groaned and leaned back against the pillow.

Linda tugged one of the takeaway cups free and held it out. 'Two sugars?'

'Yep.'

'Oat milk?'

'Yep.'

'Shot of whisky?'

'No. But seeing it's nearly opening time . . .' Danielle took the cup from Linda, wrapped her hands around it and inhaled.

'Jesus. Fuck. I am dying here.'

Linda sighed. 'No shit, Danielle.'

'What's that supposed to mean?'

'It means what it means. I know we were both drinking last night, but don't go down this road, please. It's no way to regain control of your life.'

'What are you, my mother?'

'I'm a bit too young for that. Ask me next year. But seriously, Danielle, you need to get your shit together.'

'You must be serious; you've used my name twice in three sentences. What about your own bad habits?'

'Talk to me, Danielle. Tell me what's going on in that head of yours.'

Danielle sighed. 'Whenever I close my eyes, I see guns pointing at me. I do regret drinking so much, but since Chloe was taken, it's the only way I can get any sleep. Worse things have happened to me, but I can't seem to forget that attack, or move on. And every time I think of it, all the other times come back. It's never-ending.'

'Jesus, Danielle. No wonder you can't sleep. Can I do anything to help?'

Danielle shook her head. 'It's all dog-eat-dog, who's the most powerful, who's the most violent. It's wearing, and it's not my style. I don't operate like that.'

'Couldn't you find another way to maintain the business, be in charge but not compromise yourself?'

'That'll take some work.'

'It'd be worth it, though.'

'Yeah.'

'You've been through so much. And then the fucking guards taking the apartment from you. What the hell?'

'Who knows, Linda.'

'Did they seize any other Lewis properties?'

'No, just the apartment. It wasn't in Ged's name.'

'Ann will not be pleased,' Linda said.

'Fuck her.'

'Never in my worst nightmares.'

They both laughed, but Danielle's mirth was short-lived. 'It's all fucked.'

'That's the drink talking. It's beginning to get to you. It's fucking with your mind, and you can't see your way forward.' Linda looked around the room. 'And the I in this place doesn't exactly make you want to break into song, does it?'

'At least it's somewhere to lay my head. I'd have been out on the street if you hadn't taken me in,' Danielle said.

'Well, it is your place, after all.'

'Yeah.'

'You could have gone to London. I could always send money to you.'

'What if the cops notice money being moved? I can't have my assets seized, too. And what about Chloe?'

'She's not your baby, Danielle.'

As if I don't know that. 'But she is Ged's, and I can look after her.'

'So can her family. Let her go,' Linda said. 'Seriously, it's gotten out of hand. It's since—'

'Don't say it.'

'I will say it. Since you returned to Dublin, things have gone a bit . . . well, you seem to have lost track. You have to face reality, Danielle. She is back with her family — Hazel's family.'

'She's not gone. They're just looking after her until they realise I'm a better fit.'

Linda shook her head. 'You'll be hardly fit to stand at this rate, not to mind looking after a baby. How you thought you could just take her over without anything official, I don't know.'

'It happened to me. Ged took me under his wing and more or less raised me. According to my mam, my father died before I was born. She never spoke of him. No one did.'

'Did Ann have an input in raising you?' Linda asked.

'She was always off somewhere, either on holiday, on the lash, or with her family in Limerick. No, it was Ged I had the bond with. Dean was always the annoying fucking addition, no sense or business head about him.'

'Ged saw you as the brains of the operation, so.'

'The reluctant heiress,' Danielle said, 'and look at the hassle it has drawn on me.'

'And you want that life for Chloe?'

'They only wanted her because they thought she'd be coming with money.'

'Do you really think that?'

Danielle shrugged. 'I don't know what to think.'

'But I thought Hazel's parents were decent, hardworking people.'

Danielle sighed. 'Yeah, Hazel's father runs — no, owns — a taxi firm.'

'You really think she'd be better off here, in this crappy place?'

Danielle shrugged and took a sip of the coffee. *Perfect.*

'At least you have answers now,' Linda said.

'That's little consolation when I came close to being killed — again.'

'So, what are you going to do? Head back to London?'

First Saoirse, now Linda. What's with everyone trying to get rid of me?

'I don't know what to do.'

'If you want my opinion, there's too much to be done here,' Linda said. 'You can't let the guards take apart everything Ged put together.'

'What if I can't help that happening? What if they've already put it in motion? I'll be here, broke, homeless . . . though I suppose I do have the business in London. They can't take that.'

'Danielle, do you actually realise how much money we're talking about here? What Lewis Holdings actually controls?'

'Millions, I guess. I really have no idea.'

'If you consider the properties, the business interests and the drugs, you are talking billions, Danielle. That's surely a sum worth fighting for.'

'Christ. I can't even begin to get my head around that amount.'

'With your brains, Danielle, and my technical know-how, we can control the city's drug trade,' Linda said.

'We could, couldn't we? And maybe do some good,' Danielle said.

'No good can ever come out of the drugs trade, Danielle. You need to get into the accounts, assess what is there, and decide what you want to do with it.'

Danielle sighed. 'There is little point in running away, is there? I can be a fuck-up in France, pissed off in paradise or a loser in London; the location won't make any difference to the hurt and loss. Nothing will fill the big empty hole in my heart.'

'You need to get the hell over it. Hazel's immediate family are entitled to custody of the baby. They are more closely related to her than you, and there's nothing you can do about it,' Linda said.

'At least I can trust you to tell it to me straight, Linda. You don't know how important that is.'

'Thank you. And that is what I am doing now. I'm not going to abandon you when you're most in need of support.' Linda smiled ruefully. 'And speaking of telling you straight, I came across two dead bottles of red wine this morning. I take it you didn't have company after I went to bed, seeing as there's only one glass on the counter. You necked them all by yourself? No wonder you don't remember me introducing you to Lee. You were really out of it, weren't you?'

Danielle felt something on her cheek. Only then did she realise that she was crying.

'Jesus, Danielle, maybe that was giving it to you too straight. Sorry, love.'

Danielle melted into Linda's embrace.

'This really has been a shit few months for you,' murmured Linda.

'It doesn't get easier, you know, the loss of my own baby.'

'I can't even begin to imagine what it's like to lose a child, but I care about you enough to try to understand.'

Danielle swiped at a tear that had reached her jaw.

'You need to take action,' Linda said. 'You need to not only take charge, Danielle, you need to *show* those out there that you are in charge. You can't spend every night hiding here flicking fag butts out of the window at the pigeons and drinking whatever you pick up at the off-licence.'

Danielle pushed her hair back over her shoulders, knots and all.

'Staying in here doesn't make you any safer. You need to get back out there. But you also need to stay alert. There could still be someone waiting to take you out of the picture.'

'Don't . . .'

'You need to hear this. You need to show all those others how indestructible you are. Show them that when Danielle Lewis is in action, they better watch out. There are plenty of funds coming in, so you won't have that worry while you build yourself up again.'

'What do you mean, funds coming in? I thought everything had ground to a halt since the funeral,' Danielle said, beginning to show an interest.

'No, there are some pubs, and income from rents.'

'I hope you've been taking a wage,' Danielle said.

'A little. But to do anything major with the money, I need your approval. Anyway, that kind of spending is beyond me. It needs you to carry out those dealings.'

'Have you more details?' Danielle said.

'There are quantities of cash on hold for you. It's being kept in storage, and is not easy to get access to. There are brokers that need your approval, some as far away as Somalia. There are several businesses in the company name, but there's also some property around the city — including a block of apartments along Spencer Dock — that is in your name. Then there's buildings like the one in Harcourt Street. The renovations are complete and it's up and running.'

'Jesus. Really? Why didn't you tell me all this earlier?'

'You weren't ready to hear it earlier. You are now. And remember, this building is also yours. You need to show the city that you are managing the businesses Ged left, or someone else will move in.'

'You think?'

'Yes.'

'Who have I to back me? I'll need muscle.'

'There are still guys who're running things.'

'I need to get myself straightened out, so, Linda.'

'Yes, and I have just the thing to get your mind off your distress.'

'Really?' *What? Some guy about to enter and do a strip?*

'Finish the coffee. There's a protein bar and a croissant in the bag, and then get yourself into your fanciest sweats.'

'Why?'

'I'm taking you to the gym.'

Oh. Is that all? 'Are you off your head?'

Linda smiled. 'A little, but I'm not taking no for an answer.'

'You must be joking,' Danielle said. 'Apart from the state I'm in, the last place I want to be is around a bunch of stupid men lifting weights, filling the room with their alpha-male bullshit.'

'Hmm, yeah.'

'Hmm, yeah. You'd love that, I suppose.'

'Maybe, but back to you, I've booked a couple of exclusive hours in Love Your Curves women-only gym. The guy is onside and he's discreet. I'll keep an eye on everything else.'

'Are you talking about this Lee guy?'

'Exactly, and you saw my hands around his dick last night, so you're already familiar with him.'

'Well, I didn't see much.'

Linda laughed. 'Yeah.'

'So, your boyfriend is going to train me?'

'Fuck, no, when did I ever say he was my boyfriend? He's just a convenient distraction, someone who's all right in the sack.'

Danielle grinned. 'Only all right?'

'I've had better, but he'll do for now.'

Danielle sniffed. 'Jesus, I stink of alcohol.'

'You can lick your sweat while you're working out, then you won't need to hit the bottle tonight,' Linda said.

'Talking of bottles, what about a shot of whisky? Hair of the dog and all that,' Danielle said hopefully.

'The state of you, you'd need a whole dog. No, replacing your electrolytes and getting some decent food into you will do the trick.'

Danielle made a face. 'But I haven't put on any weight to work off.'

'It's not intended for losing weight, it's to build your strength — which is what you need right now.'

'Ooh, listen to you. Don't you go all personal-trainer on me.

'Stay there, so, and wallow.'

'Remind me again why I need your help, Linda?'

'To keep you from fucking yourself over. You need to get out there, Danielle. I know you need someone to love, but that baby wasn't the answer. Maybe you need . . . I dunno — a partner?'

'Well, I'm not going on some dating site, that's for sure.'

'Maybe you just need the ride, then. You know, several inches of hard silicone with a pulse attached.'

'Well, you're no good to me for that.'

They both burst into laughter.

'You have a point, though, Linda.'

'What? About getting the ride?'

'About the hurt,' Danielle said.

'When did I say that?'

'Jesus, will you just take the compliment and listen?' Danielle picked at the croissant.

'Go on.'

'You see, when Chloe got taken, my heart shattered all over again. In London, I ran the business, kept my head down and drew no one's attention. Here, I've been thrust

111

into the heart of the criminal world, and people have their eyes on me. Yes, someone to love would be great, but it would also make me vulnerable. You're right, I need to toughen up, because there's no place for sadness in our world. It gets you killed.'

'And the ride . . .'

Danielle broke off flakes of pastry and flicked them at Linda, sending them scattering across the duvet.

'Then get your arse out of that bed and into the gym. Lee Thompson is waiting. And, please, get someone to change those sheets.'

'Is it, like, a workout or personal training?'

Linda grinned. 'Whatever you need.'

They both laughed again.

As soon as Linda had left the room, Danielle hauled herself off the bed and made for the bathroom. She picked up a towel from a pile by the shower, buried her face in it and released a scream.

She had no experience of the kind of empire her uncle had left her. Running a high-class beauty service company, with all its petty demands, had been a cinch compared to the violence of the world she was about to become immersed in.

'Here.' Linda appeared at the bathroom door with a small box in her hand.

Inside, Danielle found a bracelet with a small locket hanging from it bearing an image of Chloe. 'I don't know what to say, Linda.'

'Look, I'm not completely out of tune with the bond you had with the kid. This way, you can keep her close. I got it made from the photo you sent me. It's gold, so you can even wear it in the shower. And, here . . .'

'My lipstick?'

'Your favourite. It was on the kitchen counter. You always say you can face anything once you have your favourite lippy on. It's like your armour.'

Danielle tucked her lipstick in her pocket, while Linda helped her with the clasps on the bracelet.

'And do me a favour, get something done with that hair. A deep conditioning treatment and a trim. I wondered how you used to keep it looking so lush.'

'I had extensions when I returned, but what you see is all my own now.'

'I'll make an appointment for you.'

'Thanks, Linda.'

Danielle changed the clothes Linda had found for her and followed her to her car. A gym session in Drumcondra was the last thing she wanted, though the workout might help to get her head straight.

CHAPTER 16

On the morning of the funeral, Dwayne lay in bed, the light slicing the bedroom gloom like a dagger. The death of his younger brother had pierced his heart, but he wasn't letting it show. Instead, he buried his sorrow beneath a mass of resentments. Now Bird was dead, it seemed like everyone wanted a piece of him. Well, they weren't getting it. Not Marion Aherne, not Danielle Lewis, no one.

He'd make his enforcers and hatchet men prove their worth like never before. Brendan Aherne, for example. That craven idiot had proved he'd do anything Dwayne asked of him, including evicting his own mother from her home. That buddy of his, Anto Doyle, was another story. Where did Anto's loyalties lie?

Everything was in place. The coffin had been loaded onto the black carriage with its gold and silver trimmings. The four black horses, each wearing ostrich feather plumes, were harnessed and ready.

On leaving his house, Dwayne spotted a Garda Emergency Response Unit vehicle, followed by a couple of unmarked patrol cars. If they were there for the funeral, they'd better keep a low profile. The last thing his brother would have wanted was a bunch of scumbag cops watching him with smiles on their faces. He got into the black stretch Mercedes Maybach immediately behind the carriage. His brother had said he'd be making his own way there. Fine, so long as Jason wasn't planning some stupid stunt.

As the funeral cortege readied itself for the journey to Glasnevin Cemetery, a guttural growl heralded the approach of an Aprilia RSV. It drew up alongside Dwayne. Jason raised the shield of his helmet and gave him a nod.

Behind the Merc, a crowd of people had assembled. Cars joined the procession and the sound of horns filled the air, soon to be joined by the rumble of motorbikes. There were whoops. Someone began to sing.

At the junction of Botanic Road and Finglas Road, guards were directing the traffic, their faces impassive as the crowd of mourners jeered.

The shops along Finglas Road and Prospect Avenue had their blinds down. People going about their daily business stopped and blessed themselves. Here, all traffic had come to a halt, apart from the many dirt bikes that zipped in and around the waiting cars. As the procession neared the entrance to Glasnevin Cemetery, the noise rose to a crescendo.

The horse-drawn carriage came to a halt outside the chapel. Here, the sound of the horses' hoofs on the cobbles echoed in the silence that fell. Jason dismounted and stood at Dwayne's side, ready to shoulder the coffin into the church. Bosco Ryan and Sal Fogarty stood just behind them. Two Louisiana-based associates followed — Bill Frisco and Larry Shine — who had travelled from the States to be included in both the bearer party and to talk business.

Outside, supporters of the Flynn family continued to make their presence known. They caused disruption, brought traffic to a standstill. The cops were obviously unprepared for this much chaos, and were simply overwhelmed. Dwayne could hardly restrain his glee. The Flynns ruled Dublin. With another couple of million euros' worth of drugs to distribute, no one would be able to touch them. No one.

CHAPTER 17

The empty gym resounded with the rhythmic beat of some nameless tune. Danielle latched onto the bar, drew back her shoulder blades and pulled. The weights budged very slightly, leaving her hanging, toes just off the floor, feeling weak as shit. The dirty look she threw in Lee's direction didn't appear to faze him one bit. She didn't want to be here, in this gym in Drumcondra. Her bed had been comfortable. Burrowed under the covers, she wasn't reminded of how weak she'd become during her escape from reality.

'You can do it,' he said. 'Get out of your own way.'

With gritted teeth and a strong urge to punch him, she pulled again. The weights lifted a little further.

'Great. That's a good start.'

A few more deep breaths later, her mind had cleared. By the time she reached the eighth rep, her muscles burned. But by the time she got to the ninth, her thoughts had drifted again. Meetings she must set up — with the solicitor and business manager, and anyone else she had to keep onside to ensure the smooth running of the businesses.

'Do you want me to spot you for a bench press after this?' Lee jolted her back to the present.

'Nah,' she said. She struggled but managed to hit the tenth rep. 'I think it's time to head. I'll let you open up for your other members.'

'That's okay. I don't mind exclusive clients. It gives the place a better reputation.'

Linda joined them, slick with the sweat of a workout that had clearly been more productive than Danielle's.

'Did you speak to her?' Linda said to Lee.

Lee shook his head. 'Too busy trying to get her motivated.'

Linda grinned. 'I told you it would be a challenge.'

'I am here, you know,' Danielle said.

'Lee wanted to ask you about your plans for this place.'

Lee nodded.

'My plans? Oh, I get it. You want me to join and pay out huge sums of money not to come in?'

'No, it's not that,' Lee said. 'I'd be keen to work with a talented businesswoman such as yourself. Someone who can help me get the best out of this place.'

Danielle raised an eyebrow. 'Jesus, you're all flattery. What's your take on this, Linda?'

'What's yours?'

'If I was sticking around, maybe.' She looked around her. 'I can see how the place could be developed and improved. I can even see myself getting use out of it.'

Linda gave her a nudge. 'I think he wants to work with you.'

'I do,' he said.

'This place is already yours to run, Danielle,' Linda said. 'Ged put it in your name.'

'Really?'

'Yep. I didn't just bring you here for a workout. I wanted you to get a tangible feel of what's yours.' Linda tapped the machine Danielle had been using. 'If I can persuade you to come, think how many people we can get who actually want to work out.'

'Christ.' Danielle turned to Lee. 'Okay. Sounds like a good plan. I think we could work together.'

Smiling broadly, Lee walked away from them.

'Didn't it feel good even getting a bit of a sweat on?' Linda asked.

'Okay, I admit it. It did help, yeah.'

'Did it help take your mind off things?'

'A bit. But I still can't help wondering how Chloe is. If she's missing me . . .'

A burst of loud revs and horns broke the silence of the empty gym. Linda and Danielle went to the window, but couldn't see where the noise was coming from. They turned away.

'You'd have given her a great life,' Linda said.

'Yeah, fuck Hazel's family coming out of the woodwork like that. All they're after is cash. I'm convinced of it.'

'But you could move on. You could still have your own baby,' Linda said.

'Don't even go there.'

'Fine.'

'Maybe if the social workers did get involved, they might decide to give her back to me,' Danielle said.

Linda sighed. 'I keep telling you, Danielle, the Bradys are Chloe's blood relatives; you're not. You're torturing yourself here, Danielle.'

'But, Christ, that estate. You wouldn't bring a dog up there.'

'It isn't great, that's true. But Hazel's parents are solid.'

'Really? After they got someone to do this to me?' By now the bruises on her face had faded somewhat, but they were still evident.

'If they were behind it. They don't seem the type to me,' Linda said.

'Yeah, my gut is telling me the same thing. As I said, when Frank drove me from the hospital, he seemed genuinely shocked to hear I'd been assaulted and Chloe taken.'

'Sounds to me like he really didn't know,' Linda said.

Danielle sighed. 'But still, their relatives only live a few doors away from Bosco Ryan, and we all know who he is. Running drugs wholesale for the Flynns and getting all the kids in the estate to do his dealing for him. Scumbag.'

'Yes, and I heard that Bosco got a big promotion from Bird and is now working side by side with Dwayne,' Linda added. 'People who grow up in places like that, it's all they know.'

'Hmm.'

'What about Hazel's place? Ged set her up in a nice spot,' Linda said.

'He sure did. You mean get the family to move in there?'

'Why not?' Linda bent and touched her toes. 'Although, they'd probably be afraid of getting evicted at some point.'

Keen to divert the subject away from Hazel, Danielle said, 'Throw me the towel from my bag, please.'

Linda rooted through the backpack and tossed a small blue towel at her. Danielle wiped sweat from her face and arms.

'I need more. I need a run.' What was she saying? Her body ached at the mere thought of it.

'Jesus, Danielle, what the fuck? I don't think I'm up for a run right now.'

'Did I say I wanted you with me?'

'Well, no.'

'Second thoughts, maybe I'd be better with a fast walk.'

'You do what you need to do. I think Lee is waiting to talk to you. Meet me in about an hour on Summerfield Avenue. I'll ring you when I'm there. Will I take your bag?' Linda said.

'Do.'

'Are you sure you're okay to go alone?' Linda said.

'Despite the assault, it's been a while since anyone has tried to shoot me. I'll keep watch and run like fuck if I get even a sniff of a threat.'

'Okay, if you're sure?'

'I am. And you're right,' Danielle said. 'I've been cooped up too long, not living my life. I need to get away from those feelings, set the businesses up so that I have options.'

Linda smiled. 'That's what I like to hear.'

Lee came back into the gym. He smiled at Linda and dropped a small bunch of keys onto the bench in front of Danielle.

'For here, boss.'

'Thank you. You know, this place may not be a bad little earner,' Danielle said.

Linda, who had been looking at Lee, turned to Danielle. 'I agree.'

'Let me know what the showers are like.' Danielle winked at Linda.

'I will. Oh, and make sure the door is locked when you leave,' Linda said. 'I might be otherwise occupied.' Linda followed Lee to the changing rooms.

'Have fun,' Danielle said.

CHAPTER 18

Red and gold maple leaves floating around her, Danielle marched on, unseeing. Along with her thoughts, her feet had carried her back to the past without her knowing it. It was tempting to turn back. The Grave Diggers Pub was just around the corner. She could down a few vodkas and not have to face it all yet again. Instead, she continued past the pub and under the stone arch and metal gates of Glasnevin Cemetery.

She stood before the grave of her son. It seemed like every time she was about to make a new beginning, she was drawn back to this headstone. It seemed more like a way marker than a resting place, and her life an endless series of wrong turns, missed opportunities, what-ifs.

She heard footsteps and only turned round when they came to a stop behind her.

He seemed to emerge out of her thoughts — another what-could-have-been.

Danielle turned to face him. 'I thought we'd said all we had to say the last time we met here, Jason.'

'Well, I didn't come here to meet you, Danielle. I'm at my brother's funeral.'

'Today? I thought you were waiting until Dwayne came back.'

'He has, so he decided to bring it forward.' Jason hesitated. 'He isn't delaying making his presence known, either.'

'How?' Danielle asked.

'Never you mind.'

'Well, I do mind, if it could affect me.'

Jason sighed. 'Stick with me and I'll make sure it doesn't.'

She looked searchingly at him. 'Jason . . . What are you not telling me?'

He said nothing.

'Is Dwayne keeping things from you?'

They stood side by side, staring at the headstone. Danielle noted irrelevantly that the teal colour of her top was reflected in the granite.

Life continues, she thought. *Look, traffic passes by, the birds fly in and out of the trees. Other people are going about their business.* Danielle watched the clouds move slowly across the sky. There was a weight in her chest, words she wanted to say but couldn't. He'd done too much damage for her to join her path with his. Another what-if. If she hadn't walked in on him and that woman . . . But she'd been through that before.

Jason broke the silence. 'What happened to your face, Dani?'

'I got mugged.'

'Who by?'

She'd guessed that would be his next question. 'No idea, yet.'

'Will you let me know when you find out?'

She looked at him. 'Why would I do that, Jason?'

'No one should get away with doing that to you.'

'I can look after myself.'

'I know you can.' Jason looked around. 'We should get out of here.'

'What for?'

'To talk.'

'But I've nothing to say to you.'

'I think you might.' He gripped her elbow.

'No.' She yanked her arm free.

'I heard you went into hiding,' he said. 'Everyone's saying you're throwing in the towel and leaving the Flynns to run this city. The way it should be.'

'Fuck you.'

He gripped her arm again. 'Come away with me, Danielle, please. There's a Flynn burial being held; the place is crawling with people who have a very bleak opinion of the Lewis family. You can't stay here. You'll be in danger.'

'When am I *not* in danger, Jason? Okay, I see your point. Give me a few minutes longer here, then I'll go with you.'

It seemed like a small thing, accepting a lift. But Danielle knew it was more than that. She was embarking on a journey, taking a new road.

CHAPTER 19

Dwayne gazed bitterly at the mound of freshly-dug earth. His younger brother, cut down at the burial of his greatest rival, and just as control of the city was within his grasp.

The noise outside the gates continued, and would do so well into the night. Here, those wishing to express their sympathies did so quietly, then left, one by one. Once the coffin had been lowered, Jason had taken himself off, leaving Dwayne with the two businessmen with whom he was keen to broker a deal.

'Do you want to stay a bit longer, or are you ready to head for pints?' Bill Frisco whispered.

Dwayne turned from the grave. 'There's nothing more to be done here. Let's go.'

'Should we wait for Jason?' Larry Shine added.

'Nah, he'll be along when he's ready,' Dwayne said. 'You two men ride with me and we'll chat on the way.'

Dwayne, Billy and Larry settled themselves in the plush leather seat of the limo. The three of them sat facing a well-stocked bar beneath the window. Dwayne produced a bottle of Midleton Very Rare Whisky, that year's release, and poured them each a measure.

Dwayne raised his glass. 'To Bruce "Bird" Flynn. May he rule the clouds the way he ruled the city.' Solemnly, they clinked glasses.

Dwayne gave the driver his instructions and the limo glided forward, so smoothly the whisky in the bottle didn't move. 'So,' began Dwayne, 'how's things in the Deep South?'

'It's like picking daisies over there,' Larry began. His smile revealed very white protruding teeth, like piano keys. 'Women, children, men, all desperate for a better life, deep in debt and working their asses off to make enough money to get away.'

'Have you carried out a risk assessment?' Dwayne asked.

'Yes, the last consignment landed safe and sound, and they've a month's work done already. We've contacts at a large number of ports. New Orleans is proving very convenient. Then there's Port-Au-Prince. It was getting pricy to pay the gangs in Haiti, so we just employed them.'

'Good call. Right. Any escapees so far?'

'They'd be brave to dare. Anyway, if one or two do get away, they're soon back. Some have little or no English, and they're too shit-scared to talk anyway, since we've put the frighteners on their families back home.'

'Where do you source the stuff?' Dwayne asked.

'Haiti, mainly, and New Orleans. Haiti's a gold mine, with all the disasters. We're also thinking of checking out Romania.'

'Right. Sounds like you've that side all in hand,' Dwayne said.

'And what about your end of it, Dwayne?' Bill asked.

'Going well so far. I'll only use my own trucks, once we've a regular influx of the cargo. I'm in the process of taking over a freight company that's in debt. The drivers won't be told of the new arrangement, since it'll be operating under the name of the previous owners, and they'll carry on as before, but with a few additional consignments. Anyway, I wanted to talk to you about something else.'

Bill raised his glass and drank. 'Go on.'

'Five million euros' worth of coke.'

'Okay. And you want to transport that without human cargo?' Bill asked.

'No, it's already here.'

'Well,' Larry said, 'that should make a tidy profit.'

'Do you know what will make more of a tidy profit?' Dwayne looked from Bill to Larry. 'Crack.'

'Fuck. Are you serious, Dwayne?' Bill said.

'Very. Dublin's never seen crack, it will upend the city, make zombies of the addicts. The crime rate will skyrocket as people scramble for a taste. The cops will be so busy trying to crack down — 'scuse the pun — that we can move our cargo much more easily. I already have a guy lined up to convert it.'

Larry held up his hand. 'Wait. Just so we're clear, you want to flood the streets with crack, and you want us to invest. That it?'

'We've gone beyond that type of trade now, Dwayne. Here in Dublin, anyway,' Bill said.

Dwayne smiled. This was what he'd been hoping for — they weren't interested in competing. 'I understand that, gentlemen. I'm not looking for your money. I don't need you to invest. It's already paid for.'

'Then why are we even discussing it?'

'Because how's about ten percent of the profits for doing nothing?'

Larry shook his head. 'If a thing sounds too good to be true—'

'I know. Let's just say its previous owner no longer has any use for it. It's, er, tied up somewhere.'

The two men looked at each other across Dwayne, who sat between them, looking modestly at his shoes. After a few seconds, in which they wrestled in silence with the offer, he decided it was time to put it to them straight. 'I want to use your network of contacts. I need a list of all the Lewis properties in Dublin and the surrounding area.'

'I still don't get it,' Bill said. 'What are we investing in exactly?'

'That information will net you ten percent of any revenue from the sales of the product,' Dwayne said.

'Really? No cash, just information?' Larry asked.

'Yes.'

Larry narrowed his eyes.

'And how are those details gonna help you, Dwayne?' Bill asked.

'That's a conversation for another time. Let's just say that if I have that information, the stuff will get onto the streets that much more easily, meaning the profits should be immediate. The source I had proved to be . . . worthless, so I need to look elsewhere. I understand you and Ged Lewis shared a business consultant.'

'Woah there, Dwayne. What are you asking here?' Larry said.

'Perhaps the information I'm looking for can be got through this business consultant.' He looked from one man to the other.

Bill finished his drink. 'I don't know. If we press them to hand out confidential information to all and sundry, we could find that they no longer want to deal with us.'

'Come on, gentlemen.' Dwayne was growing impatient. 'There are plenty of business consultants out there.'

'Not with the connections this company has. Your dealings are obviously still pretty low-level, if you don't understand the rules of that part of the game.'

How dare they? Low-level, indeed. Dwayne searched his mind for a suitable response, to show them he was as much in the know as they were. He came up with nothing. 'I understand. I'm hoping this consignment will get me some way there.'

'Only a fraction, Dwayne, and we can't be recommending anyone with hidden agendas here.'

'What hidden agendas? I'm just looking for a bit of info.'

Larry leaned forward. 'But that "bit of info," as you call it, would create problems for us that a measly five million wouldn't even begin to compensate for.'

'Your business consultant is that good?'

'Yes.' Bill glanced at Larry, who gave a slight nod. 'They're the ones with the Somalian connection. They're experts in the transfer of funds in the absence of actual cash. Their word is worth not just millions, but billions, Dwayne. Like I said, even at a hundred percent of the profits, we cannot compromise them under any circumstances.'

Dwayne looked from Bill to Larry and shrugged. 'Okay. Plan B then. Can you reach out to any of your other contacts and see what they can come up with?'

'We'll do that,' Bill said, after another nod from Larry. 'And it'll still cost you.'

'Right, that's a deal.'

'We'll guarantee to get you the information for twenty percent,' Larry said.

'That's a bit higher than I budgeted for, gentlemen.'

'Well, that's our price, Dwayne,' Bill said.

'Fifteen percent of the wholesale price, not the street value,' Dwayne added.

'We want nothing to do with the streets. So, yeah, the percentage on the wholesale price.'

'Deal.'

They shook hands, and Dwayne refilled their glasses.

They pulled up outside the Bakerman's Pub on Phibsborough Road. This was a high-class bar almost hidden away between a garage and a row of red-brick houses. Dwayne noticed that two out of the five shutter doors of Phibsborough Fire Station were raised, though the fire engines didn't look poised to respond to any emergency. He remembered his father taking him there to see them when he was a kid. He'd been hooked on lorries and couldn't wait to get his HGV licence, so he could drive one. Now he owned a fleet of them. He hoped he'd done his dad proud.

He let Larry and Bill out of the car just outside the pub, directing them to a VIP area at the rear. He felt flushed with satisfaction at having concluded a deal with such top-quality businessmen, even though it had cost him more than he'd anticipated. The drugs would net him a fortune, and that business consultant would be begging for a share. There'd be no sneering at his status then. As if them two lads weren't born in the heart of Dublin, dragged up until they were lucky enough to spot an opportunity and profit from it.

'Just two hundred yards along,' Dwayne said to the driver. He needed to pick up his other phone from Jason's apartment.

As the car pulled up outside, Dwayne checked his personal mobile. There were five missed calls from Bosco. Dwayne called him back.

Before Dwayne could ask what was going on, Bosco blurted out, 'It was the wrong guy.'

'What? Who?'

'Yesterday morning, outside the—'

'Quit talking. Where are you?'

'Near the Bakerman's.'

'Don't say another word. Get into the car as soon as it pulls up beside you.'

* * *

The limo still moving, Bosco hopped in and sat across from Dwayne.

'Now, go on,' Dwayne said.

Bosco wrung his hands. 'The wrong guy got shot yesterday.'

'What? You mean you didn't shoot Ian Gallagher?'

'No. It's all over the headlines,' Bosco said.

'I didn't see it. I've been busy with the funeral. Some other guy, you say.'

'The photo on the front of the papers is the spit of Gallagher, so it would be easy to mix . . .'

'Easy to mix him up. That what you're trying to say?' Dwayne glared at Bosco.

'Well, yeah.'

'Well, no, actually. If a job has to be done, it has to be done right. Fucking hell, the wrong guy. Who was shot, so?'

'Well — killed, actually. Some fella from Dundalk who was in visiting his da.'

'Jesus Christ. Who'd you get to do it?'

'The new fella,' Bosco said.

'This cannot be happening, not now. The cops will be all over it.'

'Yeah.' Bosco's voice was almost a whisper.

The driver drove alongside a row of apartments in King's Inn Court, towards Kelly's Row, performed an almost miraculous three-point turn and parked in front of the Court.

Dwayne chewed on the inside of his cheek. Where the fuck was Jason? He needed his input on this.

CHAPTER 20

Strands of Danielle's hair, escaped from beneath her helmet, whipped around her mouth. Jason's broad back felt familiar, catapulting her back to their teenage years as they sped through the traffic, zipping between the cars, past the trucks and buses, back to the days when she was deeply in love with the tough, rebellious Flynn.

They made plans to run away together, and Jason began working for his older brothers so as to earn enough money for their escape. Meanwhile, she waited, watching him buy expensive watches, more powerful bikes. He became embroiled in the drugs trade, and there was no more talk of escape.

Back in the present, her initial sense of adventure evaporated. Was she fated to make the same mistakes over and over again? What was she doing on this bike, with this man? She looked over his shoulder and saw a traffic light on red a short distance ahead. She could jump off, run. In an agony of indecision, Danielle saw the light turn green. The choice had been made.

They arrived in front of a metal garage door, which immediately slid open, closing again behind them. They descended into a vast underground car park. Jason brought the bike to a halt and switched off. The silence that fell seemed eerie. Somewhere in the depths, water dripped slowly.

Now what?

'Are you coming up?' He was standing in front of an open lift door. She followed him in. When it reached the third floor, he took out his keys and opened one of three doors. He led the way through an empty hall into a living room flooded with light. Danielle saw they were in the corner apartment. She went to one of the windows and looked down on the North Inner City. *Somewhere down there,* she thought, *is five million euros' worth of coke that could net me a whole lot of money if it were found and distributed.* Dismissing the thought, she turned her gaze on Blessington Street Basin, a former reservoir, now a park. Jason and she had had their first kiss on one of the picnic benches in that park. He had etched their names in the wooden table.

She turned from the window. 'Point me towards the bathroom.'

He smiled. 'You've a choice of two en-suites, or there's the main bathroom by the front door.'

In the main bathroom, she repaired her face and went to find Jason. He was in the kitchen, his back to her, staring out through the window.

'You don't spend much time here, do you?'

'Why do you say that?'

'If you did, you'd hardly notice that view, but you're gazing at it as if you'd never seen it before.'

'Am I?' He turned to face her. 'Danielle, why have you been avoiding me?'

'I didn't know who I could trust.'

'That's a fair point,' he said.

'You could have told me what you'd found out about the shooting that cost us so much. I know you did find something.'

'I couldn't get near you. You'd have swiped the head off me if I'd tried. Wouldn't you?'

'Well, yeah. Not surprising, considering what I caught you doing.'

'So you've said.' He walked towards her. 'That time I saw you at the grave, I thought I might be able to persuade you to give me another chance.'

'What? With your brother breathing down our necks? Bird would just have got in the way. He never would leave me alone.'

He said nothing.

'Sorry,' Danielle said. 'I shouldn't have mentioned it, not today.'

'Yeah. Well, I know what he was like, but he was still my brother.'

'Look, maybe this is the wrong day to be talking about all this stuff.'

He nodded, and said wistfully, 'This was one of his places. He gave it to me about a month ago.'

'This apartment?' So that was why it was so bare. 'He owned quite a bit of property around, didn't he? There's that place in Ranelagh where Marion Aherne is staying.'

'She thought she'd be staying there forever, get ownership even.'

'Why? Did herself and Bird get hitched in secret or something?' Danielle asked.

'Bird and Marion? Christ, no,' Jason said. 'He had no intention of settling down with anyone but you. You were always on his mind, Danielle. He was over the moon when he heard you were back.'

She shuddered. 'But she moved in with him.'

'Yeah, she kept on at him until he had to give in. She knew too much about his business, and he didn't dare piss her off.'

'But,' Danielle continued, 'does she still not know too much? I mean, surely, Dwayne would be better off keeping her onside?'

'He doesn't care. She opens her mouth, he'll kill her, and she knows it.'

'Anyway, she's still there for the moment, what with the funeral and all,' she said.

'Nope. Not anymore. Dwayne evicted her.' Jason grimaced. 'He even got her son to help do it.'

'What? Brenno?'

'Yes. She never saw it coming.'

'I'm surprised she let him do it. I thought she had more fight in her,' Danielle said, recalling how Marion had got Bird to help her try to take the baby away.

'You know Dwayne,' Jason said. 'At the very least, he'd have taken all the windows and doors off and frozen her out.'

'Just before the funeral. That's cruel, Jason.'

He shrugged. 'That's Dwayne for you.'

Danielle shook her head. 'Getting her own son to help. Fuck. Where is she now?'

'Back in her house with her son, most likely. Anyway, I don't feel too sorry for her. If she didn't do what she did, Bird would still be alive.'

There was no answer to that. 'And what about the baby?' she said.

'Baby? Oh, Ged's. Why are you even worried about her. She's not yours.'

So everyone keeps saying. 'I fucking know, but she is blood, and she's the reason I got attacked.'

He moved closer to her. 'Attacked?'

She pointed to her face. 'This wasn't just a random mugging, you know.'

'What? Who attacked you?'

'I don't know, do I? Whoever it was, they took the baby. She ended up with Hazel's parents and I ended up in hospital.'

'I'll find out who it was.'

'And do what, Jason? More attacks, more murders? It's just an endless cycle of revenge. I am sick of it.'

'But you ended up in hospital. Don't you even care who hurt you that much?'

'Well, I'm out now, and there's no lasting damage. Apart from the heartbreak.'

'She's—'

'Not my baby, I know. But I had her so long I began to love her. As if I was fostering her or something. I don't mean she was a substitute for Sam, but when you have a mother's love to give and nowhere to place it, the longing can crush you.'

'I'm starting to understand . . . but I didn't bring you here to go over all that. I wanted to talk about us.'

'Then why didn't you do that months ago?'

He looked confused. 'What do you mean?'

'Why didn't you tell me that there was evidence to prove who tried to murder me ten years ago?'

'Answer me truthfully — would you have believed me if I'd told you what I'd learned? Especially after I'd hurt you that much?' Jason said.

Danielle sighed. 'Probably not.'

'Then that is why I left it to Saoirse. I could see she wasn't like others. She'd lost a lot too, and I knew you trusted her.'

He stood close to her, so close his familiar smell of leather mixed with mint and lemon sent a wave of desire coursing through her body.

'You've got to face it, Danielle. With Dwayne back, the Flynns are running the show. Think how powerful we could be if we combined our efforts.'

Her body cooled and her head cleared. 'You know perfectly well that the revenue from our legitimate businesses far exceeds what the Flynns earn by . . . alternative means. Why should I join forces with you and risk ending up in prison?'

'I'm talking about big money, Danielle. Not millions — billions. There are new opportunities coming up. Dwyane is working on an international connection, something new, big. Get in on the ground with me.'

'I'm doing okay on my own, Jason. I don't need you.'

'I have a good crew,' he said. 'Take Bosco — the man would go through iron for me.'

'Yeah? How sure are you of that?'

'One hundred percent.'

'You can't rely on just one good man. What if something happens to him? Bosco is too like Dwyane; he's volatile. Besides, he thumped one of my girls once. I had to bar him from Berkley Street.'

'You never liked him, did you?' Jason said.

'It's not that. I just wouldn't want to work with him.'

'You wouldn't be working with him,' Jason said. 'He works for me, does what I say.'

She looked sceptical. 'More like what Dwayne says, now that he's back.'

'No, Bosco is loyal to me.'

She shook her head. 'You'd want to be sure of that. And I am still not sure how working with you would benefit me.'

'Me, for one.'

'You?'

'You'd get my devoted attention.'

'I didn't get your attention when I really needed it, did I?'

'I've changed. It's always been you, Danielle, and always will be.'

He reached out and ran his thumb lightly over her lips. 'I've always loved the shape of your lips.'

All her resistance gone, she stepped forward and they kissed. He lifted her onto the counter, and at once, her legs were around his waist. She shrugged off her jacket. He slid his hands up under her top. They were cold, and her skin rippled. He ran his fingers over the scar left where the bullet had grazed her. They froze there, and then he pulled away.

'What's wrong? Is it the scar? Too much of a reminder for you?'

'No, no, Danielle. I just . . . forgot.'

'Forgot? How the hell could you forget that?'

'Sorry, I—'

Danielle pushed him away. He held out his arms, but something made him stop. She heard a phone vibrate. He took it out of his pocket and looked at the screen.

'It's Dwayne. I have to get this.' He turned away from her, the phone to his ear.

She swore, but the call gave a chance to catch her breath. Was this what she really wanted? She slid from the counter and planted her feet on the floor.

Then her own phone rang. It was Linda, probably worried that she hadn't called since leaving the gym. She rejected the call and stuck the mobile back into her pocket. Jason, his eyes on her, was listening to Dwayne. Her phone rang again, and this time she did answer.

'Where the hell are you?' Linda yelled.

'An apartment in Phibsborough.'

'Good, 'cause I'm nearly there.'

'Wait. How did you—'

'Lee said all that noise we heard came from Bird's funeral. I didn't know it had been brought forward. I guessed you'd head to the graveyard, so I went there to check. I saw you get on Jason's bike, and since I knew where he'd been staying, I followed. Get out of there now.'

'Why? What is it?'

'Dwayne Flynn is on his way there, and he's in a rage. He is not to be messed with, Danielle.'

'Why? What's up?'

'Ian Gallagher — you know who he is, right? A Lewis family employee — was targeted in a shooting yesterday as he left the hospital.'

'What?'

'Yes. The word on the street is that the Flynns are behind it. Now get the fuck out of there.' Linda ended the call.

Jason was still staring at Danielle. Neither of them spoke.

With a crash, the door swung open. Kicking it shut behind him, Dwayne made straight for Jason, and before he had time to react, had him pinned to the wall. He took hold of Jason by the collar of his jacket and shook him slightly.

'What the hell, Dwayne?'

'It's all gone to fuck. The wrong man got shot yesterday.'

'What the . . . ?'

'I gave them a precise description, and they still got it wrong. The cops are going to be all over it. We don't need this attention.'

Danielle shrank back, not daring to move. Dwayne obviously hadn't seen her, but what was he saying? Was it Jason who'd fired the shot?

'But I had nothing to do with that.'

'It's still your fault. If things hadn't gotten so bad while I was away, I wouldn't be dealing with all this shit, and we certainly wouldn't be burying our brother. Where the fuck did you get to anyway? What about staying close in case I needed you?'

Jason glanced towards Danielle. Slowly, Dwayne followed his gaze, his hand still on Jason's collar. He'd looked hard and rugged when they were younger but now, he still looked hard, but in a worn-out way, and much older than his forty years. Dwayne was always jealous that Jason got the good looks.

'What's that bitch doing here?'

Danielle reached for her jacket. In a flash, Dwayne was beside her. He grasped her arm and pushed it up behind her back. Christ, his strength. 'I said, what the fuck are you doing here, bitch?'

'Let me go. You're hurting me.'

'I am not having you worming your way back into our lives, profiting off our hard work.'

'Fat chance of that, Dwayne Flynn. Now, let me leave.'

The knife block was almost within her reach. If the only way she could save herself was by burying a knife in Dwayne Flynn's chest, that was what she would do.

She lunged forward, knocking him sideways. She drew the largest knife from the block and held the blade to his chest.

'Move one step closer, Dwayne Flynn, and I will drive this into your heart.'

'My brother was buried today. I come to his apartment, and what do I find? You, trying to get back in with our family. Well, it won't work, Danielle Lewis.'

Danielle glanced over at Jason. So much for his undying love. He remained glued to the wall, watching his brother push her around. The chickenshit.

The knife still pointed at Dwayne's chest, she felt around on the counter for her jacket. 'Let me the fuck out of here, Dwayne.'

As she backed slowly away, Jason stepped forward. Dwayne elbowed him out of the way, connecting with Jason's nose. Then, with a sudden jerk, as if he were emerging from a dream, Dwayne turned and headed to the hall. The door latch clicked.

'Get the fuck out, slut,' Dwayne shouted.

Jason struggled to his feet, holding his bloody nose. 'Just leave, Danielle.'

As she headed out, something fell from her jacket, but she daren't stop to pick it up. At the door, she turned and looked from Dwayne to Jason. 'Are you going to let him speak to me like that?'

Jason didn't answer.

'Well, there's only one slut here, dickhead, and it's not me. Stay the hell away from me, Jason, unless you are willing to stop being his puppet.'

Danielle then turned to Dwayne, the knife blade pointed at his throat.

'If you come within a hundred feet of me, Dwayne Flynn, I will take every bit of your business from you and destroy it — but I'll destroy you first.'

She backed out of the apartment, pulling the door behind her.

CHAPTER 21

Danielle stood with her back to the lift wall, breathing heavily, while the potential consequences of what she had just done began to seep into her brain.

Lost in her thoughts, she forgot she was holding a large knife. Only when the lift doors parted to reveal a horrified-looking Linda did she realise she must look like some deranged killer.

'What the fuck have you done?' Linda said, staring at the knife.

Danielle looked down, mildly surprised to see it. 'Oh, nothing. Though it did help to stop me making one huge mistake.'

'Let's get out of here,' Linda said.

'Absolutely.'

'How the hell did you know this was where Jason hangs out?' Danielle asked, as they made their way out.

'I keep my ears open and my mouth shut. You'd be surprised at what you hear when you do that.' Linda unlocked the car and Danielle got into the passenger seat.

'How did you get here so fast? Last I saw, you were about to get rather busy.'

'Lee's uncle drives for the undertaker, so he knew about Dwayne's return, and that the funeral had been brought forward.'

Danielle grinned. 'So Lee gets you all horny by discussing funeral arrangements, does he?'

'Imagine. No, he just asked if I'd heard about it. I hadn't, and I knew you hadn't either, or you'd have mentioned it.'

'Not a dickie bird. It makes me wonder who I have on my side, if no one gives me important information like that.'

'You have a lot of people on your side, Danielle. They're just waiting for directions from you.'

'Well, I'm glad I have you, Linda.'

'I'm glad I got here. You realise that everyone affiliated with the Flynns is in the pub two hundred yards from where you just were. So, whatever you did or did not do with that knife, you may not have got away unscathed.'

'I told Dwayne Flynn to watch himself, and not to ever cross me again or I would kill him myself.'

Linda stared at her, open-mouthed. 'You did what?'

'Yes, and I meant it too.'

'And what about Hammer Flynn? Wasn't he there too?'

'He hates that nickname.'

'I couldn't give a shit. It's his own fault; he earned it. I just want to know why the fuck you are carrying that large knife. Did you do any harm with it?'

'No, but I was prepared to. And I came close to doing something else really stupid. Strange as it may sound, I was lucky Dwayne landed on. He reminded me that when push comes to shove, Jason has no balls. He'll always be at Dwayne's beck and call.'

'Let's get out of here, and then we can talk.' Linda pulled away from the kerb. Only when the Bakerman's Pub was several miles behind them did they relax and begin to talk.

'That shooting outside Blanchardstown Hospital . . .' Danielle began.

'Yeah.'

'It was Dwayne ordered it. It was a case of mistaken identity, the bullet was meant for Ian Gallagher. He was Ged's driver, one of ours. If that is not a declaration of war, I don't know what is.'

'Fuck. What do you plan to do about it?'

Danielle sighed. 'Not let that happen again. I mean to keep my people safe and make sure Dwayne Flynn knows I'm not backing down. When I do have a plan, you'll be the first to know.'

'Good. So tell me, Danielle, how the hell did you end up going off with Jason?'

'Rush of blood to the head.' *A rush of something, more likely between my legs.*

'Where to now?' Linda asked.

'Berkley Street. I need security — CCTV, locks, and alarms.'

'Rightio. And when we get there, I'll give you a picture of who we have on our side. Also, I've made you an appointment with Ged's solicitor. You have to see a Jacob Desmond, also — whatever that's about. Maybe he's an assistant or Ged's business consultant, who knows. That's tomorrow morning at nine. For now, it's back to the sanctuary of Berkley Street. I reckon you need to get something strong into you after your encounter with the Flynns.'

'Drive on, so, Linda.'

Once they were inside the red-brick building, Linda set the alarm and they sat in the kitchen, sipping whisky. After the day's events, it took four shots of Dingle's finest to put Danielle to sleep.

CHAPTER 22

Bosco Ryan sat with a can of cider on the weed-infested slab of concrete he was pleased to call his patio. He pulled back the ring with a crack and a fizz, and took a long swallow. A blade of grass tickled his calf and his leg jerked reflexively. A fly ventured from the black refuse bag that had been tossed in a corner. He batted a hand at it, while the dog jumped up and snapped. Both missed.

'Dirty yokes,' he muttered to himself. 'Fucking council. Was it my fault I missed the bin collection? Now I've to look at that dirty pile of rubbish for the next two weeks. It's not right. They should be on call for the likes of me. I mean, you only bury a man once. And it's not every day a fella buries the only decent boss they had. Now we've Dwayne, God help us, and Jason's useless. Hasn't the balls to keep him in hand.'

The fly landed on one of his Gucci sliders and he flicked it away, his thoughts on the previous night at the Bakerman's. Bosco had been dreading having to give Dwayne the bad news about the shooting. Getting the wrong man is one of the biggest fuck-ups a shooter can make. No wonder Dwayne had been furious.

Despite the bottomless shots, the endless lines of coke, Bosco had taken note of what was going on. Bill Frisco and

Larry Shine had driven from the cemetery in the limo, but Dwayne hadn't been with them when they arrived at the pub. Bosco watched them being whisked away upstairs, where they spent the rest of the evening with the more important guests.

Eventually, Dwayne appeared, wearing a face like a slapped arse, and no wonder, since he'd just found out about a failed hit. Jason was with him, his face bruised, and with a cut across his nose. No one dared comment. Dwayne moved among the guests, making a big thing of how the Flynns were in control — complete control.

Bosco sighed. The only thing to sort a hangover from hell was more alcohol. He took another gulp of cider.

His bloodshot eyes settled on the Beemer. His pride and joy was looking a bit cruddy. He'd have to get one of the kids to polish it. Last time he asked, they'd said they wanted fifty. Extortion. They could have a tenner, lazy little fuckers. He glanced at his watch. Where the fuck had Anto got to?

Anto Doyle had rung, saying he had important information that he refused to discuss over the phone. He'd be a good lad to have on their side, Anto would: hardworking and determined. Sure, there was that bother with getting Marion evicted, but it showed he had principles, and you got to respect a man for that. So, where had that fucker got to, if the matter was so urgent?

Bosco was also due to get a call from Jason to arrange the handover of a bag of cash that was now sitting in the boot of the Beemer. He wondered vaguely where they would meet. Jason's apartment in Phibsborough? Maybe he'd have to go to Bird's place in Ranelagh. It would be weird going back there, what with Bird being dead and buried. It was a class place. Maybe Dwayne would let him and Michelle move in there. She'd enjoy being able to put that address on her deliveries. Who knew?

Meanwhile, there was a ball of cash for Jason from collections he'd made, and if it wasn't delivered when Jason asked for it, it'd be his testicles in the wrench. Bird's death had fucked up everything. Bosco had been Bird's man.

Sure, he'd keep working for whichever Flynn came out the boss, but while the two brothers were at loggerheads, things could go badly wrong. They needed to find Ged's coke. That would sort out a lot. Dwayne's plans for it made sense. It would keep the cops busy, and then the Flynns would take over and Dublin would be theirs.

Anto had inside knowledge of the Lewis family — he had known Dean. So, where the fuck was the little bastard?

Bosco leaned forward, grasped the pit bull's snout and shook it. 'Grrr, you gorgeous little animal.' He let go his grip and rubbed her head. She licked the back of his hand. 'Good girl, Lola. I'm going to miss you when Dwayne takes you back.' She began to lick his jeans, where some of the cider had spilled. 'Don't go getting drunk now. Dwayne would not be impressed.' He laughed and Lola, who had obviously got the joke, barked. He took a treat from his pocket and threw it to her. She pounced on it, wagging her stump of a tail furiously. He grinned. 'I wonder, would Dwayne let me keep you and take the missus instead?'

Looking up from the dog, he spotted his neighbour strolling past the gate. 'Well, if it isn't Kym Brady.'

'What do you want, Bosco?'

'How's your boyfriend?'

'Still alive, if that's what you want to know, but he's a great big hole in his hand.'

'Glad to hear that, pet, glad to hear it.'

'Oh, really?'

Bosco got up and went to the gate. 'If I were you, I wouldn't get smart with me now, pet.'

Kym took a breath. 'I asked you what you wanted, Bosco.'

'You'd never take Lola to the green over there for me? She's due a crap, and you'd be doing Dwayne a favour, since she's his dog. You'd want to be keeping Dwayne onside now, so you would.'

'That so?'

'Yeah, go on. What else are you good for, but taking a dog for a shit.'

'Piss off and do it yourself. I'm heading to work.' Kym started to walk away.

'Do you kiss your daddy with that septic mouth, you slapper?'

Kym stopped and turned to face him. Arms crossed. 'I'll call Shelly out here, and you can repeat what you said to your young one of a neighbour.' She opened her mouth to holler.

Bosco reached over the gate, grabbed Kym's face and squeezed, hard.

'I'll slice you from ear to ear. How would that look on your pretty slapper face now, Kym, eh?' He had to have been hurting her, but she stared back at him, defiant.

With his free hand, he rooted around in his pocket, bringing out a fifty euro note. This, he shoved down her top. Lola jumped at the gate. Bosco let go of Kym's face.

'Down, Lola. Sit.' Lola whined, lowered her back end and raised a paw. 'That's how a bitch should behave. You should take notes, Kym. Oh, and that fifty your tits are keeping warm, head to Costello's and get me forty Bensons with it.' She opened her mouth for a retort, but he cut in. 'It wasn't a request, Kym. Just get on with it and don't take all day.'

His arms resting on the gate, he leaned over it to watch her walk away. 'That's sorted the bitch.'

Kym wasn't like the rest of them round here. She was sharp as a tack, knew how to look after herself. He'd once offered to give her drugs in return for a quick blow job. Those full lips locked around his lad . . . She'd thrown him a look that said she'd bite it off if he put it anywhere near her. She would, too. He'd have to take it slow, break her down bit by bit. Once Ian Gallagher was out of the way, Kym would be fair game.

As she approached the end of the street, she put her phone to her ear and glanced back for a moment. He waved at her. She turned away and was soon out of his sight.

Bosco plonked himself back into the chair, which wobbled ominously. He took out his phone and called Anto. It rang out, so he sent him a message.

Whr r u?

Bosco stared at his screen. The message was delivered, but hadn't been read.

'He'd better be here soon,' Bosco muttered. He had clients waiting for gear and tablets. It wasn't good business to make them wait. Nor was it good business not to rake in the cash. Dwayne had better have a good plan to make up for the mix-up with the shooting.

Lola dropped a toy into his lap. She wanted to play tug. He grabbed one end of the rope and she almost pulled him upright.

'Fuck it, Lola. You've some jaws on you, you beautiful dog.'

Dwayne had sent her to a trainer, so she had a great temperament. She had papers, too. Any puppies she had would make at least three grand a pop. Dwayne had sourced a decent male. All that remained was to put them together when she came on heat. But Dwayne wasn't ready for that yet.

He gave in and released the toy, sat back and watched her run around the yard shaking it and growling. When she tired of this, she began to sniff along the wall and around the tyres of the Beemer.

'I knew it. Shell . . . Michelle?'

No answer. He shouted louder.

'What do you want now?'

'Lola needs a run, and I've just opened my can. I need my down time, after all I went through yesterday.'

'Piss off and do it yourself. I just got my nails done. You're the one looking after her, not me. I hate mutts — though I made an exception when I married you.'

'And I made an exception by marrying a bitch,' he retorted. 'Fucking useless.'

Lola squatted and deposited a huge turd in the middle of the path.

'For fuck's sake. Who's gonna clean that up?'

No longer playful, Lola had begun to snarl menacingly in the direction of the gate. Bosco got up to look, but there was nothing there.

A cat, probably, though he couldn't see any. 'Calm down, Lola.' He bent and patted her on the head. 'It'd better not be Kym coming back and getting me all horny again, just when I'm relaxed.'

He straightened up, his thoughts on a nice chicken and cheese toasty, when something struck him from behind, with such force that he was propelled towards the bonnet of his car. He slid to the ground, his face in the weeds. He turned his head slightly, the movement making him catch his breath. He could just see a pair of boots on the other side of the gate, while Lola barked frantically. His side felt crushed, he couldn't breathe, to cough was agony. Something warm and damp spread under him, across the loose stones on which he lay. They dug into his skin. Slowly, he reached out an arm and scrabbled at the concrete, trying get a purchase, to rise, his face contorted. This wasn't happening. Shot on his own estate, in his own front yard. Bleeding out next to a steaming pile of shit. Fuck that. He wasn't going to die. He wasn't. It wasn't his time. With a supreme effort, he got his face about an inch or so from the ground. 'Show your face, you coward.' The words sounded loud in his ears, but they emerged in a whisper. He coughed, his mouth filled with blood and he lowered his face to the ground.

Any minute now, Lola would jump the gate and drag the bollocks from the gunman. The gate creaked. Bosco almost smiled; now he'd be sorry. But Lola whined, fell silent. What had he done to her? She wasn't shot, so what the fuck?

He gasped out, 'You'd better not harm her, or I'll fucking kill you.'

The voice that answered seemed to come from far away, but sounded familiar.

'The dog is fine, Bosco. Don't you worry about it. You should be more worried about yourself.'

A pair of black boots appeared. They stepped over him, and Bosco heard the boot of the Beemer open and close.

Bosco spoke into the concrete. 'Don't touch that money. That belongs to the Flynns, you stupid fuck.' Where was his wife when he needed her? 'Shell, Shelly? Someone call the cops.' But no one came; no one heard.

The gunman came and stood beside Bosco, hunkered down and very briefly, lowered his mask.

'Why?' Bosco croaked.

'You know why.'

They were the last three words Bosco would ever hear.

CHAPTER 23

The offices of Danielle's solicitor were situated close to the three-arena concert venue, overlooking Dublin Port. As soon as she arrived, she was ushered through this building and into another adjoining glass-fronted one. Here, she was shown into a room almost bare of furnishings, hung with two striking paintings. One showed a blindfolded woman in a vivid blue dress, looking out towards the viewer. A bearded man in a strange outfit — he wore flippers — stood in the background, while at the woman's feet were a child and a mouse, both looking upwards. The other painting depicted two androgynous figures seated back-to-back against a vivid green background, beneath a full moon. A toad at the bottom of the painting looked poised to hop away. Danielle went over to examine them more closely.

There were times when she felt like those animals, small, insignificant, alien, staring up at the mysterious figures above her, and, like the toad, ready to escape.

'Incredible, aren't they?' The woman spoke quietly. 'They're by a Cork-based artist — Mary St Leger.'

Danielle remained staring at the paintings. 'Yes, amazing.'

'The title of that first one is *Warrior Queen*.'

'And the other?' Danielle asked.

'That one is called *Heaven and Earth . . . Sanctuary.*'

'Beautiful.'

Tearing herself away from the paintings, Danielle turned to see a tall brunette in a dark floral dress. 'I'm waiting to see Jacob Desmond.'

'Yes, that is me.'

'Oh.' It wasn't just the gender; the lady looked more like a schoolmistress leading a bunch of schoolkids on a tour than a top business maestro.

'It's actually Jasmine. Jacob is a code name by which we can identify each other. You are Ged's niece, Danielle. I've been waiting for you to make contact. It's good to finally meet you.' Danielle offered her hand, but Jasmine didn't take it. Instead, she indicated the marble desk in the middle of the room. She sat across from Danielle and put down an iPad in front of her.

'So, anyone who uses the code name "Jacob" gets access to you?' Danielle asked.

'No.'

'Then how do you know that I am who I say I am?'

'There's a facial recognition system at the main door and a fingerprint ID when you press the buzzer.'

'How did you get my fingerprint?' Danielle asked.

'Ged provided them.'

'Has anyone else tried to gain access to Ged's holdings?'

'Only you have that code name, and it could only have been given to you by Ged's personal solicitor. Did you come to this address alone, as instructed?' Jasmine said.

'Yes, I had someone drop me at the solicitor's offices, and I made my way in from there.' Danielle smiled. 'It felt like I was on a treasure hunt.'

'Well, that is exactly what it is. Ged set up his business in his thirties, and went on to amass a vast fortune. Not long before he died, he set up a trust fund for you and instructed me to assist you in his business dealings in the event of his death. There are accounts in a number of different countries that I can give you access to, should you need it.'

'The penthouse in Clonliffe View . . . I thought that was his too.'

'No, that belonged to Ann Lewis, and I understand that the Criminal Assets Bureau has seized it.'

As if I didn't know. 'All my stuff was there. I only found out when I was discharged from hospital and found the officers there.'

'Well, at least you weren't inside at the time. It wouldn't have been nice having them all piling in on you.'

Danielle made a face. 'I'm not sure if that is much of a consolation.'

'Will it not give you a clean break?'

'What? Losing access to all my belongings?'

Jasmine gave a little smile. 'What did those belongings consist of anyway? Whatever you brought from London in one suitcase, and the few things you might have bought after you got here. Were they that valuable to you?'

'Sounds like I've lost it,' Danielle said.

'Does it?'

'A clean break, eh?'

'That property wasn't in Ged's name for a reason. It was tainted with criminality long before you stayed there. It needed to go.'

'But it was in his wife's name — Ann. And wouldn't she be able to claim automatic right to his property? As in, will I have a fight on my hands? Can she drag me to court or something, because Ged left everything to me?'

'They weren't legally married,' Jasmine said.

'That's ridiculous. Of course they were.'

Jasmine shook her head. 'No, the marriage was never registered. Ged had set about initiating divorce proceedings when we discovered that there was no record of the marriage in the first place.'

'Jesus. Did Ann know this?'

'Ged was our client, not Ann.'

'She'd have been royally pissed when she did find out,' Danielle said.

'It is not our place to take account of feelings and emotions. Our concern is our clients' business interests, and nothing else.'

'Right.' *So we'll keep our feeling to ourselves then.*

Jasmine continued: 'Also, any revenue liability is fully discharged. Funds were set aside for that as well. This kept any eyes from peering too closely at Ged's business affairs. It should keep them from taking too much interest in yours, too.'

Danielle was silent. She was finding this a lot to take in.

'Is there anything in particular I can do for you today, Danielle?'

'Um . . . Yes, there is, actually. What I'm looking for is a list of properties that Ged owns — owned, rather. Garages, storage yards, industrial buildings, places like that. I could check the Companies Registration Office for a list of all of Ged's businesses, but that would be a big search. I don't have all the names of the companies he'd registered, and anyway, Ged layered and complicated his legal files so much that nothing is straightforward. And beyond that, I need a solicitor to do a thorough land registry check on anything in those businesses' names.'

'He owned properties both here in Ireland and abroad.'

'Really?'

'Yes. Your property in London, for one.'

'My business premises or my flat?'

'The flat is yours, but the business premises are another thing,' Jasmine said.

'What about my business?'

'He was your landlord,' Jasmine said.

Danielle shook her head. 'But the Lewis name isn't on the paperwork.'

Jasmine merely smiled.

'So, are you telling me that he knew where I was all along?' Danielle said.

'Yes. And during that time, he was ensuring that you remained safe.'

'Pity he didn't reach out and let me know.'

'According to Ged, you didn't want anyone to "reach out" to you, as you put it.'

'True, I suppose.' Danielle wanted to cry. *But there must be no feelings and emotions here.* She swallowed her grief.

'For now, I'd like just the properties in Dublin, please, Jasmine.'

Jasmine tapped out something on the iPad. Danielle's phone pinged. Her latest message had a PDF file attached to it. Listed were various addresses and locations that Danielle recognised as warehouses and garages. Also included was the building on Berkley Street, registered as a beautician shop, and the house in Clontarf, the family home that Danielle thought belonged to both Ann and Ged. Even this was now in her name.

The gym in Drumcondra was also listed. Linda had been right.

'That house in Clontarf, the locks have been changed,' Danielle said.

Jasmine produced an envelope and set it down on the table. 'The keys are in there.'

Danielle pocketed the envelope and returned her attention to the list. 'What are numbers seven, eight, nine and ten?'

'Car parks. Actually, one of those is in London — number ten.'

'Jesus, the turnover.'

'And the other three . . .' Jasmine ran her finger over the iPad. 'One is beneath the gym, another is under a block of apartments at Spencer Dock, and the other is at the end of Berkley Street.'

'So, people park in them every day, do they?'

'The one in London, yes. The other three are still in use also. Even when Ged died, it was good to keep them open, earning. We had thought about closing them the moment we heard. It's mostly passing trade for the uncovered car park at the end of Berkley Street — churchgoers, people wanting to park close to the city but not right in the city centre. Some spaces in the ones beneath Spencer Dock are leased to two nearby hotels. The gym car park was also leased to a nearby hotel, but has been temporarily closed while that hotel is undergoing renovations. There was some anti-social behaviour nearby, and we felt it was too accessible. The shutters were damaged. They've since been repaired, according to the management company. It should be open again next week, when the hotel owners complete their renovations — or sooner, if you think the gym patrons may need to use it. Have a think and let us know your decision on that.'

'How . . . ?'

Jasmine stared at her. 'How, what?'

'How did you learn of Ged's death?' Danielle said.

'We make it our business to be aware of our clients' movements at all times.'

Danielle didn't like the sound of that. 'But that will affect my privacy, won't it?'

'It won't. You have full control over what I have access to,' Jasmine said.

'Okay.'

'However, we do on occasion have to act on behalf of our clients, but there's no need to worry. Any decisions we make will always be in your best interests.'

'Can you expand on that?' Danielle said, looking up from the list.

Jasmine met her gaze. 'No.' She looked down at the iPad. 'You'll need entry codes to some of those properties, as well as the car parks.'

Danielle's phone pinged again. She opened the message and gasped. The code consisted of three letters and six numbers. *SAM*, followed by his date of birth.

'It's the one code for all of them. Ged insisted on that,' Jasmine said.

'Thank you.'

Jasmine smiled briefly. 'Contact me again, after you've had a chance to let this all sink in. You can leave the way you came in, via my colleagues' office in the building adjacent to this. It's safer and more discreet that way; harder to trace you to me. Use the name Jacob Desmond whenever you wish to request a meeting, but do so only through your solicitor.'

'So I mustn't share this information with anyone at all?'

'Ged never had a problem with that,' Jasmine said. 'If you think about it, most of us have very few people we can trust with absolute certainty.'

Danielle had to agree.

'Oh, and you might also want to consider who to leave all this to.'

This hadn't even crossed Danielle's mind. 'Like a family member?' There was no one, apart from Chloe, and Ged had set up a trust fund for her.

'Or anyone else you think appropriate,' Jasmine said. 'It's entirely up to you. Anyway, have a think and let me know.' Jasmine stood up. 'Take the lift to the ground floor and go through the rear exit.'

'Thank you,' Danielle said. But Jasmine was already gone, leaving Danielle alone with Mary St Leger's dreamlike strangers.

CHAPTER 24

Dwayne woke with a start, feeling something stir in the bed beside him. The girls must be getting up. Good. It was time they went. They had already been paid, so he pulled the covers over his head intending to go back to sleep. The noise of their chattering in the kitchen put paid to that. Muttering curses, he pulled on his jocks and marched out of the bedroom.

He stood in the kitchen doorway with his hands on his hips. Jason was standing at the table drinking coffee, while the girls giggled at him.

Dwayne glared. The two girls gathered their things and scuttled out past him.

'You're up early, Jason.'

'Couldn't sleep. I've a lot on my mind, so.'

Dwayne grunted. 'Well, I can, and I want more of it, so don't go disturbing me again.' Dwayne turned on his heel and headed back to the bedroom.

He was in the midst of a dream when he felt Jason shake him. 'What the fuck, Jason? Didn't I tell you not to disturb me?'

'I gave you an hour. But something's come up, and it's serious.'

'It's always serious with you. This better not be more of your bullshit drama.' Dwayne rubbed at his eyes.

'There's been a shooting at Bosco's.'

Dwayne bolted upright. 'Whadyer mean there's been a shooting? Did he shoot someone? What're you trying to say?'

'Word is he's been shot,' Jason said. 'I'm trying to find out more.'

'Well, do. Fuck off out of here while I get dressed. And have some answers by the time I get to the living room.'

Dwayne snatched up his phone from the locker. There were eight missed calls from Sal Fogarty. He called back, but couldn't get through, so he looked online. The breaking news spoke of a shooting in Blanchardstown, with more details to follow, along with a generic photo that showed crime scene tape but not the crime behind it, which was fuck-all good to anyone.

He scrambled into his clothes and went into the living room, where Jason was pacing the floor, his phone to his ear.

Dwayne waited, chewing on the inside of his mouth.

Finally, Jason ended the call. 'That was Sal. Bosco's been shot. He's trying to find out where he's been taken — if he's in the hospital, or still at the scene waiting for the pathologist, which means he's snuffed it.'

'I know what that means, dumbo.'

'Should we drive by and see for ourselves?' Jason said.

'Where is your brain, Jason? The place'll be crawling with cops. Cops who know who we are. You want us to get pulled in?'

'Right.'

'Oh my Christ — Lola. Any word about her?' Dwayne said.

'No one would shoot an innocent dog,' Jason asserted.

'Depends,' Dwayne said. 'There are some evil fuckers out there. I'll tell you something though, if there is a hair on her coat harmed, I'll hang, draw, and quarter the fuckers.'

'Trust that she'll be okay.'

'She'd better be, unless someone has harmed her to get to me.'

'No way,' Jason said.

Dwayne shook his head. 'She'd be fair game for any enemy of ours.'

'True.'

Dwayne rubbed his chin. 'I'll tell you who I think it was.'

'Who?'

'Danielle fucking Lewis, that's who.'

'What? No. No way.'

'Why not? She was here with you yesterday evening, wasn't she?'

'Yeah, but what's that got to do with the shooting?'

'Trying to get you into bed, was she?' Dwayne leered.

'Well . . . no, she wasn't. It was me trying—'

'That's what you think. Who's to say she wasn't angling to see how fucked up we were after Bird's funeral, so she could strike while we're grieving. She surely knew Bosco would have been with us, and that he'd be hungover and vulnerable.'

'She's not a murderer, Dwayne,' Jason said.

'Really? Had you your eyes closed, did you, when she held a knife to my throat and threatened to kill me?'

'Yes, but you threatened her first,' Jason said. 'She was only acting in self-defence.'

'Good to know you have my back there, baby brother. She threatened me, and that's that. Doesn't matter what happened beforehand. It was enough that she dared.'

'I swear, Dwayne, this sort of thing isn't her style.'

Dwayne bit on his bottom lip. 'But surely she knows someone whose style it is. Shaking that tight arse of hers, promising them a bit of pussy. Isn't that what she did to you yesterday? What was she hoping to get, if not information?'

'That's not the way it happened, Dwayne.'

'I don't care how it happened. She was here, wasn't she, on our patch?'

Jason sighed. 'Now you're being paranoid, Dwayne.'

Jason didn't see it coming. In a flash, Dwayne's hands were around his throat. 'Whose side are you on, little brother?'

'Ours,' Jason croaked, clawing at Dwayne's hands.

Dwayne watched Jason's face darken. Felt his pulse slow. Took a breath, and then released him. Jason slumped to the floor, coughing and wheezing.

'More coffee?' Dwayne asked, raising a mug. His expression became serious. 'Look, Jason, she needs getting rid of.'

'Why? She's no threat to us,' Jason rasped.

'Taking advantage, she was. Sneaking back while I was out of the country . . .'

'That's not why she came back,' Jason said. 'It had nothing to do with you.'

'How do you know? Anyway, for someone who is only back in Dublin a short while, she seems to attract death like a cloud of flies. And now one of my men is gunned down in cold blood. She likes to give the impression she's all alone, she and that Linda from the whorehouse, but she's not fooling me. Danielle has to have someone doing her bidding for her. The only way I'll be happy is if she's out of the picture altogether.'

'And do you think that will get rid of all opposition? There'll be plenty of others willing to take her place.'

Dwayne shrugged. 'We can worry about that after she's gone.'

'You mean . . . You're talking about killing her?'

'What else do you have in mind?'

Jason said nothing.

'I've had someone watching her,' Dwayne continued, 'from a distance like, just to see what she's doing, who she's meeting.'

'Really?'

'I was hoping she'd lead me to something I'm keen to get my hands on. I need it for our overseas ventures.'

'Like what?' Jason said dully.

'Five million euros' worth of coke is what.'

'Why are you only telling me this now?' Jason said.

'I had thought to get you to bring her onside, bleed her for information. But then I got news of the drugs.'

'As if I could ever get her onside when you act like that around her.'

'She just makes me see red. Besides, I was already fired up when I came in, then to see her here, getting her feet under the table? Nah.'

'She wasn't getting her feet under any table.'

Dwayne just ignored Jason's last remark and carried on speaking. 'But after the fuck-up with the shooting, she'll be wary. And I wasn't sure if I could rely on you to work her the way I needed you to, while I held my patience.'

'And you were sure I'd go along with this ridiculous plan?'

'Ah, you wouldn't have had a choice. I'd thought about it when I had another source that didn't work out.'

'Who? Ian Gallagher — the guy the hit was meant for?'

'Yeah.'

'He might be so shit scared he'll still come through with the information,' Jason said.

'Let's see.'

'Look, Dwayne. Suppose you got your hands on the coke. Would you be willing to leave Danielle alone then?'

'Dunno. It would certainly ease the pain, or at least stop me thinking she's out to get me.' Dwayne looked hard at Jason. 'Unless Bosco dies. Then this shit will progress to a whole other level.'

'Let me speak to her. Maybe I can persuade her to give me the information. I'm sure she still feels something for me . . . I'll work on her.'

'What, like you were working on her yesterday?'

Jason looked at the floor.

'The only thing you were working on yesterday was getting into her knickers, and look how that turned out.'

Dwayne's phone rang. Sal. He listened, his face slowly clouding over. He ended the call without a word.

'What is it, Dwayne?'

'He's been taken to hospital.'

'He's still alive, so?'

'Yeah, but he's critical. Michelle was told to get herself there as soon as possible.'

'Shit.'

'He'd better fucking live.' Dwayne looked at the mug of coffee in his hand and smashed it against the wall.

CHAPTER 25

Danielle walked away from her meeting with Jasmine straight into a wall of rain. She spotted Linda's car parked across the road and, taking advantage of a break in the traffic, darted across and threw herself into the front seat.

'How'd it go?' Linda asked.

'Interesting.'

'Right. Did you get that list?'

'Not immediately. They'll get it to me after I email them proof of identity — you know, my passport or something. The trouble is, it's stuck at the apartment and CAB won't give me access to it.' The lie fell easily from Danielle's lips. In fact, Saoirse had promised to get her passport to her, along with a few other things.

'Why do you need to prove who you are? The dogs on the street know you, Danielle. That's ridiculous.'

Danielle shrugged. 'Formalities, they said. You know what lawyers are like.'

'And how are you going to get your passport back? It's not as if you can rock up at the CAB offices and ask them for it, is it?'

'Um, no. I must find out.'

'I really don't know why they can't just give you the details now.'

Linda is awful anxious for the information. 'Well, they can't. They won't send anything by email either.'

'And he didn't give you any idea whatsoever of where they might be?'

'Nope.' *Woah there, Linda.* 'Why the sudden panic, anyway?'

'Why the panic? Think, Danielle. Who else might know about five freaking million euros' worth of blow and be looking for it? The driver? Even Ian Gallagher? I heard he was the target in that shooting at the hospital.'

'Fuck.'

'Yes, exactly. Fuck. Now, come on, Danielle. If there's any way you can press the solicitor to give you the information, or anyone else we might try, then you should do it.'

'Okay, Linda, I hear you. I'll ring the solicitors and get them to see it's urgent.'

'Good. Now, you look like you could use a drink, because I certainly can.'

'Absolutely.'

Linda pulled out into the traffic.

'So, tell me about the shooting, Linda. Who got shot instead of Gallagher?'

'You probably know more than me,' Linda said.

'Dwayne barged in and started mouthing off at Jason, not realising I was there, but all he said was that an innocent man got shot and killed.'

'Did he actually accuse Jason of carrying out the shooting?' Linda asked.

'I was too frightened at the time for it to register, but now I think about it, Jason seemed surprised.'

'Yeah, 'cause they got the wrong guy.'

'No, more than that. As if he didn't know anything about it. It seemed like Dwayne was just using him as a punching bag, someone to take out his frustrations on.'

Linda shook her head. 'Jesus.'

'Yeah. Dwayne always treated Jason like that. Bird used to protect Jason from the worst of it, and now he's out of the picture.'

Linda signalled to turn left.

'No,' Danielle said, 'don't go back to Berkley Street. Take me to Blanchardstown.'

'Blanchardstown? Why?'

'I was thinking that if we drove by Hazel's parents' place, I might catch a glimpse of Chloe.'

'What? Park up like a pair of weirdos and stare at the house?'

'No, of course not. I'll decide what to do when we're closer.' Danielle glanced at Linda, whose face wore a set expression. So, Linda didn't approve. Well, tough. Danielle didn't have to justify her actions to her or anyone else.

They drove on in silence. When they were nearly at Roselawn Drive, Danielle said, 'Pull in and scoot across. I'll take over the driving.'

Linda brought the car to a halt at a bus stop. Danielle got out and walked around the front of the car. She was about to get in when a pit bull in a studded collar came bounding towards her and began to sniff at her legs.

Linda reached into the back seat of the car and emerged carrying a hurley. She raised her weapon, ready to strike.

'Wait, Linda. Don't hit it,' Danielle said. The animal whimpered and licked Danielle's hand. She bent to pat it and noticed a smear of red on its coat.

'This dog is injured. It needs help.'

'Danielle, it's one of those dangerous dogs. If it's injured, it'll be even more aggressive.'

'Look, Linda.' The dog licked Danielle's hand, and she stroked its smooth brown and white coat. 'Is that an aggressive dog? We need to help it.' She bent further to check. 'Her.'

'What? You mean put her in the car?'

'Yes. The seats are leather; they're easily cleaned.'

'Suppose she decides to chew something?' Linda said, eyeing the dog warily.

'She'll be fine. I'll buy you a new fucking car if you like. Come on. Let's get her to a vet.'

'Jesus Christ, Danielle. You're not helping yourself here.'

'Humour me, Linda. It'll help take my mind off what happened yesterday. I ended up threatening Dwayne with a knife, which is something he'll never forget. Who knows what's going to happen to me now?'

The dog pawed at Danielle's leg. She scratched her under her powerful jaw. 'She needs help.'

Linda gave an exasperated shrug. 'Fine. You're the boss.'

'I sure am.' Danielle opened the rear door, and the dog hopped in and lay on the back seat with her head on her paws. Still wielding the hurley, Linda sat in the front passenger seat.

Danielle glanced at the hurley. 'Where the hell did you get that?'

'Like many other women, I happen to enjoy playing camogie.'

Danielle raised an eyebrow. 'And I suppose you have a sliotar to go with it.'

Linda popped open the glove box and took out the little ball.

'And could you puck the ball across that green there?' Danielle nodded towards the stretch of grass next to where they were parked.

'I'd do my damnedest.'

Danielle smiled. 'Well, it makes a handy weapon, and it's perfectly legal.'

'I know.' Linda tapped her own head. 'So. Where to?'

'Do you know of a good vet round here, Linda?'

'There's one just at the end of this lane. Take a right, then a left, and you'll see it next to the playground.'

Mindful of the dog in the back, Danielle pulled slowly away. As she did so, an Emergency Response Unit motor zipped past them, missing them by centimetres. She braked hard. The dog yelped.

'Shit!' Linda cried out. 'That's the fucking guards. You know what the emergency response crew are like. They'll secure us first and ask questions after.'

'At least the only weapon we have is that thing.' Danielle nodded at the hurley.

'More's the pity.' Linda looked at Danielle. 'Do you know where we could get hold of a gun?'

'I'm not sure. I wonder if there would be one or two in the consignment of coke,' Danielle said.

'Shit. Right. More reason to find it.'

Linda's phone rang. She looked at the screen and frowned. 'Who is it?'

'It's Claire. She runs the bar off Harcourt Square.' Linda answered. 'Yep. You're on speaker, Claire. I'm here with Danielle. What's up?'

'A couple of detectives were having lunch here. They got a call and left without finishing their food. From what I could make out, there was a shooting close to Roselawn Drive in Blanch.'

'That explains the ERU,' Danielle said.

'Sorry?' Claire said.

'We're in Blanch right now.'

'Oh, right. You didn't see anything, did you?'

'Just the cops. They came racing past us just now. Go on, what else did you find out, Claire?'

'Well, I made a call, and the word is that Bosco Ryan's been shot outside his place. I thought you should know.'

'Jesus Christ,' Danielle said.

'Wait, there's another call coming through. Hold on,' Claire said. A minute or so later, her voice came through again. 'Hello?

'Yes, we're still here, Claire. Go on,' Danielle said.

'That was a friend who works at the hospital. Apparently, he was shot in the chest and the side of the head. He was still breathing when the cops landed on, but according to what my friend heard, he died in the ambulance on the way there, and they took him to the morgue. But it's not been made public yet.'

'Right, Claire,' Danielle said. 'If you hear anything else, you let us know straightaway.'

'Of course, Danielle. And . . . I just wanted to say that it's good to have you back, and especially good to have a woman in charge for once.'

'Thank you, Claire, and thanks for being loyal and having our backs. That's very valuable information.

Linda ended the call.

'You know what this means, Linda.'

'No. What?'

'After the way I threatened Dwayne yesterday, guess who'll get the blame for the shooting?'

'No. Surely not.'

'Yes, surely. Think about it. One of our men is targeted, and then two days later, Bosco is shot dead. Dwayne is going to assume I'm involved. Linda, the threat to me just went up a few notches.'

'We need to get you to safety. Come on, let's go.'

'Not before I get this dog looked at.'

Linda stared at her. 'Are you off your head?'

'You heard Claire. Bosco's death hasn't been made public yet. Let me get the dog seen to first, and then we can think of a plan.'

'You're not being sensible here, Danielle. Until we know who is responsible for this shooting, we're at risk from others besides Dwayne Flynn.'

'You're right. And an invisible enemy is a dangerous thing.'

'Dump the dog, so, and let's get ourselves sorted.'

'No. We can't just abandon the poor animal.'

'Jesus, Danielle, you can't look after every stray and orphan that comes your way.'

'If we don't do it, who else is going to round here?'

Linda shook her head. 'Your sympathetic streak could get you — us — killed.'

CHAPTER 26

The dog was lying with her chin resting on Linda's bag. She reached back to draw it away.

'Leave it where it is,' Danielle said. 'No point disturbing her when she's settled.'

She pulled into the car park of All Animals Veterinary Service.

'Hang on,' Danielle said. 'Do we know if this crowd are okay?'

'Yep, I know a guy who works here — Tiernan.'

Danielle smiled. 'Is there anyone you don't know?'

Linda grinned back. 'There must be someone, I suppose.'

'He's easy on the eye too, Cillian Murphy eyes with arms like Henry Cavill.'

'I don't give a crap about how easy he is on my eye, I need to know that I can deal with him.'

'You can.'

Danielle parked up. Linda ran inside and out again. 'There's no one around.'

'Linda?' A man stood in the doorway, wiping his hands on a towel. 'Come on in. My new receptionist is late again, so it's just me.'

Linda waved and gave him a thumbs-up.

'Is that Tiernan?' Danielle asked.

'Yep.'

'Will you see if he can give you a lead, so I can bring this lady in?'

Linda went in again and returned carrying a lead. All three of them went back inside.

'Good girl.' Tiernan patted the dog, who wagged her tail. 'I'm sure I've seen you before.'

'Can you check her for a chip?' Danielle asked.

'Absolutely.'

He slipped a muzzle on the dog and began to examine her. He parted her fur where it looked like she'd been bleeding. The dog rested her chin on her front paws and let out a sigh.

'There's no wound here,' Tiernan said.

'What?' Danielle said.

'Look.' Tiernan showed her. The skin beneath the fur was unbroken.

He reached for a wipe and cleaned her off. 'It could be paint, I suppose,' Tiernan said, 'but it really does look like blood. Where did you find her?'

'She was running loose near the junction at Roselawn Drive and Summerfield Avenue.'

'Oh, right. I might know whose dog this is.'

'Oh?'

'I'll scan the chip just to be sure, but I'm pretty sure this is the lovely Lola.'

At the mention of her name, the dog looked up and wagged her tail stump. He moved her collar. A disc that was wedged underneath the leather now hung loose.

'Yep, look.' He put his palm under the disc. Inscribed was her name.

'So you must know her owner, then,' said Danielle.

'Well, I do know who looks after her. It's Julian Ryan.'

'Who?' Danielle and Linda said in unison.

'Yeah. I think they call him Bosco.' The vet stared down at the dog, then at the wipe in his hand. 'Jesus Christ, Linda. What the hell have you brought me?'

'What do you mean?'

'If that's not her blood, it must come from something or someone close to her.'

Linda stared at Danielle. 'Shit.'

Danielle took hold of Linda by the elbow and led her aside. 'Could it be Bosco's blood? It could well be, if he was looking after her. She may have run away when the shot was fired.'

'Shit, that's evidence the vet just wiped off,' Linda whispered back.

Danielle glanced back at Tiernan, who was still examining Lola. 'We can't tell him what we suspect. Are you sure he's onside, Linda? He'll hear about the shooting and — you know — report it or something. The last thing we need is to be implicated in a crime we had nothing at all to do with.'

'Fuck me, Danielle. Yes, yes, he's onside.'

'I couldn't have left her there. That ERU yoke could have hit her or something.'

'You're a sucker for the abandoned, Danielle. Jesus. First babies, now dogs.'

Danielle's jaw clenched. If anyone else had said that to her, she'd have punched their face in. 'I'll have to believe you when you say this guy is onside. What about the other people working here though? I don't like the sound of this new receptionist. I mean, she still hasn't turned up. She can't be very reliable.'

'I'll find out,' Linda said.

Someone banged on the door. Startled, Danielle looked at Linda.

'I locked it after us,' Linda said. 'I thought it'd be safer.'

'That's probably my receptionist,' Tiernan said. 'I'll go and check.'

The vet disappeared, returning seconds later. 'Yep, it's only her. I've locked the door again and instructed her not to let anyone else in until I say so.'

'Shit. Now we have another witness,' Danielle whispered.

Linda went to the door and peered out. 'She seems more interested in her Shellacs than whoever's in here.'

'You say you trust him,' Danielle said. 'Okay.' She walked over to the examination table. 'Tiernan, we've just realised whose blood that may be.'

'Oh.' He looked from Danielle to Linda.

'If we share that information with you and you report it,' Linda added, 'your surgery gets shut down while the forensics go through it with a toothcomb.'

Tiernan opened his mouth, then closed it again.

'We had no idea whose dog this was.' Danielle rubbed Lola's neck. 'We just saw an animal in distress. But it could just be possible that the person you mentioned may have been shot, and—' she glanced at Linda — 'Lola here may have been close by.'

The vet shuffled from one leg to the other.

'As it stands, you have a dog who's run off into the wilds of the estates. What evidence she may have had on her is likely to be of little consequence. So, it's up to you — ring the cops to say you found her wandering and brought her in for treatment, or we take her away and decide what to do with her.'

He stared at them, alarm written all over his face. 'You're not going to—'

'What? Kill her? No way. We'll look after her until we know more about her, er, situation, leaving you entirely out of the equation.'

'Actually, I'd prefer that.'

'You're sure now?' Danielle asked. 'You won't be ringing the guards as soon as we're gone?'

Tiernan shook his head emphatically.

Linda put her hand in her pocket, pulled out a roll of cash and peeled off a number of fifties, which she laid on the examination table. 'For your trouble.'

Danielle put on the lead and led Lola out through reception.

'The bill has already been settled,' the vet said to the girl at the desk, who seemed to be lost in a daydream.

'Uh, okay.'

Once Lola was settled in the back seat of the car, Danielle called out the phone number inscribed on the reverse of Lola's name tag and asked her to call it from her phone. 'I saw it when Tiernan looked at the file. I don't want them to know it's me who's calling. I just want to see if I recognise the person that answers.'

'What if it is Bosco's phone, and some cop answers? It would lead them to us, and we'll find ourselves implicated in his shooting?' Linda said.

'It's no problem. We'll just dump the SIM card,' Danielle said.

Linda put the phone on speaker and entered the number, which was answered after two rings. The voice was unmistakable. Dwayne Flynn said, 'Yeah?'

Linda hit "end call."

Someone rapped on the car window, causing both women to jump. The vet's receptionist was mouthing something. Danielle buzzed the window down.

'Jesus Christ. Do you have to sneak up on people like that?' Danielle said.

'Sorry.' The girl sounded out of breath. 'I wonder if I could have a word with you?'

'The bill's been sorted,' Linda said at once.

'Yep, I know.' She looked at Linda. 'With just you, Danielle, please.'

Danielle looked at Linda and shrugged. 'I'll just be a sec.'

'Well, we don't want to hang around too long,' Linda said.

The girl led Danielle a short distance from the car and glanced back at it. 'You need to know whose dog that is.'

'I know whose it is,' Danielle said.

'No, you don't understand. Bosco Ryan always minds Lola for Dwyane Flynn when he goes out of the country. He's back, but hasn't collected her yet.' She made a face. 'He's been too busy throwing his weight around and generally causing chaos.'

'Listen, I know whose dog it is, and I don't need your advice.' Danielle turned to walk away but the girl grasped her arm.

'You need to help me.'

Danielle stared at the hand until the girl released her grip. 'Why should I? I don't even know you.'

'Because I have something you want.'

Danielle turned to walk away. 'Look, I don't have time to play stupid games. So, if you don't mind—'

'Chloe. I can get you access to her.'

Danielle rounded on her. 'Are you trying to be a smart arse?'

'No, not at all. I'm Kym Brady, Hazel's niece. When I'm not working here or out with my fella, I look after the baby. I can easily let you see her when she's with me.'

Danielle's heart leaped. 'Really?'

'Yes, I swear.'

Chloe. Images of the child being snatched away from her rose into Danielle's mind. She glanced down at Kym's feet, encased in pink Fila runners. 'Wait a second. Do you own a pair of wine-coloured runners?'

Kym stared at her. 'What? No.'

'How about a stun gun?'

'A stun gun? Why are you asking me these things?'

'Someone attacked me the day Hazel's parents got Chloe back. Do you know who it was?'

'Attacked you? Hell, no. What I heard was you were spoken to and persuaded to hand her over to be with her family.'

'Persuaded, huh? With a little help from a taser, and a lot of punches to the ribs. I nearly lost my mind with worry, until the guards told me she was with the Bradys.'

'You rang the guards?' Kym said.

'I was taken to hospital, and they called them. The guards followed it up after I said Chloe was taken during the assault. They confirmed she was there.'

'I'm sorry.'

'Why would you be sorry, if you'd nothing to do with it?' Danielle said.

'I'm just sorry you got hurt like you did.' Kym took a deep breath. 'Danielle, I swear I knew nothing of this. All I was told was that my aunt and uncle organised someone to speak to you and get you to give Chloe back.'

Danielle shook her head. 'Why did they choose the name Chloe?'

'Because that's what Hazel called her.'

'Well, I never heard her call the baby by any name. She always referred to her as "the baby," or "the kid." It was like Chloe was nothing to do with her and just an unnecessary burden.'

'Yeah,' Kym said. 'She was bitter that Ged wouldn't leave his wife for her. She'll come round eventually and be a good mother. And if she doesn't, we — the family — will make sure she's looked after. Anyway, I'm sure she'll think differently when she decides to come back.'

But Danielle knew Hazel was never coming back. 'I looked after the baby for nearly three months.'

'Yeah. You did a good job of it; she's such a contented little thing. I'm sorry you were assaulted. That wasn't right.'

Danielle nodded. 'No, it wasn't. You know Hazel was taking drugs, don't you?'

'What do you mean, "taking drugs"?'

'Oh, nothing. It's just that I heard she got back on them after having Chloe, and then Ged rejecting her. She couldn't cope with it all, it seemed.'

'And then our cousin being shot dead,' Kym added. 'That was cruel. Hazel found it hard to get her head around all the shit that was going on.'

'Yes, she had a lot to contend with,' Danielle said. 'By the way, do your aunt and uncle still have the buggy I used to put Chloe in?'

'Yes, I take her out in it when I have her.'

'Did you find anything . . . unusual in it?'

'Unusual like what?' Kym said.

'Oh, nothing.' *Shit, so who did take it? My attacker? Or was it Kym?* 'You said you needed my help in return for access to Chloe. What do you want from me? Money?'

Kym shuffled her feet.

'Jesus, Kym, will you just spit it out.'

'Well, Dwayne Flynn broke into our apartment five days ago and threatened to kill me and my boyfriend. He was convinced Ian had some information that he needed. When Ian told him he didn't have it, Dwayne plunged a knife through his hand. He gave him forty-eight hours to get the information to Bosco Ryan. But Ian really doesn't have it. After the forty-eight hours was up, Ian was at the hospital having his hand looked at when someone tried to shoot him. They ended up killing someone else.'

'Hang on. Your boyfriend is Ian Gallagher?'

Kym nodded. 'Yes.'

'And an innocent man was shot instead of him?'

'Yes.'

'How did that happen?'

'Some guy nicked Ian's jacket, and the shooter mistook him for Ian. He looked a bit like Ian, too, by all accounts.'

'What else do you know about the shooting?' Danielle asked.

'All I know is that Anto Doyle ran into Ian in reception. They hung around in there talking. Next thing — bang, some other lad is lying on the ground, blood pouring out of him. Anto went to help the poor guy when he saw the gunman take aim. Just as he was about to fire another shot, a doctor got in the way. Anto pulled the doctor out of the way, and yer man was . . . well, you know.'

'Yeah, shot dead. Fuck.' *So, Ian and Anto are buddies? And Anto works for the Flynns. What's going on there?*

'The Flynns are not going to be happy they got the wrong guy, and they'll still come for Ian,' Kym said.

'What was Anto doing there?' Danielle asked. 'I thought he worked for the Flynns.'

'Anto? No. Anto is his own man. He's doing jobs for the Flynns to pay off some debt they say he owes them.'

'And you're sure he wasn't there doing one of those jobs?'

'No. He was there for a completely different reason. He drove Brenno to the hospital after his mam tried to top herself.'

'Marion Aherne?' Danielle recalled how Marion had threatened her at Clonliffe View, all bluster and balls, while Bird hovered in the background. Danielle had had to pull out a gun to get her to back off.

'Yes. Dwayne kicked her out of Bird's house and told her not to come to the funeral.'

'Why?'

'Does Dwayne Flynn need a solid reason to be a prize prick?'

Danielle gave a wry grin. 'No.'

'Well, Marion took an overdose. She was serious, would have been gone — as in dead — if Anto hadn't called to the house. He saved her life, apparently.' Kim smiled briefly. 'Who would have guessed that Anto was capable of something like that?'

'Who knows what anyone is capable of when they see someone dying in front of them.' *Fair play to Anto Doyle. Imagine him being hero of the day.*

'True.'

'Okay, but where do I come in?' Danielle said. 'You still haven't said what help you want. I don't have any inside information, and whatever Dwayne is up to has nothing to do with me. You said Dwayne was looking for information from Ian. What kind of information? Was it about me? Where I'm staying, or my plans?'

'It's not you personally, but rather something you have control over.'

'Go on.'

'Before Ged died, Ian did a run across the border for him, to collect a delivery and bring it back south. Some other fella — Mark, I think his name was — was meant to do it, but Ged changed plans at the last minute and Ian did it instead. Dwayne seems to think there's over five million euros' worth of coke just parked up somewhere, ready for the taking.'

How the hell did Dwayne figure that out? 'Does he now? And he wanted Ian to tell him where it was?'

'Yeah, but Ian hasn't the faintest idea.'

'But he brought it down, didn't he, so how come he doesn't know?' Danielle said.

'He did drive it down, but was told to swap vans with Ritchie Delaney when he got back to Dublin. Ian didn't even see Ged after the run, he went back up to Belfast to sort out some business or other. He never got paid.'

'And . . . ?'

'If you tell me where it is, I'll make sure you get to see Chloe — as often as you like — as long as I'm looking after her.'

'Hang on. You want me to give you information that will enable Dwayne Flynn to get his hands on a shitload of drugs in exchange for access to Chloe?'

'Well, I have to do something. It's a question of saving our lives. And if that's what it takes . . . what is access to Chloe worth to you?'

What is it worth to me? Five million euro? Fuck.

'Look, he threatened us both, not just Ian,' Kym continued. 'You don't want Dwayne carrying out his threat when Chloe is with me. We've already seen how reckless they can be — getting someone shot in a hospital, of all places.'

Danielle fell silent, pondering, while Kym watched her anxiously. This was Chloe's family, those who were caring for her, right in Dwayne's crosshairs.

'Then wouldn't you be better off to stop minding Chloe for now?' Danielle said.

'Until when?' Kym said. 'How would I explain that to my aunt and uncle? And you'd never see Chloe, that way.'

Kym was right. She so badly wanted to see Chloe — hold her, cuddle her, smell her comforting newness, and see her wonder as she discovered the world. According to Jasmine, Danielle now had control over a fortune without having to resort to violence of any kind. She didn't need the money from the coke. Flooding the streets with a Class A drug would tie the guards up completely . . . Shit. It would leave Dwayne free to build up the empire Jason had spoken of.

Decide which side you're on, Danielle.

There was a course of action open to her that would benefit both sides. But first, she had to find those drugs, and soon, before anyone else got hold of them, especially that psycho Dwayne.

'No, I certainly don't want that animal to do anything to harm Chloe, or her family.' *And I owe it to Hazel to make sure that baby is safe.*

Danielle held out her phone to Kym. 'Put your number in there for me.'

Kym did so and handed it back. 'Does this mean you'll help me — I mean us?'

'It means I need to have a think, work on a plan.'

'I'm babysitting Chloe tomorrow,' Kym said. 'It's my day off. I'll take her to the playground near Costello's. Say about lunch time?'

Danielle nodded. 'Day after tomorrow, lunchtime . . . Thank you.'

Back at the car, Linda made no comment about Danielle's lengthy conversation with Kym. Instead, she said, 'I've been thinking, Danielle.'

'Did it hurt?'

'What? No, smart wagon.'

'Sorry.' Danielle let out a laugh; it had eased the tension a bit. 'Go on, what's weighing down your mind?'

'You're not seriously taking Dwyane Flynn's dog home with us, are you?'

'I sure am.'

'Jesus Christ. Would you not just release her? Let someone else pick her up.'

Danielle looked over the back of her seat. Behind her, Lola lay patiently, head on her paws.

'I'm not leaving her to the mercy of the streets. Dwayne doesn't even care about his own brother. Imagine what he'll do to the poor dog when he gets sick of her. Besides, if we leave her to run around the streets, she'll likely get hit by a car.'

Linda sighed. 'What are you like? Fine, let's get the hell out of here, so.'

Danielle put the car in gear and headed for Berkley Street.

CHAPTER 27

The walls of Marion's sitting room turned a warm peach colour in the morning sunlight. Anto had spent the night staring at those same walls, thinking about what he'd done. The life didn't leave Bosco's body straight away. He'd a bit of fight left in him. If Bosco survived a bullet to the brain, he deserved to live to a ripe old age. Though when Anto pictured him as he'd last seen him, face down on broken concrete, surrounded by a pool of blood and cider, such an outcome seemed highly unlikely.

The scene replayed itself over and over in his head. There was one part that always stuttered and slowed, like a reel of old film caught in the teeth of a projector. It was the point where the bullet struck Bosco's head, sending him to the ground. The point where Anto realised what he'd just done and what he couldn't take back — a man's life.

He hadn't even known that this was what he was going to do until he found the gun Kym had dropped in the grave-yard. Then Marion had ended up in hospital. It was like a sign — fate had handed him his revenge. Finding a hundred thousand euro in the boot of Bosco's car had been an unexpected bonus. Thanks to Kym, who not only agreed to let him borrow the gun but also did a walk-by to make sure Bosco was at home.

Anto was now three hundred thousand euro in debt to the Flynns. Two they knew about, and one they had yet to discover, the money from the BMW. Maybe they'd think the cops had seized it while they were at the scene. Whatever, it meant he had the readies to strengthen his position. A hundred thousand euro wasn't much in the gangland world. What he really needed was to get his hands on the five million euros' worth of blow that Dwayne was looking for. Then he'd be sorted, especially now that Bosco had been removed from the picture.

He heard a key turn in the back door lock. Anto quickly stuffed the gun into the outer pocket of the backpack beside him. Brenno appeared, dark shadows under his eyes. The sight of him snapped Anto out of his dream of gangland domination.

'How is she, lad?' he asked.

'She had a good night.'

'You didn't, by the looks of you.'

'Yeah, I slept in the car in the car park. I had to go out through a back entrance. The whole reception part was blocked off — some shooting or another.'

'Yeah, they got the wrong guy.'

'Who did?'

'The Flynns, probably. Some tosser robbed Ian's Grey Goose jacket and next thing, he's lying in the hospital doorway, blood pouring out of him. Couldn't be saved.'

Brenno looked confused. 'Ian or the tosser?'

'The tosser.'

'Were you there, Anto?'

'Yes. I saw the whole thing — though if anyone else asks, I wasn't there.'

'Right. Hang on. You're talking about Ian Gallagher?'

'Yeah.'

'What was he doing at the hospital?'

'Getting his hand examined. Dwayne Flynn broke into his apartment, threatened him and stabbed him through the hand.'

'Is there no stopping them Flynn bastards? Why? What was it all about?'

'Dwayne wanted to know where Ged Lewis had hidden five mill worth of blow.'

Brenno's eyes widened. 'Get the fuck out of here! You serious?'

'As cancer, lad.'

'And Ian knows where it is?'

'No, he doesn't. It was him drove it down from the north all right, but then he swapped vans and has no idea where it ended up. That's what he's claiming, anyway.'

'Do you believe him?'

'Yeah.'

'And Dwayne is pissed off at him for that?' Brenno asked.

'No, Dwayne wants him to find out where it is. He threatened to kill him and Kym if he doesn't come up with the goods,' Anto said.

'Fuck.'

'Yeah. It looks like they tried to take him out anyway,' Anto said. 'I can't think of anyone else who'd want to shoot him. Anyway, he'll be okay now. I've neutralised a major figure in their network.'

Brenno stared at him. 'What are you on about?'

'I shot Bosco Ryan.'

'No. The fuck you did.'

'Yep.'

'He dead?' Brenno asked.

'I shot him in the head, so even if he lives, he'll be pretty fucked up. There was a few quid in the boot of his car, too, so I took that for good measure.'

Anto landed the backpack on the coffee table and opened it up.

Brenno gaped. 'Woah. I must be dreaming. Must be.' Brenno ran his finger over the bundles of notes.

'No, Brenno, you're not dreaming. This is real cash.'

'You count this, lad?' Brenno asked.

'Yeah. A hundred grand, give or take.'

'That so?'

'Yep. There's a gun, too — in the side pocket.'

Gingerly, Brenno opened it up.

'It's okay, I took the magazine out and there's nothing in the chamber. We can wipe it, if you want to handle it.'

Brenno pulled his sleeve over his hand anyway and took the gun out. He turned it over in his hand. 'This is a Beretta.'

'Well spotted, lad.'

'Where the fuck did you get hold of one of those?'

'Mulhuddart graveyard.'

'Hang on, I'm lost. You found a gun in a graveyard?'

'Yep. Ian and me legged it from the hospital after the shooting and went to the flat. We did a few lines of coke, just getting chilled when his phone rang. It was Kym. She was in a right state, but we just about managed to get an idea of where she was — Mulhuddart graveyard. She'd gone there with a gun — don't even ask — fired off a few rounds then dropped it. Silly wagon couldn't find it anywhere in the dark. I had to help, and guess what — I found it.'

'And you kept it.'

'She let me borrow it.'

'Just like that?'

'Yeah, I have some info on her that Ian doesn't know about. I saw a clip from the party she was at that night. Kym, coasting some other lad's knob, silly bitch, and more fool her to think that same lad has any time for her. Anyway, that's a story for another day. I might still tell Ian, though. He is my buddy, and she's looking to make a fool of him.'

'Jesus. All this is frying my brain.'

'Sorry, lad, you've enough to be dealing with.'

'No, no, I'm grand. But I'm confused. Surely you don't think the solution to it is to start a war with the Flynns?'

'Yes and no. Is a war really a war, if you've no idea who has made the move against you?'

Brenno blinked. 'I suppose not.'

'For now, they've no idea it was me, and while that's the case, let's see what we can get away with.'

'You want to cause them a bit of damage?'

'Yes, undermine them. After all, they owe you for sending your ma into such a state that she's in the hospital.'

Brenno's whole face contorted in anger. 'They owe me their lives for that, but I need to protect her at all costs.'

'Exactly, and the only way to do that is to eliminate the threat,' Anto said.

Brenno nodded. 'Yeah, you're right.'

'So, you concentrate on making sure your ma recovers, and leave the heavy stuff to me — but only if you're up for it, mind.'

'What? You and me against the Flynns?' Brenno whistled. 'What have we got to lose? Bird treated me like shit, but Dwayne is a hundred times worse. Yeah, let's do this. Once Ma is back on her feet, just tell me what you need me to do.'

'I will. And until then, trust me to know what I'm doing and back me, no matter what.'

Brenno nodded vehemently. 'Absolutely, Anto, absolutely. It's you and me all the way.'

'Right. Now that's sorted, what do you fancy? Cuppa? Line of coke? Nap, or all three?'

Brenno smiled faintly. 'I'll start with the cuppa.'

'Good lad, Brenno.'

Anto patted Brenno's shoulder and went out to the kitchen, leaving his friend staring at the cash and gun.

CHAPTER 28

The bar at the café was crowded with people, all ordering complicated lattes with alternative milks, along with beverages that weren't even listed on the menu. After putting in her order, Danielle took a table in the far corner, close to the toilet, whose door required a code which, according to the sign, could be found at the end of the till receipt. She had a clear view of the main door from behind an artificial palm tree in a huge pot.

With a smile, Danielle recalled the surprise on Linda's face when she found her up and ready to head for a workout. They'd spent the previous night finishing a bottle of Single Pot Still Batch Four, which hit Linda like a truck. Her head was stuck firmly to the pillow when Danielle came in to ask her to join her in a workout. Danielle didn't insist. There was someone she'd arranged to meet.

Danielle sipped at her decaf cappuccino with oat milk, which had arrived with a small tasty-looking shortbread.

Five minutes after the arranged time, she saw Saoirse standing at the counter, her jacket spattered with raindrops. Saoirse said something to the barista and glanced around. Danielle wondered if this was an act, given Saoirse's profession. Maybe she really hadn't seen her. Saoirse's hair hung loose across her shoulders and she wore a denim dress. She looked as if she was about to set off somewhere, because she had a small suitcase on wheels and a large tote bag over her shoulder. She looked nothing like a Garda detective who was about to meet the head of a notorious criminal gang.

She took the seat next to Danielle and dumped the bags on the one opposite.

'Force of habit?' Danielle said.

'The only way to ensure there's no one coming up behind me is to sit with my back to the wall.'

They smiled at each other.

'How have you been, Danielle?'

'Busy rediscovering myself.'

Saoirse nodded. 'Where are you staying?'

'Berkley Street.'

'Is that not busy with clients coming and going?' Saoirse smirked. 'I hear there's a big demand for tanning and waxing among the male population.'

Danielle laughed. 'No, that side of it was shut down after Ged's death.'

'Okay. Well, don't you want to know what's in the bags?' Saoirse said.

'I'm not in the habit of rooting through other peoples' bags, especially if they belong to a detective — they'd have me in an arm lock in a blink.'

They both grinned.

'Go on,' Saoirse said. 'Unzip it and tell me if you're happy with what is inside.'

In the small suitcase, Danielle found a pair of black leather trousers, various tops, jeans, a tracksuit, and some underwear. 'I'm impressed. How did you manage to get all this?'

'It's not a whole lot, when you think about it. Luckily for me, you've only been back just over three months, so you haven't accumulated loads of stuff. I got them all from the press in the bedroom. The case was there, too.'

'Oh, yes, of course. I didn't recognise it.'

'Have a look in the tote bag.'

Danielle unzipped the bag and found a large brown envelope sitting on the top. Inside was her passport and a photo of her uncle Ged. She looked at it and a warmth spread through her. He had her back all along, and she never knew.

'Thank you for these. The passport gives me more freedom.'

'Did you decide to stay in Dublin, or are you going back to London?' Saoirse asked.

'You mean, did I decide which side I'm on?'

Saoirse sighed. 'I guess the answer to that one will become apparent in the course of time.'

'Maybe. Maybe not.' Danielle didn't even know herself yet.

The next item in the bag was a carefully folded pink baby blanket. Danielle held it against her face and breathed in the scent of baby. She recalled how settled Chloe would get when she swaddled her in that blanket. There was also a yellow babygrow dotted with white bunnies – Chloe was wearing the matching one, green with white bunnies, when she was taken from her — and a little dress, jacket and matching hat, as well as more blankets and babygrows. Some of them still had labels attached, and were too big for Chloe as she was now. Danielle had bought them in the hope of seeing her grow into them. The most heart-wrenching item was Chloe's comfort blanket.

'I thought you might like to have them . . . I mean, the baby might like them. You bought them for her.'

'I did. I appreciate you getting them for me.'

Saoirse's order arrived, and they fell silent until the server was well out of earshot.

Danielle took a breath. 'I have some information that might be of help to you.'

'Go on.'

'I believe the Flynns are behind the shooting at the hospital three days ago. It was a case of mistaken identity.'

'We know about the mistaken identity part,' Saoirse said, 'and have a number of theories we're working on.'

'Can you share?'

'Some. One of them being that Ian Gallagher reported the theft of his jacket.'

'He reported it to the guards?' Danielle said.

'No, the hospital reception. There was no sign of him when we arrived at the scene. CCTV shows him and another male exiting via a side entrance just after it happened.'

'The other male was Anto Doyle,' Danielle said. 'He was there with Marion Ahearne's son. Dwayne Flynn kicked her out of Bird's place and told her she wasn't welcome at the funeral. She took an overdose.'

'Jesus Christ. The scumbag.'

'Absolutely.'

'One theory we have is that Anto Doyle is aligning himself with the Flynns. Have you heard anything about that?' Saoirse asked.

'I couldn't say, but he is Brendan Aherne's best buddy, and he also seems to be friendly with Ian Gallagher. How deep that goes, I'm not sure. They say Anto did CPR on Marion and saved her life.'

'Jesus. We had heard a bit about that, but not all of it.'

'Your turn, Saoirse. How come this innocent guy got a bullet?'

'He was wearing the stolen jacket, which was quite expensive and very distinctive. There wouldn't be many of them around. The guy was also of a similar build to Gallagher and even had hair the same colour. He just happened to be in the wrong place at the wrong time.'

'Shit.' *So, Kym was telling the truth about that. She must be telling the truth about the rest, so.*

'His sticky fingers got him killed, poor guy.' Saoirse took a sip of her coffee. 'We're looking for Gallagher to give us a witness statement. And now we know Anto was there, too, he'll be asked for one as well.'

'Good luck getting them anywhere near a cop-shop, or signing anything implicating the Flynns, especially the way Dwayne is throwing his weight around at the moment,' Danielle said.

'Are you sure the Flynns were involved?'

Danielle bit her bottom lip. 'Don't ask me how I know—'

'That goes without saying.'

'Gallagher was in hospital to get a wound to his hand looking at. Dwyane broke into his apartment, threatened him and stabbed him through the hand with a knife.'

'Jesus. Why?' Saoirse asked.

Danielle shrugged. This was verging on giving away too much information. The last thing she wanted to do was have the heat turned in Kym's direction, and risk losing her one avenue of access to Chloe. And she absolutely could not tell Saoirse about the drugs. 'I'm not sure what the beef is, just that Dwayne is not happy with him.'

'Right. Maybe Gallagher might spill if we talk to him.'

Danielle shrugged again. Hopefully, Ian wouldn't be that helpful. The dilemma with Kym had kept her awake the previous night. And then there were the guards. Saoirse had proved herself to be trustworthy. Her colleagues, however, were another story. They'd be happy to see her homeless.

The café door opened. Two more people came in, but they seated themselves over by the entrance. Danielle fiddled with her mug of coffee, while she worked out what to say to Saoirse.

Decide which side you're on, Danielle.

She took a breath and repeated what Saoirse had once said to her in London. 'I have a plan. I cannot tell you everything yet, but you have to trust me, knowing I have both our interests at heart. Will you do that?'

Saoirse regarded her for what seemed like an age. 'Yes, Danielle, I will.'

Danielle released her breath. With it went the weight of months of accumulated tension. Now she knew what to do.

CHAPTER 29

Having dumped her gym bag in an empty changing room, Danielle went into the main area of the gym. Lee was busy showing a client the correct stance for a deadlift and hadn't noticed her come in. There were three other women in the room.

She was twelve reps into her first round of lat pulldowns when one of the women came up to her and exclaimed, 'Is it really you?'

Danielle hadn't recognised her, but the voice was unmistakable. 'Aimee!'

One of the most reliable girls working out of Berkley Street, Aimee looked almost plain without her make-up and sexy clothes. 'How are you doing?' Danielle asked.

'Linda gave us all some money to keep us going, and told us we were to wait to hear what was happening with the place.'

'Good of Linda to look after you,' Danielle said.

'Yeah, she's sound, she is. So, does this mean Berkley Street is back in business? I'm earning a bit, but it's tough without the Lewis name to keep me safe.'

'I haven't got the place back to where it was yet,' Danielle said.

'Oh, right. I see.' Disappointment clouded Aimee's face.

'You'll be the first to know when we do. You're top of the list, don't worry.'

Aimee gave her a brilliant smile. 'Fantastic! I'm a good earner, and Ged always made sure we were well looked after. You must miss him.'

Danielle smiled. 'I do, Aimee.'

'Oh, gawd, I just realised you're all on your own now. I'm sorry.'

'I'm fine, really.'

'Oh, right, okay. Anyway, I'll leave you to your work-out.' Aimee turned to go, then stopped. 'Oh, I think it's only right to tell you . . . I mean, you always said you prefer us being straight with you—'

'Go on, Aimee, what is it?'

Aimee looked about her, leaned closer to Danielle and whispered, 'I got a weird booking recently. Well, my friend did. She is seeing Lee here, and only takes on high-class, well-paying clients.'

Danielle wondered if Linda was still seeing Lee. She might need to know she was sharing him with someone.

'Anyway,' Aimee said, 'my friend needed one more for a booking she had, and she asked me along. The money was huge. I wouldn't have done it if I'd have known who it was, and by the time I got there it was too late to back out. He has a reputation for violence. Hazel and Linda used to screen our customers for us, but it's hard to do it ourselves. Look, I don't usually discuss my clients, but just this once—'

'I understand, Aimee. Go on.'

She lowered her voice even further. 'Dwayne Flynn.'

Danielle's whole body tensed. It took all the will she could muster to keep her expression neutral. 'Really?'

'Yeah, the night of his brother's burial.' She scrunched up her face. 'He was a bit pathetic, really. He ended up falling asleep on the job. Anyway, Jason was there, too.'

'Oh?' Danielle was itching to ask if he was one of the customers.

As if reading Danielle's mind, Aimee said, 'Well, Jason was having none of it. All he was interested in was sitting on the couch and drinking. He's not gay, is he?'

'No, Aimee, he's not.'

'Jane tried with him, and he totally ignored her. And Jane is hard to ignore, if you know what I mean.'

Danielle smiled briefly. 'I can imagine.'

'Anyway, he was grand — Jason, that is. He even had coffee with us the next morning, while Dwayne just wanted us gone. Mind you, we're used to that. I just wanted you to know I had no idea it was going to be Dwayne, in case you hear something. And don't forget, ring me, so, if you need me. I'm a good earner.' Giving Danielle a huge wink, Aimee left her to it.

Meeting Aimee made Danielle think. She hadn't intended starting up the Berkley Street business again, but if it provided the girls with a safe place from which to work, maybe it was worth considering. Jesus, though — a *madame*? Danielle almost smiled. Perhaps Linda would consider it, if she went back to London? They'd have to discuss it. The biggest surprise of all was that Jason hadn't partaken. Maybe he had changed.

'Back for more punishment, I see.' Lee was grinning broadly.

'Something like that.'

'Your sidekick not with you today?'

'You mean Linda?'

'Yeah. I've been texting her, but getting no replies. I hope she's okay. She seemed a bit distant the last time we were . . . um, together.'

'She's sleeping off a hangover,' Danielle said.

'Right. Tell her the cash should be ready tomorrow.'

'Cash? What cash?'

'The fee I pay.'

Danielle frowned. 'For what?'

'Um . . . tax on trading.'

'You must be joking. Why would we charge you tax on trading? Surely we're not charging protection money on one of our own businesses? When did this start?'

He looked down. 'Just over a month ago.'

'And Linda is collecting this?'

'Yes, of course. That's what she was here for the other day.'

'Really.' So, were they seeing each other or not? It's not the impression Linda gave. Maybe Linda had told her that to cover up what was really going on.

'Are you and Linda, well, seeing each other?'

He shrugged. 'Now and again. She keeps me at arm's length most of the time. She comes and goes; even has her own personal locker in the changing room. She keeps the key to it.'

'What's in it?'

He shrugged. 'I dunno. Her stuff, I suppose.'

'How much "trading tax" are you handing over?' Danielle asked.

'Ten percent. I wouldn't mind, but I can't even park here anymore. The hotel that was using it is being renovated, the carpark shutters got damaged, next thing the carpark was closed up too. I don't know what's happening. That car park was one of the perks of working here.'

'What do you do for transport now?' Danielle asked.

'I cycle.'

'Right. Look, it should be opened up again soon and you can park here again.'

'Sound. Anyway, I'd better let you get back to your workout. Give us a shout if you need any help.'

'Wait. Who are those other women?' Danielle asked.

'Um, well, there's Jane, and you were talking to Aimee.'

'So they are members?' she asked.

'Yeah, all regular members. I can give you their details if you want, but they're no threat, I assure you.'

Lee wandered away. She watched him chat to one of the women, who was using the leg press. No threat. It was an odd way to refer to the women. No threat to what? Her? The business? And Linda had never mentioned taking money from the place. What else was Linda keeping from her?

Lee had finished chatting and was heading to the reception desk. Danielle called him over. 'This locker that Linda uses, can you show me which one it is?'

'Of course. Follow me.'

He led the way into the changing room and pointed to locker number seven.

'There.' All the other lockers had keys hanging in their doors.

'Is there a master key?' Danielle asked.

'Um, I don't think so. I've never needed one,' he said.

'No one has ever left their stuff here and not come back for it?' she asked.

'Nope. Wait, I'll check the office.'

Danielle followed him into the small corner space just behind the reception area that served him for an office.

Lee searched through various drawers, eventually finding two keys under a jumble of papers. He held them up.

'Worth a try?'

'Sure.' She took them from him and returned to the changing room.

After a number of tries, the door to locker number seven swung open. Inside was a navy canvas holdall. Danielle pulled it out and put it on the bench. She unzipped it to reveal a rolled up blue towel, which she pulled out. Underneath was a white envelope containing a wad of fifty euro notes.

Lee whistled. 'Few quid there by the looks of it.'

'Yes,' Danielle said. 'Maybe you'd like to check on your customers, Lee?'

'What? Oh, yeah, course. I'll leave you to it.' He backed out of the changing room.

Danielle closed the door behind him and returned to the bag. Beneath the envelope she found a piece of cardboard, the kind usually found at the bottom of the bag to keep it flat. She pulled it out. Wrapped in another blue towel was a pair of red runners with dark blotches on the toes. Next, a charger lead with an unusual plug. The last thing in the bag was a purple device, roughly the size of a mobile phone. It had an on/off switch on one side, and a USB port. The front of this device bore a label with a picture of a viper on it. The charger fitted neatly into the USB port. Danielle lifted her top to reveal the burn marks below her rib cage. They had almost faded to nothing, but were still faintly visible. She measured the distance between the marks and compared it with the metal flanges at the top of the device. They matched exactly. She was holding the taser used to knock her out when the baby was taken.

Her head spun. She had been living under the same roof as her attacker, who'd all along been pretending to have her back, to support her. No wonder Linda hadn't asked about her discussion with Kym. Christ. How could she have been so stupid?

Danielle put the items back in the bag, picked it up and stormed out of the gym.

CHAPTER 30

Still seething with rage, Danielle parked Linda's car by the church on Berkley Street. From the boot she took out her suitcase and the bag from Linda's locker, leaving the tote bag where it was. She slammed the boot shut so hard the car shook with the force of it.

Waiting for a gap in the traffic, she took a breath, telling herself to calm down. What to do next? First, she had to confront Linda with what she'd found. Handing it over to the guards was out of the question; this was something she'd have to handle herself. While she stood mulling it over, someone came up beside her and touched her arm.

'Are you moving house?' Jason asked.

Danielle glared at him. 'What the fuck are you doing here? You're not following me, are you?'

'What? No. I was just hoping to meet you. I wanted to explain.'

'Explain what? How you let Dwayne walk all over you as usual? How you didn't stand up for me when he barged in and insulted me? Or how you killed an innocent man while trying to shoot Ian Gallagher, who, by the way, was working for my family. I think that's about it, or is there something

I'm forgetting? Do let me know if there is. Nothing can make me feel worse than I am already.'

'I didn't shoot that guy. I knew nothing about it until Dwayne came in and charged at me. He takes everything that goes wrong out on me.'

'Why?'

Jason shrugged. 'I don't know. He just does. And there was no way I could fight back. He'd have beaten the shit out of both of us.'

'Would that have been before or after I buried that knife in his neck?' Danielle said.

'Yeah, he is well pissed off about that.'

'What the fuck do you want, Jason? I have things to take care of.'

'Dwayne has someone on the inside,' he said.

'What? Inside where?'

'Someone close to you. I don't know who. I just over-heard him talking. I'm worried about you, Danielle.'

Linda. How nice she'd been. So considerate and tactful. Finding my weak spots and then running to Dwayne. Lee was just a smokescreen. It was Dwayne she was with.

Fuck, that's the only thing that makes any sense. Why else would she be taking money from the gym?

'Dwayne is capable of worse than I thought,' Jason said.

'If you are that worried, why aren't you being more open with me?' Danielle said. 'All I get from you is some vague shit I can do nothing with.'

'What do you mean, Danielle?' he said.

'What I mean is, I need something concrete, not half-ar-sed warnings that only serve to make me paranoid. Is it a man or woman, this person on the inside?'

'I told you, I only heard part of a phone conversation.'

She stared at him. 'What's in it for you?'

'What do you mean?'

'Could it be a certain large quantity of blow that every-one seems to be looking for?'

Jason glanced around furtively. 'Yes, Dwayne knows about that. He spoke to me yesterday, wanted me to get you onside.'

Maybe it was the way he looked at her, but for some reason, she believed him. 'You're serious, aren't you?'

'Yes. He suggested I try to get you to tell me where it was. But I know you, Danielle. You'd have seen through me like a pane of glass. And I have more respect for you than to even try.'

She raised an eyebrow. *He's not getting out of it that easy.*

'I still love you, Danielle. Can't you get that into your head?'

'Not while you are under Dwayne's thumb. It was the same when we were younger, I wanted to get out of Dublin, go somewhere and make a better life, you and me. But you always did what they said. You got hungry for the money. Dealing. Dragging us into this criminal bullshit.'

'And what about your family, Danielle? Do you think Ged built his business out of the goodness of his heart? Come on, Danielle, get your head out of your pretty arse and see the reality of the situation. You are now in control of the family finances. You can't keep hold of your fortune without, at the very least, using the threat of violence. Doing it any other way makes you vulnerable.'

She inhaled. 'And what? Here you are, the knight in shining armour come to protect me. That it? Don't tell me it's not about that blow Dwayne is after.'

'Fuck's sake, Danielle. No, it's got nothing to do with those drugs. I'm telling you, the first I heard of it was yesterday. Even Bosco knew more than me.'

'So, who's the rat?'

'I can try to find that out. Whoever it is, I think they also had a hand in Ian Gallagher's shooting.'

'Shit.'

'Come on, Danielle, there's still that spark between us; you know there is. I miss you. I still love you. We still have a chance of a life together. If you want to leave, I can go with you to London or somewhere sunny. Spain maybe, just you and me like we used to talk about.'

'Oh yeah? I don't think Dwayne would be very impressed with that.'

'No.' He glanced around. 'Can we get off the street, please? Go inside and talk?'

Danielle looked across the road to the door of the building she was currently calling home. 'No. I am not going to find myself alone with you again, not after what happened in the apartment. How do I know you're not setting me up?'

'I'm not, I promise,' he said.

'Fuck this.' Danielle spotted a gap in the traffic and ran across the road.

Jason caught up with her as she was about to ascend the steps. 'You are in danger, Danielle.'

'So what's new?'

'Listen, this is a credible threat.'

'From who?'

'Dwayne. I told you. Someone close to you who's working with him.'

'So you keep saying, but who? Be straight with me, Jason. I am sick to death of having to constantly watch my back.'

'I don't know. Dwayne is treating me like one of the fuckheads that run his errands. He tells me nothing. Isn't that obvious? You saw how he treats me.'

'He was always a prick, even when we were younger,' Danielle said.

Jason nodded. 'Yeah. At least Bird could handle him, but now Bird's gone . . .'

'I know. But how come this has suddenly come to a head? Why's Dwayne out to get me now all of a sudden?'

'Bosco Ryan was shot. He's dead.'

'Yes, I heard.'

The sound of a dog barking came from inside the building. Jason glanced up at the window. 'When did you get a dog?'

'Never you mind, Jason, we've more important matters to discuss.' *Shit. I'll definitely be a suspect in Bosco's murder if Jason sees Dwayne's dog in my house.*

But Jason was already going up the steps. He peered in the window.

'Jason, wait! Don't.'

He turned back and looked down at Danielle. 'That's Dwyane's dog, Danielle. If he gets to know you have Lola, you're well and truly fucked. He's been looking for her everywhere. What are you doing with her? She was with Bosco.'

Danielle sighed. Jason would never believe her if she tried to explain. 'She was locked in the kitchen. She must have got out.' It sounded lame, even to her.

'She'll jump and pull at handles, she's very clever. I'll take her back, and tell Dwayne I found her.' He put his hand on the door.

'No you won't. The way he treats humans, what he must do to animals doesn't bear thinking of.'

Jason lowered his hand. 'Yeah, it doesn't, does it?'

'Then leave her here.'

'It really will be your funeral, Danielle, if he finds out that you have her.'

'According to you, I'm in danger from him anyway. I might as well be hanged for a sheep as a lamb.'

'No. Having Lola puts you in real danger, because right now he just suspects you're responsible for Bosco's shooting. If he finds out about her, he'll be certain you are.'

'But I was with you yesterday. Surely he'll think I couldn't have done that and have a hit planned.'

'He thinks you were giving yourself an alibi,' Jason said.

'But didn't you have other company on the night of the funeral? That's what I heard.'

'What? No. Whoever told you got it wrong. I stayed up drinking all night.'

So Aimee was telling the truth.

'Oh, for fuck's sake, Jason, he is crazy. I had no idea you'd be at the cemetery.'

'I was at my brother's funeral.'

'Which I didn't know was happening.'

'Try telling Dwayne that. He thinks whoever shot Bosco stole his dog, and now I find her at your place. How does that look?'

'Dwayne is paranoid. I knew nothing about Bosco being shot. I only heard about it later. I found Lola running around the streets, terrified, covered in blood. I thought she was injured and . . .'

'Go on.'

'Doesn't matter.' *Best not drag the vet or Kym into this.* 'She's sorted now, and safe.'

'Just be careful, that's all.'

'Story of my life. It's about to rain again. I'm cold and I want to go in. Alone.'

Jason reached for her hand. 'If that's what you really want . . .'

She pulled back her hand. 'At this moment, Jason, it is.'

He nodded, and turned away.

She watched him walk slowly away. Despite her words, she felt like crying. She so desperately needed a little human warmth, a hug. But she daren't let down her guard. He never saw the tear land on her cheek.

Danielle marched into the kitchen and shook herself free of her burdens, shoving the bag from the locker under a chair. Lola bounded towards her. Danielle petted her and opened the door into the back yard so the dog could go out.

Realising she'd left her gym bag behind, Danielle frantically searched her pockets for her phone, which was in the back pocket of her jeans. Lola wandered back in and nuzzled Danielle's thigh.

She was busy petting Lola when she heard the front door bang. She jumped and Lola barked. Linda stood in the doorway with a takeaway coffee in each hand and a paper bag hanging from her mouth. It met the floor with a slap.

'What in the name of fuck was Jason Flynn doing here?' Linda plonked the cups on the table and picked up the paper bag.

'That's the end of the croissants anyway.' Danielle said, regarding her coldly. Maybe Linda was worried that Jason had come to warn her — which he had. 'He didn't come in, even though he wanted to. Where did you see him?'

'I spotted him walking away. How long was he here? What was he trying to talk you into doing now?'

'What do you mean? Do you think I don't have a mind of my own?'

'Not when it comes to Jason,' Linda said.

'Just shows how much you really know me, Linda.'

Looking surprised at Danielle's sudden unfriendly tone, Linda pushed one of the takeaway cups across the table to her.

'He wanted to warn me.' Danielle searched Linda's face for a reaction. All she saw there was surprise.

'Threaten you, you mean?' Linda said.

'No, warn me about someone close to me.' Danielle watched her closely.

Frowning, Linda removed the top of the takeaway cup and stirred her latte. 'Did he say who it was?'

'No. Who would you say was close enough to me to harm me or put me in danger?'

'Unless you've been meeting someone else, I'm the closest person to you at the moment, and I'm no threat. We're friends.'

'Really?'

Linda was about to take a sip of her coffee. She put it down again. 'What are you trying to say, Danielle?'

Danielle reached for the gear bag and hoisted it onto the table. She stood up and pulled open the zip. One by one, she took out the contents and put them down on the table in front of Linda. First, the envelope of money. 'Trading tax, eh? A tax on our own business. What the fuck is that about, Linda?'

Linda stared blankly at a bunch of fifties that had fallen out of the envelope.

'And that's not all,' Danielle said. She pulled out the runners and landed them on the table. 'Remember these?

Oh, look.' She pointed to one of the dark stains. 'You know what? I think that might be my blood.'

'What are you—?'

'Sufficient evidence for a charge of assault, I believe. But what's this?' Danielle pulled out the taser. 'Illegal possession of an offensive weapon. I should charge this up and show you exactly how it feels to get tasered.'

'What is going on?' Linda asked.

Danielle was about to explode. 'The person Jason warned me about, the one working with Dwayne, is you. What did he promise you in return? More of this?' She picked up a handful of banknotes and scattered them over the table.

Linda stood up, sending her chair crashing to the floor. 'What shit was Jason feeding you, Danielle? Did he say I was working with Dwayne?'

'He didn't need to. I found all this,' Danielle said, indicating the bag and its contents. 'In your locker at the gym.'

'I don't have a locker at the gym. What else did Jason say?'

'That this person was also involved in Ian Gallagher's shooting.'

'I was nowhere near that shooting. I was here. We both were.'

'You could have got someone else to do it,' Danielle said.

'Danielle, take a breath and think.'

'I'm too angry to take a fucking breath.'

'So, Lee showed you a locker and said it was mine. What exactly did he say to you, Danielle?'

'He said you're taxing him. You keep stuff in one of the lockers in the changing room and hold onto the key.'

'First off, why would I keep stuff at the gym when I can hide it in my room?' Linda said.

'Because it's evidence.'

'I know nothing about that bag or its contents. And as for taxing the business, I do the accounts, as you know. Every Friday I transfer the takings to keep the books straight. I also update the customer records — you know, people checking in, members — to ensure that they match up with the income.'

'And what's the story with you and him?'

Linda gave a faint smile. 'I've had my suspicions about him for a while. I wanted to get close to him to find out more.'

'You gave me the impression you had a thing going on,' Danielle said.

'Yeah, once, but it was never really a thing. He's seeing Jane — she works with Aimee servicing high-end clients. Wait — when did he say I put the bag there?'

'He didn't.'

'Look, I can go back over the records and check who's been in since the assault on you.'

Danielle had had cause to doubt a lot of people today. Her doubts about Jason had arisen through his own actions, but Linda was another story. Those had been put in her head by others. Her gut was screaming that Linda could be trusted.

'How do you know Jason's story about Dwayne having someone on the inside wasn't just to win you over and make you trust him? It might have been a ruse, to get you to tell him where those drugs are,' Linda said.

'While I haven't the faintest idea. Okay, Linda. Just do your checks and we'll take it from there.'

'Grand. You enjoy the coffee and whatever's left of the croissant I got for you. Meanwhile, I'll find proof of how wrong you are about all this.' Linda swept her hand over the money and taser.

She got out her laptop and started it up. 'Here.' On the screen was a video showing the empty changing room.

'Don't tell me you can watch people changing?' Danielle said.

'Well, no, not really. I'm the only one who has access to the recordings. The camera is well hidden and Lee has no idea it's there. It's not like him and his friends are sitting round gawping at it. Though he nearly caught me setting it up. I had to, er, divert his attention.'

'That was the one occasion you mentioned?'

'Yep. Which locker did you get the bag from?' Linda said.

'Number seven.'

Linda zoomed in. 'Remind me of the date you were assaulted?'

The date was burned into Danielle's mind. She gave it to Linda.

'Roughly what time?'

Danielle gave her that, too.

Linda fast-forwarded the recording. About two hours after the attack, they watched a hand reach for the locker. Linda zoomed out and they saw two people standing in front of it. One was about a foot taller than the other, but Danielle couldn't see what they looked like, or even if they were male or female. One of them stuffed the bag into the locker and turned the key.

Linda turned to Danielle. 'Do either of those people look like me?'

'No.'

'Does either of them have a similar build to Lee?' Linda said.

'Yes.'

Linda raised an eyebrow. 'And who led you to the locker?'

'Lee.'

'I'm sure he did so perfectly casually.'

'Yes.' Danielle ground her teeth. 'Fucker comes across as a thick meathead, but is always looking for the main chance.'

'That is a good way of describing him, Danielle.'

'Would he be working with Dwayne, do you think?' Danielle asked.

'A lot happened while you had yourself hidden away,' Linda said. 'Most of the people who work in the businesses are still with us, but I can't say for sure about him. It was one of the reasons I put up the camera. We have to assume the worst until we know better.'

'So, how do we prove that Lee and Dwayne are in league together?'

'Leave that to me. I can do a bit more digging into the accounts. You need to think about what you are going to do with him, if he is collaborating with Dwayne against you.'

'Would they go as far as to share Jane?' Danielle asked.

'What do you mean?'

'I met Aimee at the gym. She told me that Jane was booked for a job and needed another girl, so Aimee went along. Jane never told her it was Dwayne Flynn.'

While they talked, the video was still running. The two people began to strip off.

'Wait!' Danielle had suddenly noticed what was taking place on screen.

Lee's hands were all over his female companion. They had sex on the floor of the changing room. Linda zoomed in on the woman's face.

'Fuck,' Danielle said.

'Fuck,' echoed Linda.

What else could they say?

CHAPTER 31

The baby needed pacifying. Her crying resounded through-out the shop. Danielle guessed that Kym hadn't spotted her yet and was pleased to see that Kym responded, retrieving the soother and running it gently over Chloe's lips. Teething was a bitch. Chloe was quiet for a moment or two, and then began to cry again. Kym left Chloe to kick out, but Danielle was no good at tough love. She got to the buggy just as the soother tumbled to the floor. It was time to make her pres-ence known.

While Kym got down on her hands and knees to retrieve the soother, Danielle, unable to resist, scooped Chloe from the buggy. She walked to the end of the aisle, rocking the baby.

'What the fuck are you doing?' Kym shouted.

'Jesus, Kym, it's only me.'

'Fuck's sake, Danielle.'

Danielle put a finger to her lips. 'Shh, it's worked, she's settled.'

'I nearly shit myself with the fright,' Kym said. 'What are you doing in here? We'd arranged to meet at the playground.'

'True, yeah. Sorry. Linda drove me, the woman who was at the vets with me. I was picking up something for her before she dropped me to meet you, when I heard the crying, I just went into automatic pilot.'

'Fair enough. Give her here, and I'll settle her back in. My ma doesn't want her mollycoddled.'

'There's no mollycoddling about it. She just needs a bit of love and comfort. Besides, your mother is not her gran. She's only her great-aunt.'

'While she's in my care, she gets plenty of love and comfort, I'll have you know.' Kym prised Chloe from Danielle's arms.

'Of course. I didn't mean . . .' The last thing Danielle wanted was to tick Kym '.

'It's okay; you're grand.'

'Do you mind looking after her?' Danielle asked.

Kym shrugged. 'I expect it will fall to me quite a bit, although my aunt and uncle are pretty hands-on. They're mad about her.'

'I don't blame them. She's gorgeous.' Danielle stroked Chloe's cheek. 'Where do you look after her then? At your aunt and uncle's place, your parents' place, or your own apartment?'

'All of them. I try to make sure I'm close to her home. More so now, after Dwayne threatened us like he did.'

The mention of his name, and the potential risk he posed to Chloe, made Danielle's blood run cold.

'Do you really think Hazel is just off sunning herself somewhere and will come back for Chloe?' Kym said.

Danielle looked at the baby so she wouldn't have to meet Kym's gaze. 'Do you?'

'No,' Kym said.

'What makes you say that?'

'I just have a feeling . . . The drugs, you know. And she was flaky. The last time we spoke, she was heading to a party. I wanted to go, too, but she wouldn't take me, she said it wasn't the right sort of crowd. She told me not to worry and we'd meet up soon. I never saw or heard from her again. Where do you think she is?'

This time, Danielle couldn't avoid her eyes. 'Honestly?'

'Is there any other way to be, Danielle?'

'There isn't,' Danielle said. 'I think go with your gut. If your feeling is that she's sunning herself in Spain, then that's where she is.'

'Okay then. We'll just have to wait, won't we?'

'We will.'

Kym had done a great job of settling Chloe. A guy delivering bread bumped against her, sending her stumbling forward against the buggy. Chloe didn't stir. Kym adjusted the blanket.

'Kym? Kym, it's me.' The voice came from behind them.

'Oh, hi, Anto,' Kym said unenthusiastically.

'We need to talk, so that things don't get too complicated or fucked up.'

Kym spoke quietly. 'You know Danielle Lewis, Anto?'

'Oh, right.' He stared pointedly at Kym. Danielle wandered off up the aisle and picked up a can of deodorant. She heard the baby crying again, and, the deodorant still in her hand, returned to the others.

'It's a bottle she wants,' Danielle said. 'Have you got one?'

'Yeah.' With a sigh, Kym rooted around in the changing bag underneath the pram.

Watching Kym, something crawled up Danielle's spine. The changing bag brought back memories of the attack. It had been taken from her along with the baby. There was something else that had gone missing, too. Danielle felt along the side of the buggy where the Beretta had been, but there was nothing in the pocket.

Anto was beginning to look uneasy. He eyed the security camera in the corner above, then shifted his backpack from one shoulder to the other. Drops of sweat appeared above his lip.

'You look a bit jittery, Anto,' Danielle said. 'What's up?'

He wiped his forehead with his sleeve. 'I just need to be someplace.'

'Then head off. I'll catch up with you later,' Kym said, still rummaging in the bag. 'Ah, here's the fucker. It'll be a bit cold.' She shook the bottle.

'Stick something in her gob, for fuck's sake,' Anto said, glancing around.

'You really are on edge,' Danielle said. 'Let me look after the baby while you two have your chat. Don't mind me.' Danielle stuck the can of spray in her pocket and put the bottle to Chloe's lips. It *was* cold, but she began to suck the minute the teat hit her mouth.

Kym looked at Danielle, then at Anto. 'It really isn't a great time, Anto.'

'Look, I can busy myself in another part of the shop, if you like,' Danielle said.

'No, don't worry, Danielle,' Anto said. 'You might be able to, I dunno, help or something.'

Danielle caught the dirty look that Kym threw him.

'There's no one close enough that they can hear,' Danielle said. There was a girl in a bright pink tracksuit at the counter, a toddler at her side, pulling at bags of crisps while the cashier was busy getting cigarettes from behind her. The only other person in the shop was the bread delivery guy, whose hands were now empty of bread, and he had a mobile held to his ear. He looked in their direction a couple of times before turning away.

'If you're looking for the cameras, everyone knows the ones here are only for show,' Kym added.

'You're not looking to rob the place, are you, Anto?' Danielle asked. 'That's shitting on your own doorstep — not a good move. Not to mention it's a step down for you.'

Anto's uneasiness was transmitting itself to Danielle. The shop suddenly felt a lot more cramped than it had before he entered, and the shelves seemed to close in on her. She had a strong urge to leave. Something was about to happen.

Anto's ringtone broke the tension. He looked at the screen and cut the call. It rang again, and again he didn't answer.

211

'There's someone mad to get hold of you there, Anto. Maybe you should answer it,' Danielle said.

'Nah, it's Brenno looking for a lift to the hospital. I'm heading to pick him up anyway.'

'The hospital?' Danielle had to at least pretend she didn't know.

'Yeah. His mam.' Anto sighed. 'She tried to do away with herself, thanks to that prick Dwayne.'

'Shit, no,' Danielle said.

'Yeah.'

'How is she now?' Danielle asked innocently.

'Getting there.'

'What did Dwayne do to her?' Danielle said.

He regarded her for a moment, eyes narrowed. 'What do you care? Don't tell me you give a shit, Danielle Lewis. Up there in your ivory tower, looking down at the rest of us.'

'There is no ivory tower, Anto, and I'm not one to look down on anyone. I do so give a shit.'

Anto shrugged. 'He kicked her out of Bird's place, and banned her from attending the funeral.'

'Prick,' Kym said.

'Exactly. She's like a second mother to me, and no one messes with my family.'

'I understand. In case you hadn't heard, CAB kicked me out of my place with all my stuff inside. I only found out after I was discharged from hospital, where I'd been admitted with injuries from an assault.' Danielle pointed to the marks on her face, now largely faded.

'Oh, right, yeah. Sorry.'

The bread delivery guy thundered past them, nearly knocking over the buggy. He headed through the emergency door and stood for a moment at the rear of his small truck, glancing back into the shop. Then he shut the doors and went around to the front.

Kym looked past Danielle, then down at Chloe.

'He's in some rush, isn't he?' Anto said. He glanced around again, then turned back to Kym. 'I need to talk to you, but not here.'

'What is going on, Anto? You're creeping me out big time,' Kym said.

He leaned closer and whispered, 'I have something to give you.'

Kym jerked her head away. 'For Christ's sake, Anto. Not here.'

This time, Anto answered his phone. About to speak, he glanced over to the door, which had just opened, and a look of horror appeared on his face. There was a concave mirror in the corner of the shop, and Danielle saw the reflection of a man in overalls standing in the doorway. He wore sunglasses and a baseball cap. His mouth was covered with a mask. Not daring to turn and look, Danielle watched the slightly blurry figure step forward and raise an arm. There was a gun in his hand.

'Run!' Danielle yelled. At the same time, she pulled the can of deodorant from her pocket and directed the spray at the gunman.

Kym seemed frozen to the spot.

Anto gave the buggy a shove, sending it along the aisle in the opposite direction to the gunman. The movement galvanised Kym, who ducked and turned just as a shot rang out, sending plasterboard and fibreglass raining down on them. The gunman fired again, spun round and ran from the shop.

Anto lay on the floor, blood spreading slow as melted butter across the front of his white T-shirt. Danielle saw his chest rise and fall. He was still alive — so far. The pram was covered in white dust, but the screams from inside told her Chloe was alive. Kym was on the floor, with blood on her arm, but she too had survived.

Danielle helped Kym to her feet. She saw that the side door was still open. Snatching up Anto's backpack, she grasped the buggy in one hand and Kym in the other and made a run for it, emerging just as the delivery van pulled away in a cloud of exhaust fumes. One of the rear doors swung open, narrowly missing the buggy. It disappeared around the corner, leaving a trail of sliced pans in its wake.

Danielle looked around for CCTV and saw that the cameras were all facing towards the bank next door.

Still hanging onto Kym, who looked dazed, Danielle pushed the buggy into a nearby alley. A squad car raced past. They ducked behind a skip until it disappeared, and then hared off down the lane. Chloe was quiet. Maybe Hazel had always been on the go while she was pregnant. Mayhem had always been in Chloe's life, even when in the womb . . . Anyway, there was no time to think about that now.

Deep in a maze of alleys and narrow streets, Danielle stopped, gripped Kym by the shoulders and turned her round to face her. 'You okay?'

Kym nodded. She was shivering and covered in dust, as was the buggy. But Chloe was safe. They all were.

'Let's get the hell away from here,' Danielle said. 'Tell no one you were at that shop. No one. You hear?'

'What about our prints? DNA?' Kym's bottom lip quivered.

'Jesus, I just stopped Chloe from crying. Don't you start.'

'It's okay,' Kym said. 'I'm not gonna start snivelling. We are both made of tougher stuff.'

'Well, I grabbed anything I touched and brought it with me.'

'Good thinking, Danielle.'

'And they'd need to have your DNA on file to get a match. It's not in their system, is it?' Danielle asked.

Kym shook her head.

Danielle wondered if they had taken her DNA after the assault, but there was no time to worry about that now. While she considered how best to get them away without attracting attention, a car pulled up beside them.

'Get in.' Linda reached across and flung open the passenger door.

'How come the cops didn't see you?' Danielle asked.

'I pulled into this side street to go to the bank machine when I heard the sirens.'

Kym was fussing with the buggy. 'What do you think you're doing?' Linda said. 'Come on, just get the hell in.'

'I am getting in,' Kym said. 'I can't fold the buggy with the baby in it, can I? Jesus.'

Linda got out and took charge of the Maxi-Cosi. Danielle noticed that there was a hand-print in the dust covering the buggy. She guessed it was Anto's, left there when he had pushed it out of the way of the gun. The thought of his courage overwhelmed her. He'd saved Chloe from danger, and now he was probably dead. She swallowed her tears, shoving the folded buggy roughly into the boot of the car, and throwing the backpack into the front. She looked around. People were running past, keen to get out of the way of the approaching cops as the sirens grew louder. It wouldn't be long before the place was swarming with them. *Fuck that.* Kym slid into the back seat, the baby seat beside her. Danielle sat in the front.

Linda drove off, doubling back on herself every so often, until she reached a car park. She brought the car to a stop. 'Have you baby wipes?'

'Yeah,' Kym said. 'They should be in the bag. Why?'

'It'll help clean off most of the dust. When you get home, jump straight into the shower. Okay?'

'Okay.'

Kym took out the wipes and passed some to Danielle before scrubbing what she could from her clothes and arms.

'Were either of you cut?' Linda asked.

'Just a scratch from the edge of a shelf or something,' Kym said.

'We're in a lot better condition than Anto,' Danielle said sadly.

'Fuck, yeah,' Kym said. 'Did we do the right thing, Danielle? You know, just leaving him like that?'

'Are you off your head?' Danielle said. 'What else could we have done? You know what happens to witnesses around here. We absolutely did the right thing. The emergency services will respond and he'll be helped.'

'Yes, you're right.'

'Of course I am. Now. Not a word about it to anyone. Are we agreed?' Danielle looked at her hard.

'Agreed. Though I still feel bad about it . . . I mean, he took a bullet for us. That's no small thing.'

'He did — if the bullet was meant for one of us, and not Anto himself.'

'I told you Dwayne was an animal,' Kym said.

'You think he was behind it?' Danielle asked.

'First Ian, and now this, and while I was with the baby, too. I told you he wouldn't care if she was with me.'

'That man was the wrong shape for Dwayne. He was taller, too,' Danielle said.

'I'm sure he was behind it, though,' Kym said.

'I can't help wondering which of us really was the target,' Danielle said.

'He probably thought he'd hit the jackpot when he saw the three of you together. Maybe he was trying to decide which one of you to shoot, and that second's hesitation was enough to save you,' Linda said.

'Yeah, Linda. You could be right,' Danielle said.

Kym shrugged. 'Whichever of us was the real target, he didn't care who took the bullet.'

'That's true.'

'Where is the safest place to drop you, Kym?' Linda asked.

'Well, with all the cops around, I'd best head to my parents' place. I can ring my aunt and uncle from there and have them take Chloe—'

'No.' Danielle's sharp tone surprised even herself.

Kym frowned. 'Why?'

'If they think you've put Chloe in danger, they may stop you looking after her, and that would be the end of our arrangement.'

Danielle ignored the look Linda gave her. She'd forgotten that Linda knew nothing of the deal with Kym, and the real reason she'd sudden access to Chloe.

'Drop me close to it, so. The cops are still doing house-to-house after Bosco's shooting. I can't have my crowd thinking I had anything to do with that,' Kym said.

'Why would they?' Linda asked.

'Um, well, no; they wouldn't. I meant—'

'That might be a good plan,' Danielle interjected. 'But let's not go straight there, Linda. If it's okay with you, Kym, let's wait till the fuss has died down. We'll drive away and come from a different direction, just to make sure no one notices that we're coming from Costello's.'

'Good plan,' Linda said.

Kym nodded.

Linda switched on the engine and pulled away, only to be surrounded by a swarm of cop cars. A guard was standing in the middle of the road, blocking their way. The buggy was still covered in dust and plasterboard, and Danielle realised she'd forgotten to fasten her seatbelt. *Shit*. All this officer needed was an excuse to search them, and she'd just handed him one on a plate.

'Where are you going?'

'I'm just dropping my friend home,' Linda said.

'Address?'

Kym leaned forward and gave it to her.

'You can't go this way, I'm afraid. There's been an incident.' She peered at Kym in the back seat and across at Danielle, tutted and shook her head.

'What's happened, Officer?' Linda asked.

The cop merely shook her head. 'You need to find a different route.'

She waved a squad car through and returned her attention to Linda.

'Go on now, before I get out my notebook and start to see what I am currently much too busy to deal with.' The guard rapped on the roof and pointed back the way they had come.

'Thank you, Officer.'

Linda drove them through various housing estates, finally dropping Kym at the top of her road. Danielle got out to give Chloe a kiss goodbye.

She and Kym stared at each other for a few moments. 'Go on, Kym. Be safe. No talking to anyone, mind. You'll be fine. Like I said, we were never there. Whoever was behind it, they do not need two witnesses to target.'

Kym was just about to turn away when Danielle put her hand on her arm. 'Someone knew about that hit and I don't mean Dwayne.'

'What do you mean?'

'Just before it happened Anto got a call, and someone shouted at him to get out. Who was it?'

'Oh, did he? I don't remember that,' Kym said.

'But you heard something?'

'No, nothing.' Kym looked away.

Danielle changed tack. 'After what we've just witnessed together and survived, I won't see you wrong.'

'Thank you,' Kym said.

'Of course.'

Danielle got back into the car and watched Kym set off at a jog, then slow her pace to a fast walk. She thought of Anto as she'd last seen him, his rather ratty face smooth and placid as he slipped into unconsciousness. Three more sirens blazed past a street away from where they were parked. One sounded different — hopefully an ambulance. Anto didn't deserve to die on the floor of a tatty corner shop.

A sudden thought nearly made her groan out loud. If the gunman had come for her and she had survived, she was exposed to more danger. Well, she wasn't yet ready to bring down the shutters on her life, certainly not at the hands of an inept gunman. She needed to step up. One thing was clear: she could no longer wait and see what might happen — this mess would only be sorted if she took back control.

CHAPTER 32

Anto lay on his back amid a thick cloud of swirling dust, particles of plasterboard raining down upon him. He tried to raise his hand to wipe his face, but he couldn't move his arm. He prayed that the gunman had legged it, and wasn't waiting to put one in his skull, like he had with Bosco. He tried to roll to the side, but the weight of his pain held him down. Someone must have ratted him out to Dwayne. Why else would he be targeted like this? Fucking Costello's corner shop was the last place he'd expected to get hit.

A pair of lace-up shoes materialised in his line of sight. A woman was asking his name. A second pair of shoes appeared. Someone seemed to be pressing on his shoulder. It hurt like fuck. He wished they'd stop.

He must have said so, because the woman said, 'We're trying to stop the bleeding. The ambulance is on its way.' She held his hand, the one he could move. He was glad of the touch. 'You'll be fine, Anto, just stay with us. My name is Sinead. You know Dave.'

Dave? I don't know any Dave.

'Did you get a look at the gunman?' the woman called Sinead asked.

'Not really.' It hurt to speak. 'Balaclava. The bastard.'

'The bastard is gone now and the Emergency Response Unit are patrolling the area on the lookout for him,' she said.

As she leaned over him, he spotted the handgun. He struggled to move but couldn't.

'We're the guards, Anto. You're quite safe now.'

What? The fuckers had saved him? Nah, not the guards . . . Would they?

Someone in green knelt down beside him. Must be the medics, thanks be to . . . Jesus, the pain was unreal.

'Can you tell me your name?' the paramedic asked.

'Anto Doyle.'

'Good.' Someone shone a light into his eyes. 'You were lucky. The detective sergeant stemmed the flow of blood, bandaged you up good.'

Well, fuck me, helped by a cop. That'll be some story to tell Brenno when I get the chance.

Anto was loaded onto a stretcher and into the waiting ambulance. There was more fuss at the hospital. Couldn't they take away the pain? He was wheeled in through double doors and into a room where they stuck needles in him. Voices, beeps, Anto needed it all to go away. And then it did. As the anaesthetic took effect, he slipped into oblivion.

* * *

'How is my hero today?'

Anto opened his eyes to a haze, as if he was emerging from a three-day bender. His neck was stiff. He tried to look around to see where he was, but he couldn't raise his head. His mouth was sandy and dry. His throat felt raw. Someone rubbed his lips with a moist sponge. It felt like the best thing in the world.

'I don't feel like much of a hero, Doc,' he croaked. 'Just glad I survived.'

'Just stay still while I examine you.'

'Grand.'

'We got the bullet out. And I'm hoping there'll be minimal damage to your arm's capacity to function.'

'In English, Doc, if you please.'

'If we allow the wound to recover, along with the appropriate physiotherapy, we should have your arm back in working order in no time.'

'Mighty stuff. You're legend, Doc.'

'I appreciate that.'

She leaned closer and pulled down her mask. 'I never got to thank you properly for saving my life that day.'

He blinked a few times before it registered. 'Anytime, er, Doc.'

He raised his good arm and made a fist. She smiled, and gave him a gentle fist bump.

'Here, Doc.' Anto cleared his throat.

'Yes?'

'You know that day, the one we were just talking about? You and the life-saving and all that?'

'Uh huh.'

'Well, the cops will want to talk to me about, you know, this.' He moved his head slightly, toward his damaged shoulder.

'They will. One of them managed to pack your wound to prevent more blood loss.'

'Yeah, and look, I'll pay that back some day, but for now, they needn't know from you that it was me that day at the front door. They'll be able to solve that one without drawing me in and risking more of this.' He tilted his head again.

'I hear you. Now, don't worry about that or talking to any cops. I need you to get some rest for the moment, and to recover so you can pay those detectives back for saving you.'

'Yeah, sure. Thanks again, Doc.'

'And thank you,' Lisa whispered.

CHAPTER 33

Rounding the corner to the last stretch of her home run to safety, Kym was relieved to see her uncle's taxi parked up in the driveway. Sweaty and breathless, she flung herself through the door, certain of a welcome. Her uncle never asked awkward questions, wouldn't want an account of where she'd been. She smiled, looking forward to giving her uncle a big hug.

To her dismay, the person waiting in the living room was her mother, Audrey.

'Where the fuck did you get to?'

Deflated, Kym lifted Chloe from the buggy and, sighing wearily, trudged across. At times like this, when her uncle wasn't around, Kym missed Hazel badly. At least when Hazel lived at home, Kym had somewhere to escape to. Then Hazel started working for Ged Lewis, became his lover, and Kym had nowhere to go.

Audrey sat in a chair, wreathed in cigarette smoke, her legs crossed at the knee. One foot was swinging, slipper hanging from the toe for dear life.

Kym eyed the cigarette, now burning dangerously close to Audrey's fingers. She didn't warn her. 'Just the shops. Where's Uncle Frank?'

'How should I know? Do I look like his keeper?'

'No, but his taxi is in the driveway,' Kym said.

'He's probably out in the shed with your dad, playing with bits of wood and that. Makes a right mess, all that sawdust.'

Kym's father was a skilled carpenter, who made cribs and bespoke furniture. Audrey never gave him credit for the beautiful pieces he turned out. She never gave Ray's brother credit, either, though Kym's uncle Frank had built his taxi business up from nothing, and now owned a fleet of cars and minibuses.

'Shops, eh. Did you get me a bottle?' Audrey said.

'No, I didn't.'

'Fucking useless.' Audrey got to her feet, flicked ash into a non-existent fire, and studied her daughter from her face to her runners. 'What's that thing you've got there, stuck in your bra?'

'Fags.'

'When did you take up smoking?'

'They're for Ian.'

Her mother put her hand on her hip. 'Oh, I see. You go for fags for your fella but you can't be bothered to fetch your mother her vodka. Some daughter you turned out to be. Fucking useless.'

Useless, am I? And who does all the cleaning here? Kym.

'I was looking after Chloe, too.'

'Frank better be paying you well, that's all I can say.'

'He does.'

'Well, don't forget I need my cut out of that,' Audrey said.

'I know. Chloe is a lovely baby, Mam, ever so good. She's been well looked after.'

'I hope you're not giving that Lewis one any credit for that. Fucking baby-snatcher.'

As if she knew she was being talked about, Chloe began to cry.

Kym's mother grimaced. 'That noise. I can't stand it. Would you take her off somewhere — ouch.' The cigarette had finally burned its way down to her fingers.

'I'm only just in, Mam.' All Kym wanted to do right now was head upstairs to her old room, away from her mother.

'Bawling brat. Shit's getting on my nerves. I need a drink. Here, head away down the road to the offie and get me a naggin — anything will do. Whatever's cheapest. Go on with you.'

The off-licence was next door to Costello's. No way was Kym going back there. She had to be careful what she told Audrey, or she'd be off out to the neighbours, gossiping over the wall, delighted to have more information than the cops. Besides, she'd promised Danielle that she'd keep her mouth shut.

After a moment's thought, she said, 'Costello's is surrounded by cops, Mam.' Kym jiggled Chloe in her arms and she stopped crying. Maybe her mother would lay off, now she was quiet.

'What?'

'Did you not hear anything on the street?' She knew this comment would drive her mother mad. She couldn't bear for the neighbours to know more than she did. 'Some fella went in and wrecked the place.'

'Were you there, then?'

'Nah. It must have happened just after. I'd been and gone by then, but I heard all the sirens going off, and someone up the road said there was drama. I didn't hear the full story though.'

'I wonder does Nora next door know anything? She hears it all, nosey cow. But she'd be the most likely to have heard.' Audrey went to the window and peered out.

'I hope no one got hurt,' Kym said innocently. Her insides ached. Poor Anto. It had been horrendous to witness.

'Yeah,' her mother said indifferently.

Her mother pulled back from the window as a squad car whizzed by. She flicked the fag butt into the empty stove and shrugged. Anyway, 'tisn't you or me. Go to the other offie then.' She waved a hand at her daughter. 'Go on.'

'I can't. Look at what just passed. There's cops everywhere.'

Her mother went to the window again and glanced up and down the street. 'And how is that going to stop you going to the shops? There's free movement, you know. If they try to stop you, tell them to go fuck themselves.'

'And land in a poxy cell for my troubles? No thanks.'

In a flash, her mother's hand was at her face. The slap stung like a motherfucker. Kym held Chloe tight, thankful not to have dropped her.

'Don't talk back to me like that. Ungrateful little bitch.'

Kym's face was still burning when Frank and Ray Brady rushed into the living room. Surely they'd see her mother's palm-print on her face, Kym thought. They never did. Her mother didn't usually hit her on her face. Mostly she aimed for her back, her legs or her arms, where the weals or bruises didn't show.

'Did you hear what just happened?' Ray's face was flushed.

Frank sniffed the air. 'Have you been smoking again, Audrey?'

'Nope.'

'Not around the baby, please. It's not good for her little lungs,' he added mildly.

'Go on, Ray, tell us what happened then,' Audrey said, ignoring her brother-in-law.

Audrey had made sure to stand in front of Kym. Anyway, it no longer stung.

'Some lad went apeshit in the shop. Wrecked the place, apparently.'

'I dunno,' Frank added, shaking his head. 'Bosco Ryan dead, Costello's wrecked . . . I also heard that Dwayne Flynn is on the warpath. Lost his dog, apparently. Bosco was looking after her, and she ran off when he got shot.'

'It would be a brave man to chance taking something belonging to Dwayne Flynn. Everyone knows that's his dog. I thought he and anyone close to him was untouchable, but taking out his right-hand man.' Ray whistled. 'Now that was brave.'

'Well, he's obviously not untouchable now, is he?' Audrey said.

Audrey turned to her daughter. 'You spoke to him just yesterday, didn't you, Kym? Maybe you were the last one to do so.'

'Me?' Kym said.

'Were you not bitching about him chatting you up every time you pass his house? Makes you a star witness, Kym, that does.' Audrey raised her eyebrows.

'No way. There's loads of people around the estate he could have chatted with after me.'

Audrey narrowed her eyes. 'That bitch wife of his could have seen you flirting with him. Maybe she got jealous, told on you.'

'No, Mam. She probably wasn't even there. I never saw her.' Her chest tightened. *Suppose he had cameras.*

'Don't be bringing them filth here. I don't want people seeing a squad car parked outside. They want to talk to you, you can fuck off down to the station. And don't come back, either.'

'Go easy, Auds,' Ray said. 'She's not done anything.'

'Ah, go easy yourself. No wonder she's such a cheeky little bitch the way you spoil her.'

'Who'd mind Chloe if I didn't come back?' Kym knew she'd pay for that remark later. Not while her dad and uncle were present, though. One day, she'd escape this miserable existence. She had pinned all her hopes on Hazel, who had promised to help her get away.

'Chloe would be fine with me,' her mother said.

Kym saw Frank's doubtful expression. He knew his sister-in-law all too well.

'I have no intention of talking to the cops,' Kym said. 'They can't make me. I haven't done anything.'

'Whatever.' Her mother shrugged and headed for the kitchen.

'I'll give you a lift back to your apartment, if you want,' Frank said.

'Thanks, Frank. I'll sort Chloe first. She needs a change. Then you won't have anything to do but cuddle her.'

'You're a good girl,' Frank said.

In her old bedroom, Kym changed Chloe and settled her. After she cleaned up and changed her clothes, she dialled Lee's number. It rang out. She sent a message.

There's too much risk. We HAVE to leave Dublin. I'm heading to pack. Meet you at yours later. I'll let myself in and explain everything when I c u. Love u xx

One tick for sent. A second tick for read. It looked like he was typing something. Then stopped. No reply. No phone call back, yet.

No point delaying. Her mind was made up. She popped the baby seat into the rear of her uncle's taxi and they set off.

'We never talked about that day, did we?'

'What day, Frank?'

'The day we got Chloe back.'

'What about it?'

'I picked Danielle Lewis up from the hospital.'

Kym was astonished. What were the chances of that happening? 'I didn't know that.'

'You do now. Well, I saw the state of her.'

'Right.' A cold wave enveloped Kym from head to toe.

'Why, Kym?'

'Why what, Frank?'

Frank seemed to be waiting in silence for Kym to say more.

She let out a breath. 'It wasn't all me.'

'Who else was involved? Ian?'

'No, someone else.' *Ian wouldn't have the balls.* 'Ian had no idea.'

'And Danielle has no idea, either. So she never got a proper look at you?' he said.

'No.'

'Are you sure?'

'Yes.'

'Did you have to do that?'

'I did.'

'Why?'

'Do you really think she'd have just handed Chloe over to us without a fight? It was the quickest way. Anyway, she's only some bitch that happened to get lucky because of who she was born to.'

'When she was born, the Lewis family had practically nothing. Her uncle built up the businesses almost single-handed.'

'Yeah.'

'She'd no say in who her family was, no more than you did.'

Kym shrugged, wondering why her uncle gave a crap about Danielle Lewis.

'It's ironic that Ged did so well, seeing as Danielle's father was cast out of Dublin for his criminal activities.'

'Who is he?'

'Ah, he's in a different country, hasn't been back in years. I'm not sure she even knows who he is. But I will say this, you think Ged Lewis was powerful, you should have seen Danielle's father.' Frank came to a halt at a red traffic light.

'Right.'

'So tell me, if you think Danielle is such a bitch, why were you in a car with her just under an hour ago?'

'What are you talking about?' Kym said, her heart sinking.

'A couple of things about us taxi drivers. We see a lot of what goes on, and Danielle Lewis is hard to miss, being such a prominent figure in this city. One of my drivers was passing Costello's just after this guy supposedly burst in and wrecked the place.'

Kym said nothing.

'He saw you go in with the buggy, followed by Danielle soon after.'

'Okay,' she said, 'I felt guilty about the attack, and Danielle has done a great job of looking after Chloe. I thought she deserved to see her and maybe get a bit of a cuddle.'

'And did she?'

'Not really. She didn't get much of a chance.' Kym paused. 'She sensed what was about to happen and got us out of there. She, well, she saved us.'

'What do you mean?' The driver behind them sounded his horn. Frank pulled away.

Kym sighed. 'Anto Doyle was shot in the chest. We were nearby. I didn't know what to do. Danielle dragged us out of there before we came to harm. Anto took the bullet.'

Frank drew in at a layby, switched off the engine and twisted around to face Kym. 'What about Chloe?'

'It wasn't us he was after. It was Anto.' Kym stared straight ahead.

'How can you be sure?'

'Anto got a call to warn him, just before it happened.'

Frank let out a heavy sigh. 'That's it. We're moving out of that cursed estate and away from Dublin.'

Kym turned to face him. 'Really?'

'Yes,' he said. 'Given what you've just told me, you surely must feel guilty for your part in assaulting her.'

'Yeah.' Kym's throat was so tight she could barely get out the word. As far as she was concerned, Danielle was a means to an end. If she had to do the same thing to her again, then she would.

'I don't believe you.'

At this stage, Kym didn't care whether he believed her or not.

Frank turned back and gripped the steering wheel. 'I don't know what game you're playing, or what you are trying to do, but you need to leave Chloe out of it.'

'I'm not—'

'In fact, I don't want you looking after Chloe anywhere but in our house. We've already lost Hazel, and I'll not chance losing more of my family.'

'Hazel could be back any day now.'

'Wake up, Kym. Hazel's long gone. She may well be dead. I can feel it in my waters.'

'But Uncle Frank . . .'

He let out a heavy sigh. 'One of my drivers told me he dropped Lee Thompson to a party at this huge house in Foxrock, it was on Brennanstown Road to be precise. Dean Lewis was there, too, and my driver thinks he might have seen Hazel. The rumour is that this Thompson fella brought some dodgy drugs to it, and this girl took them — injected them or something. Either way, she is meant to have died. The thing is, the body was never found. I have a feeling that this girl was Hazel. She's gone, Kym, I'm convinced of it.'

Lee? No way. 'How sure are you about all this, Frank?'

'Very. And we've made up our minds. Dublin, and especially where we live, has grown way too violent to bring a child up in, so me and your aunt are looking to move south.'

'Where?'

'Maybe Limerick or Cork. Somewhere rural anyway.'

Shit, that's access to Danielle gone, their arrangement disappeared to bally-go-backwards. There was no way Danielle would tell her where those drugs were if she couldn't see Chloe. Now, there was really nothing to keep her here.

Kym looked out of the window. Clouds had gathered, but it wasn't raining. 'I'll walk from here. I need to think.'

'Good idea,' Frank said.

As she watched her uncle's taxi drive away, Kym decided it was time to bring her plans forward. She had to get hold of those drugs by any means possible, get the money and get the hell out of Dublin. With Danielle off limits and Hazel gone, only one person could help her now — the man she loved.

CHAPTER 34

Thanks to Bill Frisco and Larry Shine, Dwayne now had the names of five possible sites where a van containing a shitload of cocaine might be hidden. None of those location had been in Ged's name. He'd have been ages trying to link them to Ged or any of his businesses. He owed those two men bigtime. Now it was time to enjoy the spoils, once he found them. He'd visited two of them already, with zero success. He was returning from another fruitless journey when he spotted someone he recognised. The guy moved unsteadily, reaching out every so often to touch the brick wall that ran along the pavement. Then he crouched down, as if to tie up a shoelace. Dwayne mounted the pavement and drove at the guy, coming to a stop just centimetres before him.

The guy stood up, holding something out in front of him. Dwayne saw a gun, aimed through the windscreen, straight at his head. Dwayne raised his hands and indicated to the car door. Gingerly, his eyes on the barrel of the gun, Dwayne eased open the van door and got out.

'Lee, it's me, Dwayne. Fuck's sake, man, get that thing out of my face.'

Lee didn't seem to notice that he was standing on a main road in Drumcondra with a gun in his hand. He wore a dazed expression, like that of a boxer who's just hit the ropes.

'Hey.' Dwayne clicked his fingers. 'Lee, man, what the fuck?'

Lee shook his head as if he had just realised where he was. Dwayne reached for his wrist, eased his arm downward and prised the gun from his grip.

'Get in, you thick fuck.'

Lee climbed into the passenger seat. Dwayne opened up the gun, emptied the chamber and set off. They drove in silence as far as Richmond Road and the entrance to Tolka Park soccer stadium. Dwayne pulled in beside a pair of large metal gates that rattled in the breeze.

The thunderous roar of a motorbike resounded against the high brick wall of the stadium. Dwayne adjusted the rear-view mirror and watched Jason dismount and approach the passenger door.

He rapped on the window. 'Who the fuck is this?'

'Danielle's gym manager. Lee, meet my brother, Jason.'

'What's going on?' Jason said.

'I'm waiting for Lee to tell me. He seems to have lost his voice.'

Lee blinked, looked from Jason to Dwayne and took a breath. 'You never told me that Danielle Lewis was going to be there.'

'Where? What the fuck is going on?' Jason demanded.

'I thought Anto was supposed to be the target,' Lee said.

Jason flung open the door, dragged Lee from the van and threw him to the ground. 'Talk to me, you mother-fucker. What do you mean, "target"? What have you done to Danielle?'

'Fuck's sake.' Dwayne stormed around the van and dragged Jason off Lee. 'You want to draw the attention of every cop in the area? There's a firearm in that van, and Lee's acting like he doesn't know which way is up. Now, calm the fuck down and let's get the story out of him.'

'I thought you agreed not to touch Danielle until I found out more,' Jason said.

'That, baby brother, is still the case. I'm going to count to three. If Lee still isn't speaking after that, we are going to take him somewhere quiet and tear him limb from limb.'

Jason stood back, allowing Lee to get to his feet. Brushing himself down, he found his voice. 'My buddy tailed Anto to Costello's. He called me from there to say Anto was busy chatting to two women. I reckoned it was a good time to go for it, while he was distracted, like. I barged in and next thing I see is Anto talking to Danielle Lewis and Kym Brady.'

Dwayne glared at Jason. 'You see? I fucking told you Danielle had a hand in Bosco's death. I bet Anto was giving her a rundown on how he wiped him out.'

'We don't know that's what they were talking about. Besides, he could have been speaking to Kym Brady, not Danielle,' Jason said.

They both looked at Lee. He shrugged. 'No idea. They were just stood there together, talking. There was a baby there, too.'

'Go on, so,' Dwayne said.

'I fired at him, but he grabbed the baby's buggy and pushed it away. Next thing I know, I'm blinded. Fly spray or deodorant or something. I couldn't see a thing. That shot must have gone to the ceiling, because the whole thing crashed down on me. I was covered in plaster, and a beam hit my leg just as I fired off a second shot. That one did hit Anto.'

'Is he dead?'

Lee shrugged. 'Don't know.'

'Were Danielle, Kym or the baby injured?' Jason asked.

'Don't know. I'll need that gun back, Dwayne.'

'Why?'

'It's mine.'

'What happened to the one I got you to do the job with?'

'I lost it. The cops probably have it now.'

'What level of thick are you, Lee? Christ.'

'You said the gun was clean. Brand new, you said. I had gloves on.'

Dwayne began to pace. 'That's not the fucking point, man. They're not like bags of Tayto that you can just pick up in a shop.'

'I . . . I know that, Dwayne. That's why I need my one back.'

'No.' Dwayne put his face close to Lee's. 'I'll keep it. It'll replace the one you lost.'

'That means I don't have one, Dwayne,' Lee said.

'No shit.' Dwayne rolled his eyes.

'Is this the Costello's in Blanchardstown?' Jason asked.

'Yeah,' Lee said.

'When was this shooting?'

Lee checked his watch. 'About an hour ago. Why?'

Dwayne stopped pacing. 'Hang on. That's a two-hour walk away from here, so how come you got here so fast?'

'My buddy. He was delivering bread, and drove me away after it happened. Then I ran along by the canal for a bit.'

Dwayne's phone rang. It was Sal. Without waiting for him to speak, Dwayne said, 'That takeaway was delivered to the wrong address. I think we need to cancel the order.' He turned away from the others. 'Yeah, they were short a few quid for the tip, too. The whole tip.' He was saying that the target didn't die and the firearm was lost, possibly to the cops.

'Okay,' Sal said. 'I suggest we meet at the forge and get some ash.'

'I agree.' Dwayne ended the call and turned to face Lee. 'Anto survived.'

'Oh shit.'

'Yeah. Shit. Now get in the van.'

Drops of rain spattered the windscreen.

Lee looked at the ground. 'Uh-uh.'

'Get in,' Dwayne said evenly.

It began to rain in earnest. Lee shook droplets from his hair. 'Why?'

'Are you due to work today?' Dwayne asked.

'Yeah, at two. I'm not going, though. I can hardly be expected to go into the gym after shooting someone in front of the boss, can I?'

'Did she see your mug?' Dwayne asked.

'No, I had a bally on.'

'Then how is she to know it was you? What better way to throw her off the scent than to carry on as normal?'

Lee sighed. 'Okay. I'll do my best.'

'You'd better,' Dwayne said.

The rain was now pelting down, drenching the three men.

'Check those remaining three addresses for me, Jason. The stuff has to be in one of them.'

'Yeah, will do.' Jason revved his bike and sped away.

Lee waited, drenched and shivering.

'What's wrong with you, man?'

'Dunno, Dwayne.'

'You'll catch your death if we don't get out of this rain. Here.' Dwayne tossed Lee the keys. 'You drive.'

Lee caught them. He looked at them and then at the van. Slowly, he climbed in and put his hands on the wheel. Lee's ring tone sounded. He looked at the screen and didn't answer. It pinged with a message. He was still staring down as his thumbs swept across the screen typing a reply to Kym's message.

'What the fuck are you doing? We need to get going.'

'Yeah, yeah. Sorry, Dwayne.' Lee stuck his phone into his pocket without finishing or sending his message.

The engine rattled into life. 'Head for Dargle Road and keep going. I'll tell you where to stop.'

Lee drove in silence, as Dwayne directed him through a maze of by-roads until they were heading along a narrow lane on the outskirts of the city.

Lee coughed nervously. 'What's the story here, Dwayne?'

'Picking up a delivery. We won't be long. You can head into the gym after that. Go down as far as the old pump house for me.'

They travelled a few hundred metres, between a graffiti-covered fence and a stone wall blanketed in ivy.

'This is a dead end, Dwayne.'

'What better place to make a handover.'

'Okay.'

'Right. Stop here.' Dwayne opened the door. 'Give me a second. Keep the engine running.'

When Dwayne looked back, Lee was leaning forward, his arms around the top of the steering wheel, watching him.

Lee's execution was swift and almost silent, the sound muffled by the silencer affixed to the gun. Lee's life ebbed away through the hole in his neck. The shot to the head finished him. But that wasn't all. A bottle filled with petrol and stuffed with a smouldering rag landed on the seat Dwayne had, just seconds before, vacated. The van was engulfed in flames.

Meanwhile, Dwayne was roaring away on the back of Sal's motorbike. Another loose end tied; another inept minion removed. Lee had fucked up twice — first with Ian Gallagher's shooting, and now the hit on Anto Doyle. Dwayne couldn't let that sort of thing go unpunished.

CHAPTER 35

Kym had almost finished packing her suitcase when she heard the door of the apartment slam. Knowing that Ian wasn't due back for another hour, she ran to the dresser and took out the knife that Dwayne had left still plunged into Ian's hand. Knife in hand, she hid behind the door, her heart pounding.

It was with a mixture of relief and horror that she saw Ian. Now she'd have to break the rotten truth to him. She put the knife back and watched from the doorway as he stood over the open suitcase on their bed.

He turned and started. 'I thought you were looking after Chloe.'

'My uncle collected her a while ago. I thought you were at the hospital visiting Anto.'

'It was a quick visit.'

'Right, because I wasn't expecting you for another hour.'

He looked at the suitcase again. 'Clearly. You want to tell me what's going on?'

'I can't do this anymore, Ian.'

'Do what?'

'This. You and me.'

'Is it Dwayne? You know, the threat and that.'

She shook her head.

'Look, I've been trying to find somewhere else for us to go. But there's nowhere affordable, and we've got this place for practically nothing.'

'I don't love you anymore.' There. It was out.

Ian opened his mouth to speak, but nothing came out. He plonked down onto the bed and looked up at her.

'I don't understand, Kym.'

'What's not to understand? Look, when Ged moved you up, I thought you'd be earning enough to get us out of here. Instead, we're living in fear for our lives. If you'd been clever enough, you'd have found out where those drugs are. We could have taken them for ourselves and sold them, and we'd have been made.'

'It's not that simple, Kym. We don't have the contacts.'

'Listen to you, dragging me down again. I don't want to be with someone who has no ambition.'

'But things are beginning to move. I was talking with Anto. There's possibilities, a chance to promote myself. Just give me a chance.'

'See? You expect the likes of Anto Doyle to tell you what's what. Well, guess where Anto is now?'

'What do you mean?'

'He's either six feet under, or fighting for his life in hospital, with a bullet in his chest.'

'What?' Rain began to beat against the patio doors.

'Yes. He should have taken charge when he got the chance, the weeks between Bird's death and Dwayne's return. While Jason was in mourning, and didn't know what to do. But he did nothing.'

'But he did. Well, not before Dwayne's return, but as soon as he got an opportunity.'

'What do you know, Ian?'

'Everyone says it was Anto took Bosco Ryan out.'

'It's true. He did.' She looked straight into his eyes.

'You sound very sure of that. How—'

'I gave him the gun — the one I lost in the graveyard.'

'But why?'

238

'It's Danielle's gun. She had it stashed in Chloe's buggy. I was just waiting for her to tell me where the drugs were, and then I was going to frame her for Bosco's shooting.'

'Why would she tell you?' Ian asked.

'I promised her access to Chloe.'

'Christ, Kym. What are you doing?'

'A lot more than you. I also helped him make the hit.'

'What do you mean, helped him? How?'

'I made sure Bosco was at home, and told Anto. He came along and — bang. No more Bosco.'

'Jesus, Kym.'

'That is how you get things done, Ian. Not by sitting around here.'

'There's someone else, isn't there?' Ian said. 'Someone more . . . exciting.'

'Yes.'

'Let me guess. Lee Dirtbag Thompson, from the gym.'

'How do you—'

'That day I was at the hospital—'

'Yeah?'

'Me and Anto met up and came back here. You were off at that hen do.'

'So?'

'I've seen a video clip of the party you went to later.'

'What the hell are you talking about?'

'I'd heard rumours that you were doing the dirt on me. Even Anto said you were, but I didn't believe it until I saw that video.'

Kym's knees went weak.

'It was of you kissing and touching him.'

'When, where did you—'

'At the hospital. The reason it was a quick visit. It's doing the rounds. I was coming back to talk to you when you got in. Jesus, Kym. What the hell were you thinking? Did you not see who the other woman was?'

She sighed. 'Yes.'

'Jane, one of the girls who used to work at Berkley Street. She's friends with Aimee, who's friends with Brenno Aherne.'

'Yeah? So?' Kym stared him down, defiant.

'So, Lee has promised to *rescue* Jane from all this, too. Let me guess, you were all three going to head off into the sunset, and live happily ever after?'

'You're lying. I happen to know that he's doing an important job today. It'll get him a big payout, enough to cover our escape.'

'Oh yeah? You really think he's going to carry you away? There is no escape from this life, Kym.'

'There is. He'll have the money by tomorrow, and we'll be off.'

'Do you know who he is working for?' Ian said.

'Danielle Lewis. It's a cover, that's all. Really, he's working for himself.'

'You think? And what kind of important job has a big payout?'

Kym shrugged.

'You may think you're streetwise, Kym, but really you have no idea. He's working for the Flynns — Dwayne Flynn, to be precise. And the important job was a hit — but on who? You said it yourself. Who is either six foot under or fighting for his life?'

The blood drained from her whole body. 'Anto Doyle.'

'There you go.'

'I was there.'

'What?'

'I was in the shop when Anto was hit.'

'Tell me, did Lee change his mind and turn around when he saw you?'

'I don't know for sure if it was him. I had the baby with me.'

'I'll tell you right now, he confides in Jane a lot more than he does you. Aimee apparently suspected something was up and got it out of her. Aimee then told Brenno, who was frantically trying to ring his best buddy, but he wasn't answering.'

'Shit.'

'If Lee really loved you, he'd have aborted the hit, wouldn't he? To avoid putting you in danger. Sounds to me like he went straight ahead with his plan. Some lover you've got there, Kym.'

Kym swallowed. 'Yeah, but . . .'

'But what? He chose Jane, Dwayne Flynn and that hit over you.'

'No, it's not that.' Kym felt terribly weak. 'It was me who did it.'

'Did what?'

'I was the one that told Lee who killed Bosco.' Kym sat on the bed, on the other side of the suitcase from Ian. She covered her face with her hands.

'Oh, Kym. You idiot. You painted a great big target, right on Anto's back.'

Kym felt like everything was closing in around her. 'Jesus.'

'Yeah, and by the way, Lee was pimping his girlfriend out to Dwayne. She took Aimee along with her one night. Aimee had no idea where they were going until she got there, and then it was too dangerous to back out.'

Kym lifted her face from her hands. 'What?'

'Yes, so best of luck with a future life with Lee — under Dwayne's control.'

'No, it's not like that. It can't be. That thing at the party, with Jane, that was a one-off. She was the spare, not me.'

'Really? And who did you ring for help that night? Think about it. He let you walk out of that house, in the state you were in. It was me and Anto who rushed to help you, not Lee fucking Thompson.'

'But he loves me, no one else.'

'Yeah, he loved what you could do for him. I bet he loved you even more when he thought you might have something over Danielle Lewis, something that would lead him to five million euros' worth of blow.'

Kym felt flayed, stripped to the bone. Only now did she realise just what she had done.

'Off you go, now, Kym. Here, let me give you a hand.' Ian marched into the bathroom and returned with an armful of Kym's toiletries that he landed in the suitcase. Creams and open containers of make-up and fake tan smeared the interior. He pulled open a drawer and tipped the contents on top of the mess.

'There. Anything else? Oh, yes . . .' He pulled a small mirror from a nail in the wall. 'There. So you can look yourself in the eye and see what a fuck-up you are. I chose to ignore what I saw on that video. I put it down to shock, your intoxicated state. Well, more fool me. Well, I've learned my lesson. I'll not be available when you come crawling back.'

Kym opened her mouth to speak, but had no idea what to say.

'And where is your hero now? Ring him, go on. See will he come and pick you up.'

Her hand shaking, she found Lee's number. *The number you have dialled is unreachable.* She tried several more times, but he still couldn't be reached.

'Can't get hold of him, eh. Let me call a cab for you. You can head home to your mam's, so, because you're not staying here for a minute longer.'

She rang her uncle, who answered immediately.

'Can you collect me again, Frank, please? I'll need a lift back to Mam's.'

'I can, but not for another hour,' Frank said. 'I've a meeting to get to.'

'That'll do me.' She ended the call.

Ian was regarding her. He had an eerie calmness about him that she'd never seen before.

'I heard. An hour. Fine. There's something I need to do. When I return, all traces of you better be gone from this apartment, you hear me?'

'Yeah,' she said, in a small voice.

He left, closing the door gently behind him.

Lee still could not be reached. What if what Ian had said was right? What had she done?

Kym spent the next hour gathering as many of her things as she could.

Her phone pinged with a message. She opened it with trembling fingers. But it was only her uncle letting her know he was outside.

She closed the suitcase, picked up her handbag and walked, dazed, to her uncle's cab. She threw the suitcase onto the back seat next to Chloe, who was asleep.

'Suitcase? You heading home?'

'No.' Her voice cracked. 'Take me to Whitefriars Street, please, Frank.'

'Whereabouts? You mean the apartments there?'

'Yeah.' She cleared her throat. 'Yes, please.'

'Right.'

They drove on in silence.

On reaching the apartments, she retrieved her suitcase with a brief 'Thanks.'

'Wait. Do you want me to hold on for you?'

'I don't think so, Frank. Maybe you should get Chloe home. That would be best.'

As the lift climbed through the floors, Kym tried to sort her head out. What should she say to Lee? Ask him about the shooting? She wondered if he knew anything about Hazel. The assault on Danielle had been his idea; he'd even got hold of a taser. If any of the rest of what they said he did was true, then the past few weeks of her life had been a toxic mass of lies. Maybe Lee would deny it, maybe it wasn't her Lee, but some other fella. Maybe . . . The key wouldn't work in the lock. She hammered on the door.

The woman who answered was familiar, though she'd only seen her a few times — Aimee Sexton.

'Yeah, can I help you?'

Kym blinked and looked beyond her into the hallway. She checked the number again, looked at the key in her hand. 'What are you doing in this apartment?'

'What's it to you?'

'I'm Lee Thompson's girlfriend, and I want to know why you're here.'

Aimee looked Kym up and down, folded her arms across her chest and chewed her gum. 'Really?'

'Yes, really.'

'Jane!' Aimee hollered over her shoulder.

Jane came to the door. Her face was puffy. She stared at Kym through eyes red with tears. 'Who are you? Oh yeah, the third wheel that night at the house party.'

'She says she's Lee's girlfriend,' Aimee said.

'Oh, just fuck off,' Jane said, and shut the door in Kym's face.

Kym stood outside, listening to Jane and Aimee's muffled conversation.

'What if Dwayne has done something to him? He didn't want to do it, Aimee, I swear he didn't. He said he was made to.'

Jane's words struck Kym like a bolt of lightning. So, Ian had been telling the truth. Which meant that what Frank had said must also have some truth in it. She had handed information to one of the most dangerous men in Dublin, through a man she thought loved her.

Kym left her handbag and suitcase at the door of Lee's apartment and took the stairs down to the street. Dashing out of the building, she failed to hear the beeps indicating that a commercial vehicle was reversing.

The lorry was loaded with rock and gravel, and the driver couldn't have seen Kym slip and fall beneath its wheels. It carried on reversing, raining stones and gravel onto her inert body. The huge rear tyres moved towards her face.

CHAPTER 36

Dwayne was still on an adrenaline high when Sal dropped him home, but the sight of a familiar car parked outside the block of flats brought him back down to earth. He found Bill Frisco and Larry Shine sitting in the living room, Jason standing just inside the patio, facing them.

'Visitors for you,' Jason said, and made for the door.

Dwayne felt his gut grow taut — he might need back-up. 'No, Jason, stay. This is Flynn business, so you're in on it, too. Lads, good to see you both. I appreciate your support at Bird's funeral. It was a late one, wasn't it — or early, depending on how you look at it.' He let out a nervous laugh.

Jason shot him a quizzical look.

The visitors weren't laughing. 'We're here for an update,' Larry said. 'It's three days since the funeral, two since we got that information to you.'

'I'm nearly there, lads. On the cusp, you might say.'

'Cusp?' Bill said. 'Well, *cusp* isn't good enough. You made us promises, guarantees. Our contact got you your information, so where's our part of the deal?'

Larry shuffled to the edge of the couch. 'You wouldn't be planning to cut us out now, Dwayne, would you?'

'No, lads, of course not.'

'You have twenty-four hours.' Bill stood as he spoke. 'And if you haven't delivered what you promised, we're taking it over.'

'You can't. Who's going distribute it for you?'

Bill stared at Dwayne, his eyes narrow. 'We can't, eh?'

'I didn't mean—'

'There's plenty of others ready to step up and take your place,' Larry added.

'Not if it means crossing the Flynns, they won't.'

Larry stood shoulder to shoulder with Bill. 'Don't overestimate your importance, Dwayne Flynn. Twenty-four hours and it's ours.'

Larry patted his shoulder on the way out. 'Twenty-four hours.'

The two brothers listened to the door shut. Only then did Jason speak. 'What have you done, Dwayne?'

'Nothing to worry your head about, Jason. It's all in hand.'

'It didn't look like that to me. You do not mess with the likes of the Friscos, or them Shines. What the fuck are you getting into bed with them for anyway? We're fine on our own.'

'Fine on our own, are we, Jason? If you'd got the information out of that bitch of yours, then we wouldn't be in this situation. Running around, waiting for fucking idiots to give us information that we should be able to get for ourselves. I was only out of the country a few months. I leave you in charge, and come back to find it's all gone to shit and our brother is dead.'

'Fuck you. You've kept me in the dark about everything that's gone on. You only let me in when you needed to show those two a unified front.'

Dwayne closed the distance between himself and Jason. 'And who's to blame for that? Bird died on your watch.'

'Bird's death is not on me. Don't you fucking—'

'Don't what? Tell me, what is the one thread running through all the shit that's been happening?'

'Things are different now. The opposition is brutal. Everyone wants a piece of the action.'

'No, baby brother, the one thread is Danielle fucking Lewis. She returns after a decade away, and suddenly we're back dealing with shit we'd all moved on from. Her appearance on the scene made Bird vulnerable, while you've been wasting your time chasing something you'll never get back.'

Jason stood with his legs spread apart. It was a familiar stance. He was readying himself should Dwayne decide to strike. Dwayne turned and made for the door.

'Where are you going?' Jason asked.

'To sort what should have been done at the beginning, demanding straight answers, direct from the source. If they can't be got voluntarily, then it'll have to be by force. Whatever it takes.'

'No, Dwayne.'

'You heard those two. There'll be no messing this up.'

'Wait, Dwayne, please. Let's discuss this together, as Flynns. Come up with a plan.'

'It's too late, Jason.'

Dwayne slammed the door behind him.

CHAPTER 37

Danielle stood at the top of Dun Laoghaire pier, watching a ferry that was just chugging out into open waters.

Linda had driven her here, saying she needed a break. 'Sea air clears all your troubles away.'

Danielle received a call from an unknown number.

'You might remember me from dropping you home from the hospital just short of a week ago,' the caller began.

'Frank? Chloe's grandfather?'

'Yes, that's me. I want to meet with you. Where are you now?'

What should she say? Suppose this was a set-up. Was whoever shot Anto looking to clean up and remove any witnesses? Which side was Frank on?

'Um, what do you want to meet me for, Frank?'

'I believe my niece might have had some kind of arrangement with you?'

Danielle remembered the last conversation they'd had, in which Frank warned her to stay away. Her throat tightened. If she admitted to the arrangement, she could be getting Kym into trouble and might never see Chloe again. She was silent for a few seconds, torn with indecision.

'What exactly do you want, Frank?'

'Nothing. I just want to meet with you, and I swear on Chloe's life I come in peace.'

She told him they were at the pier, and Frank said he'd be there in thirty minutes.

Meanwhile, Linda had bought them a latte each and almond croissants. Danielle's stomach gurgled as the nutty aroma reached her nostrils. Her mouth full of croissant, she said, 'I think I've figured out where the drugs are.'

Linda looked up. 'Have you? Where?'

'I'll take you there after I've met Frank. You could say they were under our noses all along.'

'And if you do find them, what are you going to do then?' Linda said.

'I don't know. First, we'll have to make sure they are where I think they are. After that, we can make a firm decision.' Linda didn't need to know that her decision was already made.

'Okay.'

They sat into Linda's car as they waited.

As promised, precisely thirty minutes after his call, Frank Brady's taxi drew up beside Linda's car. Danielle waited for a few moments before she got out, in case he had been followed. No other cars drove by. Warily, she approached the taxi. Frank got out, reached in and emerged with a very alert Chloe.

'Take her for me a minute, would you.' He held the baby towards Danielle.

The child in her arms, snuggling into her, Danielle closed her eyes. All was still.

When Danielle reluctantly opened her eyes again, Frank was watching her, a broad smile across his face. Why the sudden change of attitude? she wondered.

As if he had read her thoughts, Frank said quietly, 'I believe that's what my niece promised you.'

Danielle smiled back at him. 'Thank you.'

'I don't know what she was up to . . .' He sighed. 'You see, it was Kym who assaulted you.'

'Yes, I have proof that she was involved. She wasn't alone in the attack either. I did ask her straight out if she had a hand in it, but she denied it, but there's no doubt.'

He shrugged. 'Wouldn't you deny it, if questioned directly by your victim?'

'I suppose. But I don't understand why she should do that. What did Kym have to gain?'

'She had an opinion of you . . .'

'And?'

He stared out over the grey waters of the Irish Sea. 'When Ged died, I really thought Hazel would come home to us. We kept trying to contact her — we still do — but there's been no trace of her for months. It's true we shut her out after she took up with him, but then we realised that by doing that, we were also shutting out our grandchild. We eventually found out you were looking after her, but we couldn't get in touch with you either.'

'But I was there, in the apartment. I hardly ever left it.'

'We tried the intercom at the gate, but you never answered.'

'True. I muted it.'

'How come you ended up looking after Chloe anyway?' he asked.

'Hazel asked me to look after her while she went to a funeral — it was her cousin's, your nephew — and she never came back for her. I'd collected them both from the hospital and I noticed that Hazel wasn't bonding with her, but didn't think she'd just go off and leave her own baby.'

'I know my daughter is no saint. We all knew where she worked, and that she dabbled in drugs. Then, when she told us her baby's father was not only a Lewis but married to boot, it was the final straw. Nothing personal — you'd been away for years, and Dean was dealing. We didn't want our family to be associated with what he was up to. It was bad for Chloe. We were about to contact the social workers when Kym said she'd have a word with you about it. And we thought that's what she did.'

'Until you collected me from the hospital?'

'Exactly. I worked out that it must have been her who did that to you, since the baby arrived at the same time. Sure, she was taking her to her own family, but we never intended it to be done that way.'

'Why are you telling me this now?' Danielle asked.

'You didn't deserve to have that done to you.'

'Thank you, Frank. To make you feel better about it, I think she did it for a man who works at my gym. I saw a video clip of them together.'

Frank shook his head. 'Silly girl.'

'I guess we can't always choose who we fall in love with.'

Frank grunted. 'He's a cesspit, that fella.'

'You know him?'

'Yeah, he hung around with Dean. Hazel knew him, too. He sells drugs. We think he was her regular supplier. He went to all the parties she went to. I think that's how Kym met him, through Hazel. There were rumours about a tainted batch on the streets a while back. Most were pulled, but not before some were taken to a party. Someone died, so I heard.'

'Shit.' *So Saoirse was on the right track. She needs to know about this. And I must watch Lee more closely.*

'Anyway, I let it be. Who knows, she may see sense,' he said.

Danielle nodded. 'Hopefully.'

'I can see that Chloe has been well looked after. She's a happy baby, and that can only be because of the care you gave her in the months she was with you.'

'Hang on a minute.' Danielle went to the car and retrieved the tote bag. She took out the blanket with the pink bunny and showed it to Chloe, who held out her hands, gurgling happily. Danielle passed the bag to Frank.

'Here. There are clothes in there that have yet to fit her.'

Frank took it from her. 'Thank you. Is there anything from here you'd like to keep?'

'That's okay. Everything I need is in here.' She pointed to her heart. 'All I want is to see Chloe happy.'

'I'm selling the taxi business and the buses we're moving out of Dublin,' Frank said, 'somewhere down the country. We're looking at the moment.'

'Maybe I can help,' Danielle said.

'How?'

'I'll buy you out, help you to relocate.'

'You will? What's in it for you?'

'What's in it for me is the knowledge that Chloe is safe, and you're free to care for her and raise her well. Whether I get to visit her or not is entirely up to you and her grandmother. I'm not going to make it a condition of my purchase.'

Frank looked as though he didn't dare to hope — selling the taxi company wouldn't have been easy. 'Are you serious about this?'

'Yes. Have a think and let me know what you decide. I promise you'll have no ties or obligations to me beyond a business deal.'

'I think there is something I can do for you in return.' Frank spoke slowly.

'Like what?'

'I can give you a piece of information that might be of some value to you.'

'Go on.'

He met her gaze. 'Have you ever wondered about your father?'

A shiver ran through Danielle's spine. 'Not really. My father died before I was born.'

'What if I told you that he didn't die. That he is alive and well. Would you want to know who he is?'

Did she? She'd been fine all along believing him to be dead. 'I'm not sure, Frank.'

'I knew your mother. You're very like her, you know. She had a kind smile, too. I went to school with Ged. I met your mum at Ged's twenty-first.'

Danielle shifted Chloe's weight a little. She'd grown since Danielle last held her.

Frank looked past Danielle. His eyes had a faraway look in them. 'We went on a few dates, me and her.'

'What? You and my mother? You mean to say you're my fath—'

He let out a short laugh. 'No. I never got a chance when the suave Fintan Cassidy appeared on the scene. There was a man who had notions about himself. He started off as a mechanic, did up his dad's Ford Cortina and used to drive it around. Flash Cassidy, some of us used to call him. I was gutted that your mother chose him. Anyway, he got your mum pregnant. Her brother Ged and their parents had disliked Fintan from the start, and were not having him be part of the family. I'm not sure he was even told. He always thought he was too good for Dublin and, with Ged's encouragement, Fintan left for the UK. He went to Liverpool, and then on to Wales, bought a yard and began selling and servicing cars and vans.'

This was the last thing she'd expected to be told. 'So he's in Wales?'

'Was. He then got into property development, which took him to Spain and Dubai. He's currently in Cyprus.'

'How did—'

'I've taken an interest. Myself and the wife were on holiday in Cyprus last year and came across him there. Fintan recognised me, made a big deal of showing off. Look, his business is doing extremely well, but I wouldn't think was all done exactly lawfully.'

'Interesting. And a bit pot and kettle for Ged to decide who my mother could or could not fall in love with. Do you think he'd have taken her with him if he knew . . . about me?'

Frank pressed his lips together. 'Who knows?'

Danielle wasn't sure if it was the sea breeze that caused his eyes to water a little. 'She did come back to me for a while, but her heart wasn't in it.'

'So, you were in my life when I was a baby?'

'Yes, briefly. Then she was killed in that car crash. You were still little, and between your grandparents and Ged, they raised you. But I'd have loved you like a father, if she'd have let me.'

'I had no idea. You and I have never had anything to do with each other. Not as far as I can remember, anyway.'

'No. And it broke my heart.'

'Do you think she drove her car into that tree on purpose?'

'We'll never know, Danielle.'

'Thank you for telling me this, Frank.'

'It's important to know where we come from. It tells us so much about ourselves.'

Danielle kissed Chloe on the top of her head, then handed her back to Frank. 'Let's make this sale happen and get you relocated.'

'Good plan.' They smiled at each other.

Frank put Chloe and the tote bag in the car, waved and drove away.

Danielle was staring into space, thinking about what Frank had told her when she felt something hard press into her ribs. The barrel of a gun.

A familiar voice sounded in her ear.

'Not so tough without your big knife, are you, Danielle?'

'What the hell is this, Dwayne?'

'I have an armed man shadowing that taxi. A crash is easily arranged. It may even be fatal. It all depends on what you tell me.'

'What do you want, Dwayne?'

'Five million euros' worth of coke, that's what I want. And don't tell me you don't know where it is.'

She glanced over her shoulder. No sign of Linda, or the car. *Fuck. She has stabbed me in the back, told Dwayne where I am. I should never have said I'd figured out where the drugs were.*

'Fine. If you get your hands on it, will you let me alone from now on?'

'I might. For now, I will guarantee that no harm will come to Frank Brady and his little grandchild.'

'Fine.'

'In less than a minute, a blue Audi will pull up beside us. You sit in the front. I'll be in the back. You direct the driver. When I have my hands on that white powder, I'll tell my man to let the taxi and its precious passengers go on their way.'

'Okay. Let's get this done.'

The blue Audi was already pulling up. Danielle jumped into the passenger seat, praying fervently that the drugs were where she'd guessed them to be.

CHAPTER 38

His gaze firmly on the road ahead, Sal Fogarty squeezed the steering wheel of the Audi. He'd known Ged well, had been pals with him when Ged and Bird had a decent relationship. Now he was taking Ged's niece off to her death, if that's what Dwayne decided. It was a shit situation.

'Okay, Danielle fucking Lewis. Where to?' Dwayne said, from the back seat.

'Fuck you, Dwayne,' she retorted.

'One phone call and that precious baby and her grand-pappy are toast.'

'I don't know for sure.'

'We have a list of possible locations. There are two left to check,' he said.

'Okay, where are they then?'

'A house in Clontarf and an industrial unit in Greystones.'

Could she divert him, delay him? Not with the threat to Frank and the baby.

'Head for Ballsbridge for now, or if the traffic is heavy, go towards Booterstown. Either way, you could head for the East Link Bridge, or go through Phibsborough. It's going to take us the best part of three quarters of an hour to get there.'

'Are we heading for that house in Clontarf?' Dwayne asked.

'No, it's neither of the ones you mentioned.'

'You'd better not be taking us into some trap, Danielle.'

She sighed. 'I'm not.' Seventy kilos of coke for Chloe and Frank's life. It was worth every gram. Her fate, once Dwayne got his hands on it, was anybody's guess. She was tired of hiding, tired of ducking. This had to end — one way or another.

'So, where are we heading?'

If she told him, would he just kill her and dump her body? Would he still harm Chloe or Frank? The only way she'd be certain was to see his face when he got his grubby hands on that hoard. Then she'd know.

'Drumcondra.'

'Why?'

'We need to go to the gym. Lee is on duty. If you let me ring him, I can get him to close up. That way, there will be no witnesses.'

'Nah, I'm afraid Lee won't be working for you anymore. He has officially handed in his notice — at least, what's left of him has.'

Jesus Christ, Dwayne was an animal.

Thank Christ the keys to the gym were in her jacket pocket. There was no point delaying the inevitable by pretending she didn't have them.

'Does Jason know you're doing this to me?'

Dwayne stopped humming. 'You think Jason has a say in what I do?'

They drove on in silence, away from South County Dublin towards the north of the city. Danielle watched people she couldn't call to for help pass by, drivers who had no idea of her predicament. Heavy rain puckered the sea to her right. When they neared the East Link toll bridge, the rain stopped and the water lapped placidly on the shore of Dublin Bay. The sight of the Irish sea failed to ease Danielle's tension. Sal passed through one of the unattended kiosks on the toll bridge. At least the camera would pick up her last known movements if she failed to return. But who was left to report her missing? Not Linda, judging by her disappearing act. Frank maybe, if she didn't follow through with her promise to buy his business. Though he'd be more likely to think that she'd just changed her mind.

Sal pulled up outside the front door of the gym.

'You'd better have a way in, Danielle,' Dwayne said.

'The keys are in my jacket pocket.'

'Pull them out, slowly. Sal, keep a watch. One wrong move and you'll get a bullet in the back of your skull.'

As she pulled them out, the keys caught in a thread. She yanked them free.

'So, it was in the gym all along,' Dwayne said. 'Dirtbag Thompson didn't have a clue. Idiot's surely no loss to the world.'

'Not exactly.'

'You'd better not be fucking with me, Danielle.'

'I'm too tired to fuck with you, Dwayne.'

With Dwayne's gun trained on her, Danielle led the two men through the gym's reception and on into the rear, beyond an area used as a storage room, stopping at a door with a key-pad on it.

'Here?'

Danielle nodded.

'What's the code?' He raised his hand, fingers poised to enter the digits.

'I don't know.' She couldn't even hazard a guess. 'Check the keys, Dwayne. There's a fob. That could be it.'

Dwayne hovered the black fob in front of a small screen underneath the keypad. There was a click, and the door was released.

Dwayne pushed the door open. Before them lay a hall-way, from the end of which a flight of steps descended into blackness. As they moved forward, a light stuttered into life, revealing another door at the bottom of the steps. This one had a bar across it like a fire door.

Dwayne gave her a shove. 'You go first, Danielle. I'm not getting caught in any trap. That door could be electrified or something.'

Danielle pushed at the bar and the door opened into a wide hallway, with paint buckets and a spray pack stacked against the wall. The hall led out to a small car park with numbered spaces. Some had signs on the wall indicating their use by gym members; other signs read they were for hotel patrons. Parked at the far end was a white transit van. Dwayne thrust Danielle out of the way and strode forward, followed by Sal, Danielle trailing behind. The door swung behind them.

Dwayne gave a whoop, which echoed in the deserted car park. 'What do you think, Sal? Could this be it? Our key to the next level?'

Speaking for the first time since Danielle got in the car, Sal said, 'This could indeed be it, Dwayne. Let's see.'

Danielle was considering darting back up the steps, locking them in and leaving them to it when Sal grabbed her by the arm and dragged her over to the van.

Dwayne snapped his fingers. 'Keys?'

Danielle bit on her bottom lip. 'Try the arch of one of the rear wheels.'

Dwayne took hold of her and shoved her towards the van. 'You check for me.'

At the top of the rear tyre on the driver's side, Danielle found a key and two fobs. She pressed one of the fobs, the lights blinked, and the locks were released. She looked back at Dwayne.

'The other fob must be for the exit.' She pointed towards the large metal shutter at the end of the car park.

Dwayne snatched the key and fobs from Danielle's hand and, pushing her aside, went to the rear of the van and pulled the doors apart. He let out a long whistle.

'Come and look at this, Sal.' Dwayne was almost singing the words.

Danielle could see brown boxes labelled *Tableware*, *Linens*, *Dining sets*.

Dwayne ripped the tape off the top of one of the boxes. Instead of household goods, the box was packed with white bricks covered in bubble wrap. Dwayne took a brick in each hand and held it aloft. 'Fuck you, Danielle Lewis, and all the rest of your pissing family.'

'Just make the call, Dwayne,' she said wearily.

'What call is that then?'

'You've got what you wanted. Now tell your man to stop following the taxi.'

'How gullible are you, Danielle? There never was any man following that car.'

Gullible. That was the least of it. Her mouth went dry. She had just handed Dwayne the means to become the most powerful man in Dublin. This truckload of blow would make Dwayne the dominant player in the underworld. And there was nothing she could do to stop it. She glanced at the metal door of the car park, back towards the door through which they had entered. Sal or Dwayne would kill her before she could make a move.

It was all up. She sank to her knees, unable to stand. Sal and Dwayne were too busy going through their treasure to notice.

CHAPTER 39

Danielle was still on her knees, hunched over, when she felt something touch her arm. She looked up to see Linda, her finger to her lips. Dwayne and Sal were now inside the van and pulling out the bricks to count them. Very slowly, Linda and Danielle began to step backwards, their eyes glued to the back of the van.

It was Sal who looked up first. Shoving Danielle behind her, Linda raised the Beretta and pointed it at first one and then the other of them. Sal tapped Dwayne on the shoulder and pointed. Dwayne turned, reached behind him and fired a single shot. It missed. The second found its mark, sending Linda to the ground. Danielle grabbed the gun from her hand and pointed it at Dwayne, who was just lowering himself from the van. The two of them faced off, weapons raised.

'Fuck them, Dwayne, let's get out of here.' The sound of Sal's voice and the slam of the van doors ricocheted off the walls of the empty parking area.

Smiling evilly at Danielle, Dwayne lowered his gun and turned away. He'd won. She didn't dare shoot him in the back. Unable to claim that she'd fired in self-defence, she'd have ended up behind bars.

The metal shutters began to rise after Dwayne pressed the button on the other fob. Dwayne then tossed the keys to Sal and the two jumped in. With a loud rev, the van careened from the building and disappeared in a cloud of exhaust fumes.

Danielle knelt down beside Linda. 'Where are you hit?'

'My leg. It hurts like a motherfucker, but I can move it.'

'Try not to,' Danielle said, her eyes desperately searching the cavernous area for something that might help.

Blood was beginning to soak Linda's jeans. She pressed on the wound to stem the flow. Danielle ran to the hall, returning with a pack of cloths that had been lying among the paints and brushes. She tore it open, slid the bundle of cloths beneath Linda's hand and held it there.

The door swung to with a squeal of metal. Danielle heard the distant sound of sirens. Linda smiled.

Danielle tilted her head. 'Is that you, Linda? What did you do?'

'I contacted Saoirse and told her Dwayne had taken you.'

'What? You just rang up a Garda station?'

'No. The night I picked you up and brought you to Berkley Street, you had on you a brown envelope with a phone number written on it.'

'How did you know it belonged to a detective?'

'The harp is only ever on official government envelopes. I took a chance.'

'I'm glad you did. But how did you know where we were going?'

Linda threw a glance towards Danielle's wrist, and the bracelet she had given her.

Danielle followed her gaze. 'You mean you tracked me through that?'

'Yeah. I had to give you something I'd be sure you'd wear.'

'Why?'

'When I heard Dwayne was back, and what with Ged's drugs still on the loose, I had to find a way to protect you.'

While Danielle tried to grasp what Linda was saying, there came the blast of a siren, followed by the sound of screeching tyres outside.

Linda grimaced. 'Jesus, my leg.'

'But . . . when Dwayne arrived, I turned to look for you and you'd disappeared.'

'I got a call warning me Dwayne was on his way. I wasn't able to get to you before Dwayne appeared, so I contacted Saoirse. I told her that Dwayne had kidnapped you and was using you as a shield, while he took delivery of a large quantity of drugs.'

'That must have caused quite a response.'

'Sounds like it did.' Linda's laugh gave way to a grimace, and she clutched at her leg.

Linda and Danielle both looked at the handgun, now lying on the ground beside them, and back at each other.

'Shit. Now we're screwed, too,' Linda said.

'Yeah,' Danielle began. 'Ah, but wait — neither of us let off a shot.'

'We still shouldn't have it. What are you thinking of doing now, Danielle? You can't blame it on Dwayne; the forensics will show he didn't handle it. They're right outside. We'll get caught putting it over there.' Linda looked to where the van had been parked.

It took Danielle just a second to decide. She pulled her sleeves down over her hands, grabbed the gun and ran to the hall. With her hands still covered, she wiped the gun with some methylated spirits from the stack of paint and other equipment. She checked the chamber for a bullet. It was empty. There were four left in the magazine, which took six. She didn't have time to wonder about the two missing bullets, or how Linda had got her hands on the Beretta in the first place.

Danielle took out the four bullets and cleaned them. She peeled the lid off one of the paint buckets, dropped the gun and the bullets into it and snapped the lid back on. Then she ran back to Linda, just as someone banged on the metal gate.

Danielle and Linda, huddled together in the middle of the empty car park, looked like two children caught playing some game they shouldn't. With shouts of 'Gardaí!' a crowd of black-clad police burst in. Danielle raised her hands.

While one of them knelt down by Linda and began to treat her wound, another took charge of Danielle. A woman guard told her to get onto her knees and keep her hands where she could see them. She demanded to know if Danielle was armed.

Danielle said that she wasn't, and the guard told her to stand up while she patted her down.

The rest of the unit had spread out. Some disappeared into the hall and Danielle heard them thundering up the steps. Others remained in the car park, peering into corners and craning their necks to the corrugated roof.

Soon the building resounded with cries of 'Clear!' The guards drifted back into the car park just as a paramedic dashed in and went over to Linda. As she was examining her wound, a familiar face appeared at the entrance — Detective Garda Saoirse Kelly. With her were Sinead Teegan and Dave Richards.

Saoirse walked over to Danielle. 'Tell me your version of what happened.'

Danielle gave her the story, leaving out the origin of the consignment. She also omitted to say that Linda had been armed, saying instead that Dwayne shot Linda while she was helping Danielle to escape. Which, anyway, was mostly true.

Danielle finished her account, asking, 'Did you get him?'

Saoirse grinned broadly at Danielle. 'We sure did. Along with a shit load of drugs.'

'A shit load, eh? That's quite a lot,' Danielle said.

'Subject to analysis, of course.'

'Of course.'

'Sal and Dwayne are in custody.'

'Their prints should be on the packets, Saoirse. They were opening the boxes like a pair of hungry savages.'

'All to the good. We've run a check on the registered owner of the van. It's not an address I recognise, but we've a patrol car looking for it. Somewhere in South County Dublin, I believe.'

Danielle knew it would be a wasted journey. Vehicles used in the course of committing an illegal act were usually registered to non-existent people at obscure addresses. But let the officers find that out for themselves.

'Do you need me for anything else, or can I go?' Danielle asked. 'I'd like to go to the hospital with Linda.'

Saoirse smiled at her. 'Well, you've done nothing wrong, so I can't detain you.'

Danielle caught up with Linda as she was being stretchered out. 'How are you?'

Linda managed a laugh. 'A little lighter, without a litre or so of blood.'

'Give me your car keys, and I'll follow you to the hospital,' Danielle said.

'Yeah.' With a wince of pain, Linda drew them from her pocket.

'Shit, I hope it's not inside some cordon.'

'No. I parked it a distance away in case Dwayne spotted it and sprinted from there.'

'Just a second.' Danielle leaned forward and whispered into Linda's ear. 'Where did you get the . . . ?'

'It was in Anto's bag, the one you took from the shop,' Linda whispered back.

'What?'

'There's a ball of money in there, as well. Go on, off to the car now, get yourself well away from here.'

'Just one more thing. Who rang to warn you that Dwayne was coming for me?'

'Jason.'

'*Jason?*'

'Who else? He swore on his life that you were in danger from Dwayne, and I had to get you to safety. By the time he told me that, Dwayne had already pulled up and was taking you.'

'Fuck, really?'

'Yes.' Linda said. 'I ducked out of sight in case he took me, too. We'd really have been screwed if that had happened.'

'We sure would. Hey, did you put cameras in here, too?'

'No, I couldn't get in to sort them. If I had, I'd have seen the van.'

'Of course.' Danielle shook her head. 'Imagine. Those seventy Ks of coke have been sitting here all along.'

'And now Dwayne's been caught with it in his possession.'

'Poetic justice,' said Danielle. 'He and Sal have been arrested. I've told Saoirse she should find their prints on the boxes, in case they claim not to have known what's in the van.'

'Good one.'

Danielle stayed to watch Linda being loaded into the ambulance. A few metres away, Dwayne was lying face down on the ground, his hands cuffed behind his back. Sal lay in a similar position by the driver's door.

Danielle was tempted to approach Dwayne and whisper that, to add insult to injury, she also had his dog. Lola would be with Danielle for the rest of her life — a quantity of drugs such as the one he'd been found with carried a mandatory ten-year sentence.

Danielle was filthy, and covered in Linda's blood. She needed to check on Lola and get out of these clothes. Now that Danielle had given Saoirse her version of events, all that remained was to ensure that Linda's account chimed with hers.

CHAPTER 40

Danielle spent the journey from the hospital listening to the car radio for news of the arrests. As she'd expected, the headlines were awash with stories of the large haul of drugs that had been recovered.

Back at Berkley Street, Danielle put Anto's backpack full of money on the living room floor and switched on the TV, catching the tail end of the breaking news. A reporter standing outside the gates to the Phoenix Park Garda Headquarters was saying excitedly, 'Two men have been detained under the provision of the Drugs Trafficking Act, 1996, and can be held for up to seven days.'

That should keep Dwayne quiet for a while, Danielle said to herself, as a wave of exhaustion swept over her. She switched off the TV and went to bed.

But Danielle couldn't sleep. She had never been alone here before, and she lay awake listening for noises in the vast, empty house. In the early hours she got up and let Lola out for a pee. Then she did something unprecedented — brought the dog up to her room. Lola sniffed around for a bit, and then settled herself on the large chair in the corner of the room.

Comforted by Lola's presence, Danielle fell into a deep sleep. The following morning, she awoke with a start, sensing a weight on the bed. She lifted her head and saw the dog curled up by her feet. Lola had adopted her.

Smiling, Danielle lay back against the pillows. There was a call she had to make. It rang for what seemed like an age before he answered.

'You're okay, then?'

'Yes. I called to say thank you,' she said.

'As long as you're all right.'

'Are you still in Dublin?' she asked.

'No, I decided I'd be better off out of my brother's way. I don't know when I'll be back. It depends . . .'

'But everything's okay now. He's in custody, and is sure to be kept there until he's charged.'

'Don't count on it.'

'But he's a flight risk. He has business connections in South America and the Caribbean — he was there for a few months, wasn't he?'

'Yeah, well, that's if someone else doesn't take the fall for it.'

Danielle sat up. Lola raised her head in response. 'What do you mean?'

'Don't be surprised if he manages to wriggle his way out of it.'

Lola settled again, but not Danielle. There was an uneasy feeling in her gut. 'Like what? Will he let Sal take the fall for the whole thing?'

'That's a possibility.'

'But his fingerprints . . . they're on everything.'

'Doesn't matter, Danielle. Dwayne always finds a way. He could say he did it under duress.'

'Shit.' Danielle rubbed her cheek, where a slight itch served as a reminder of the attack.

'Don't go celebrating his downfall yet,' Jason said.

'Right.' Danielle swung her feet to the floor and sat on the edge of the bed.

'And for fuck's sake, Danielle, get that dog back to him.'

268

As if she knew she was being spoken about, Lola sat up and whimpered. She hopped from the bed and rested her head on Danielle's knee. There was no way that violent animal was getting his hands on this beautiful one.

'Do you hear me, Danielle? Give her back.'

'I hear you, Jason. We'll talk when you get back.'

'Let's,' Jason said.

* * *

Lola slept in Danielle's room for the next two nights. She was great company. The bullet had taken a chunk out of Linda's thigh. It hadn't embedded itself, though it had left a deep wound whose dressings needed changing several times a day.

The three of them were in the living room, watching the news. Linda lay on the sofa with her damaged leg stretched out in front of her. Danielle sat on one of the chairs and Lola lay on the rug at her feet. This time, the reporter was standing outside Store Street Garda Station. The two men arrested and detained under the Drugs Trafficking Act had just been remanded in custody for a further period. Linda and Danielle were safe for another while. When the ads came on, Danielle stood up and stretched.

'I'm getting a coffee, Linda. You want one?'

'Yeah, go on. And stick some of that whisky you like in it.'

'The Dingle stuff?'

'Yeah, that's tasty.'

When Danielle returned with two mugs of coffee, she found Linda apparently deep in thought.

'You okay there? Are you in pain?'

'No. Anyway, pain's good; it reminds me that I'm alive. I was thinking — and don't you *dare* ask me if it hurt.' Both women laughed. 'Do you think Anto had a part in your attack, Danielle, seeing as he had your gun?'

Danielle shook her head. 'I don't think so, no, but Frank Brady said that Kym did. She must have taken my gun from

269

the buggy. Maybe she gave it to Anto. He could well have used it to kill Bosco Ryan, not knowing where it originated from. But it's not as if I can rock up to Saoirse and ask her what make of bullets were removed from Bosco's body. I'll need to speak with Kym again, and drag the truth out of her.'

Linda sat upright. 'Fuck, Danielle. Did you not hear about the fatal accident at that construction site the other day?'

'Yeah, I remember hearing something about it, but what's that got to do with us or Kym?'

'Kym ran out behind a truck as it was reversing. The driver never saw her, drove over her apparently. She was killed instantly.'

Danielle put down her mug, suddenly nauseous.

'And that's not all. They're saying there was a body in the van that was torched that day, too. The rumour going round is that it was Lee Thompson.'

'Shit.'

'Yep. Kym and Lee were having it off behind Ian's back. He knew it was going on but chose to ignore it. Then Kym walked out on him. Apparently, she turned up at Lee's place, suitcase in hand, only to find another woman there.'

'Where are you getting all of this?'

'Aimee. She was there visiting Jane. She answered the door to Kym. Meanwhile, Ian had told Jane that Lee'd had a big job on for Dwayne Flynn — a hit.'

'Anto? The shooting in the shop?'

'Bingo. Kym had no idea that Lee was working for Dwayne. According to Aimee, she was under the impression that they were running away together. She went and told Lee that Anto had killed Bosco. Yer man tattled to Dwayne, so he ordered the hit.'

'Jesus Christ. Does Anto know about any of this?'

'Aimee had been in to see him at the hospital. Marion and Brenno went, too. According to her, they brought his mam in. Poor woman wouldn't believe that he'd survived until she saw him for herself. So yeah, I'd say he's been brought up to date on everything by now.'

'So, when is Anto being discharged from hospital?'

'He got out yesterday. He's staying at Brenno's. Him and Marion are looking after him for a few days, then he'll head back home, so his own mammy can look after him.'

'Right.' Leaving her coffee untouched, Danielle got to her feet.

'Where are you off to now?' Linda said.

'I've a job to do. I'll be a couple of hours. Do you need anything before I go?'

'No, I have Lola here to mind me.'

'See you soon,' Danielle said.

CHAPTER 41

Danielle mounted the steps to Marion's house and knocked at the door. With her long dark hair freshy trimmed and styled, falling loose, leather trousers and satin bodysuit, she wanted to present the best version of herself. There stood Aimee, who greeted her with a warm smile.

'Hi, Aimee,' Danielle said, slightly taken aback. 'Can I come in?'

'Of course, Danielle. Marion's in the kitchen with Anto, just through there.' Aimee pointed along the hallway.

'And Brenno?'

'Gone to the shops for milk.'

Marion was sitting at the kitchen table. Anto was there too. He had his arm in a sling. There were lines on Marion's face that hadn't been there before, and her brown hair was grey at the roots. She fixed Danielle with a hard stare.

Danielle ploughed ahead regardless. 'Hi, Marion. I hope I'm not intruding. It's just that I never got a chance to say how sorry I was for your loss.'

Marion's expression softened. Her eyes filled with tears. 'Thank you.' Anto put his hand on Marion's arm for a moment.

'You and Bird were together a long time. It can't have been easy.'

'No, it wasn't.' Marion gave a long, shuddering breath. 'You are one of the few who have shown any sympathy towards me. I appreciate it.'

The back door swung open. Brenno stopped in his tracks and looked at his mother. 'What's *she* doing here?'

'It's okay, Brenno,' Marion said. 'Put the kettle on and let's all have some tea. Take a seat, Danielle.'

'Thank you.' Danielle took a seat at the table, putting her bag on the floor beside her.

Brenno came in and did as instructed. Aimee and Anto went out, leaving the three of them sitting in silence, listening to the thrum of the kettle. Brenno stood with his back to the women, apparently willing it to boil. Marion stared at her hands. Just as the kettle clicked off, Aimee and Anto re-entered and sat down at the table. Brenno remained standing, his back to the kitchen counter, his gaze travelling from the back of his mother's head to Danielle's face. He brought four mugs and four coasters to the table.

'Join us, Brenno. This is a peaceful table. I'm sick of all this fighting, sick of running scared. Jesus Christ, I've had enough.'

Brenno frowned, but put a fifth mug on the table and filled the teapot.

Aimee retrieved the milk from the fridge.

'Don't break the posh milk jug now,' Marion said, summoning a wan smile.

Danielle glanced at Anto's arm. 'How's the injury?'

'I'll live.'

'Good.' She turned to Marion. 'And, you? I hope you're doing okay, under the circumstances.'

'Taking it day by day, Danielle.'

They passed around the milk. Brenno took the carton from Danielle with his gaze averted.

'How are you, Danielle?' Aimee asked.

It took Danielle a moment or two to respond. Good question. How was she?

'Thanks for asking, Aimee. I'm a bit stunned, I suppose, still in shock from the assault on me, and Chloe being taken like she was. I understand that Kym and Lee were behind it.'

Anto frowned. He opened his mouth to speak but closed it again.

Danielle smiled at him. 'Go on.'

'I had no idea she was involved. Ian is our buddy — mine and Brenno's. I told him she was cheating on him with that dirtbag, Lee, but I'm not sure he believed me.'

'Don't worry, Anto, I believe you.'

Danielle turned to face Brenno. 'You've been through a lot, haven't you?'

'What do you know about it?' he said sullenly, though he did raise his eyes to her.

She was getting somewhere. 'Nothing. Just . . . tell me what's on your mind.'

'Why are you here, Danielle, here in our kitchen? What do you want?'

'I came to express my condolences to your mother. I also wanted to thank Anto for pushing the buggy out of the way when Lee shot at us. He made sure the baby came to no harm.'

'And if you hadn't sprayed him like you did, he'd have shot me in the head,' Anto said.

Brenno stared at him, and then back to Danielle. 'Really?'

'Yeah,' Anto said.

'And I also came to return something to its rightful owner.' Danielle reached down for the bag. 'It's yours, Anto.'

'What do you mean?'

'After you were shot, I took your bag. Lucky I did, as it turned out, or the guards would have had it. This isn't it; I dumped the original bag and transferred the contents to this one. It's brand new, so there's no prints or anything on it.'

'Really?'

'Yeah, it should sort you out for a while.'

Anto shoved his chair back, snatched the bag from her and left the room. Danielle guessed he was checking through the contents. By the time he came back in, he was smiling hugely.

'Cheers, Danielle.' He looked to Brenno. 'Here, lad, we've done good, you and me. Call it compensation from the Flynns.'

'Look,' Danielle began, 'Dwayne's in custody right now, but if he gets released, who knows who he'll target? What's in that bag might help you relocate, Anto, if you wanted to. Oh, and the other thing that was in there has been, er, neutralised.'

'Thank fuck for that,' Anto said.

Danielle's phone buzzed with a message. Linda, needing something, she supposed, just at the wrong moment. But no. The message was from Saoirse:

He's being released. He's calling some kind of press conference o/s Store Street GS. Other man taking fall for everything.

Shit. 'Marion, where is your telly? I just got notification that Dwayne is being released.'

Everyone except Marion checked their phones.

'Why do you need the telly? Isn't everything on here?' Brenno tapped his phone.

'He's calling a press conference, apparently.'

'Jesus,' Anto said.

'It's in the sitting room,' Marion said, pointing the way. She remained sitting at the table while the rest of them hurried through to watch.

Amid the cameras and reporters gathered outside Store Street Garda Station, the newsreader filled dead air with the announcement that a man was about to be released from custody and wanted to make a statement, adding a comment on the unusual nature of his request.

One of Dwayne's minions must have dropped a suit and shirt into the Garda station for him. It looked like the one he was wearing when he threatened her at Jason's apartment on the day of Bird's funeral.

The cameras closed in on his face, while on and off the screen his audience fell silent. Dwayne cleared his throat and began to speak.

'When an innocent man like me gets arrested for someone else's crimes, it just goes to show that this country has gone to rack and ruin. I am grateful that the cops — I mean, the guards — have seen sense and have released me. But this isn't the last they'll hear of it. No man should be kept in conditions of the likes of that cell. Those who were behind putting me there—' here, he stared into the camera, causing Danielle to pull back instinctively — 'will be hearing from me.'

'Jesus Christ, the bastard is making threats on live TV,' Brenno said. 'He should be stopped.'

'Look,' cried Aimee. On screen, a man could be seen behind Dwayne, edging closer to him. 'That's Ian Gallagher. What the fuck is he doing there?'

Ian was now standing behind Dwayne and slightly to one side. Something in his hand caught the light and flashed for a moment. A blade. Before anyone around him saw what was happening, he lunged at Dwayne and thrust it in, just below the ribs. Then he pulled it out, blood spurting from the wound.

'You ruined my life!' Ian shouted. 'You ruined everything, you animal!'

To the horrified gasps of the crowd, Ian drove the blade in again. He was just about to stab Dwayne a third time when two guards took hold of him and wrestled the knife from his grasp.

Danielle searched for an emotion. Along with many thousands of others, she stared at the screen and watched a man bleed out, live on TV. And she felt nothing.

The camera zoomed in on the knife, now lying on the ground. It had a dark brown handle, possibly leather, of a similar length to the blade, now coated in blood. The camera zoomed out and in again on Dwayne, who was on the ground, his blood pooling beneath him.

'The bastard won't be such a threat now, will he? He's no loss to the world, that's for sure.' Marion had come in quietly and was standing at the back of the living room, her eyes on the screen. 'It's a pity Bird can't come back in his place.'

A shiver ran through Danielle. God forbid. Well, at least she could be sure that would never happen. As for Dwayne

276

. . . who knew? Ian, on the other hand, was well and truly screwed.

The newsfeed cut away from the scene and back to the studio.

Marion glanced down at her slippered foot, the edge of a white bandage showing. 'Karma's a bitch, eh,' she said.

'I think I'll put the kettle on again,' Aimee said. 'Who's for a fresh brew?'

'Maybe something a little stronger,' Brenno said.

Anto was still staring at the screen as the others left the room. 'Who knew it would have been that easy to get him?' Anto said. 'But poor Ian's fucked now, with the nation as witness to his actions. Even in his demise, Dwayne had to take someone else down with him.'

Danielle hoped that Linda had been watching, too, as well as all those others Dwayne Flynn had fucked over in his time. Few people would have been brave enough to do what Ian Gallagher had just done. Thanks to his action, many people would sleep easier in their beds tonight, knowing that Dwayne Flynn would never threaten them again.

THE END

THE JOFFE BOOKS STORY

We began in 2014 when Jasper agreed to publish his mum's much-rejected romance novel and it became a bestseller.

Since then we've grown into the largest independent publisher in the UK. We're extremely proud to publish some of the very best writers in the world, including Joy Ellis, Faith Martin, Caro Ramsay, Helen Forrester, Simon Brett and Robert Goddard. Everyone at Joffe Books loves reading and we never forget that it all begins with the magic of an author telling a story.

We are proud to publish talented first-time authors, as well as established writers whose books we love introducing to a new generation of readers.

We have been shortlisted for Independent Publisher of the Year at the British Book Awards three times, in 2020, 2021 and 2022, and for the Diversity and Inclusivity Award at the Independent Publishing Awards in 2022.

We built this company with your help, and we love to hear from you, so please email us about absolutely anything bookish at: feedback@joffebooks.com.

If you want to receive free books every Friday and hear about all our new releases, join our mailing list: www.joffebooks.com/contact

And when you tell your friends about us, just remember: it's pronounced Joffe as in coffee or toffee!

ALSO BY CASEY KING

THE DUBLIN THRILLERS SERIES
Book 1: DECEIT
Book 2: EXPOSED

Milton Keynes UK
Ingram Content Group UK Ltd.
UKHW012258100524
442532UK00004B/121

9 781835 261897